MARK FROM EARTH

R. GRUSZECKI

ILLUSTRATIONS BY MARCO Q. LOPES

Praise for MARK FROM EARTH

"This book is rot."

- Harold Babbermont, stuffy critic at Orion's Belt Press

GUESS WHAT HAROLD.....

"I read it while hoverboarding to school!"

- *Julia, 8th grader at North Nebula Prep School*

"My friends keep stealing it right when I'm teleporting home."

- David, 10th grader at West Halo High

"I've read it to my kids five times already. They refuse to sleep until I read it again. My voice is hoarse. My eyes blurry. Why won't they sleep?"

- *Adam, exhausted father of two*

"Oh wow. Chapter 14. Incredible (spoiler)! Favorite part: Mark battles the (spoiler) and (spoilers) the (spoiler). (SPOILEEEEER)!"

- (Name ommited for trying to spoil it for everybody)

#1 Interstellar Bestseller."

– *The Galactic Gazette*

That's right, Harold. #1. Interstellar. Best.seller.

Earthbound Book Co.
1204 NE 146th ave
Vancouver, Wa 98684

Book Design: Amy Pogue of Irving Street Press

Library of Congress Cataloging-in-Publication Data:

Gruszecki, Rafael.

Mark from Earth, 4th ed.

ISBN 978-0-9895475-3-6

1. Fiction. 2. Science Fiction. 3. Action & Adventure

Fourth edition paperback: January 2016 (Stardate: Heelo 3031)

1 2 3 4 5 6 7 8 9 10

Printed in the United States of America

MARK

FROM EARTH

R. GRUSZECKI

ILLUSTRATIONS BY MARCO Q LOPES

Earthbound Book Co.
Crater City, Pluto

Start with a mystery....

End with a history.

CONTENTS

CHAPTER 1
SET SAIL FOR THE STARS

"Does that look like a good spot for a crash landing?"

"Aaaahhhh!"

"How about that mountain?"

"AAAAHHHHHH!"

"Perhaps the ocean?"

"NNNNEEEEAAAAAA!"

"No, you're right. I can't swim anyway!"

This nail-biting conversation was happening between two highly unusual people – especially since one of them was not a person at all, but a rather short and paranoid android.

"We're going to smash up and buuurrrrnnn!" screamed the android. His name was Lloyd. His knobbly knees were curled up to his red metallic chest and his hands were barely covering his big camera-lens eyes.

"Ten thousand thundering comets!" crowed the pilot, "what a rush!" His name was Stan Zumski – Captain Stan Zumski. And though he looked like someone's grandpappie – tall and grey with a twinkle in his old brown eyes – he refused to act like it. That's why he trimmed his salt and pepper beard into a perfect square. It was also why his right leg whirred and clacked as no normal leg should – because it was made of gears, cogs, and a teacup passing for a temporary kneecap.

"Jupiter's red eye!" said Captain Zumski as his strong hands fought the shuddering controls. "What a beautiful evening for a crash!"

And so it was. Their starfighter was shot to pieces, burning fumes pouring out both ion engines, two of the four wings rattling – and then with a screech snapping off. It was a violent mess raining like fire out of a spectacular sunset sky.

"Open your lenses, Lloyd!" shouted Captain Zumski as the glass in front of them began to crack. "Enjoy the site of this lovely little planet before we crash!"

But Lloyd kept his lenses locked tight, even though this was his first visit to Earth – and Earth is a most peculiar place. The people there still drive on the ground instead of buzzing about in hovercars; they still take out the garbage instead of having androids do it, and perhaps most peculiar, they still haven't popped off to explore the vast, uncharted weirdness of our universe, which is a real shame – because our universe is really, really weird.

"I do believe we'll be crashing somewhere in Australia this evening," announced Captain Zumski as their flaming wreckage tore into the upper atmosphere. Another wing screeched, ripped off, and swirled away behind them. They dove through cloud after cloud after cloud as they plummeted to the dusty red continent below. "That's where this kid is, isn't it, Lloyd? What's his name?"

"Mark," replied the trembling android.

"Mark," repeated Captain Zumski, gunning the ion engines. One roared to life, sending a storm of orange exhaust out the back. The other engine exploded. "Mark," he repeated with a chuckle. "I don't know who'll have the bigger surprise today! This kid Mark, who's going about his everyday life until we show up! Or you and me – if we survive this thing!"

The glass around them cracked faster. Wind began howling in. It stunk of melting plastic. The captain's grip tightened. The controls fought back. His knuckles went white. "Hold onto your bolts!"

Australia filled their vision. Gigantic red deserts. Jagged mountains. A golden coastline and the shimmering ocean beyond. Quiet towns and bustling cities burst into view. Towering glass skyscrapers. Traffic chocked highways. Sprawling mazes of neighborhoods. And somewhere down in that mess of hubbub and life was a kid named Mark.

Specifically speaking, he was in a city called Sydney. To be even more specific, he had just finished his first day at South Sydney Middle School. And to be right on the nose about it, he was already being chased away by three big mean eighth graders – whose ugly little pug he had just dognapped.

"Get back here with my dog!" shouted the biggest, meanest of the eighth graders trying to catch Mark.

"You don't deserve him!" Mark hollered back, holding on tighter to the ugly little pug – who barked happily and licked Mark's freckled face -- its floppy ears bouncing about as Mark's worn-out sneakers ate pavement.

"I'll break your twig arms and twig legs!" wheezed another of the eighth graders in the chase.

Mark ignored him and locked eyes with his furry new friend as they dashed into a nearby park. "What's your name then, huh?" he wondered. "Dog Vader? Artoo Dogtoo? Parker the Barker? Scuddles Picklebottom?"

"Woof!"

Mark's blue-green eyes lit right up! He knew what the pug's name should be! Leaping over puddles full of floating barkchips, he held up the happily barking sausage and proclaimed: "I hereby name you -- Oz! Oz the Great and Powerful!"

"His name is Spot!" protested another out-of-breath eighth grader.

Mark flipped around and began running backwards, still holding Oz the Great and Powerful up high so they could both face their enemies. "Seriously?! He doesn't even have a spot! He's one solid wrinkly brown color! Like a furry little turd!"

Oz the Great and Powerful barked in cheerful agreement.

"You dumb orphan dork!" spat the leader. "I'll smash your freckled face in so bad your own mom wouldn't recognize you! If she were still alive!"

Mark ignored that too. He'd gotten quite good at it. So he was an orphan. No big deal. He never knew his mom and dad. It was alright. Water off a duck's back. So he had way too many freckles all around his nose. Looked like he was rusting. Great. He once took a sharpie and played connect the dots in front of a mirror. It looked like a derpy T-Rex. So he was short and scrawny for his age. But he was fast. He was so fast. One time he ran away from school, flat out, full speed, for a solid hour – but that was because a girl in gym class said she had a crush on him.

Unfortunately, though Mark was curiously fast on his feet, he did NOT have eyes in the back of his head – and as he was running backwards holding Oz the Great and Powerful, his left foot snagged on an overgrown root.

WUMP.

All three overfed vultures quickly closed in.

"Take Spot," commanded the biggest one.

"No!" Mark choked, lungs flat from the impact and vision blurry.

Oz yelped as a pair of powerful hands ripped him away from Mark's arms.

The third guy slammed his palms against Mark's wheezing chest, grabbed two handfuls of Mark's baggy, hand-me-down shirt, lifted him clear off his feet, and smashed him against the same tree the root belonged to.

"Now," huffed the out-of-breath leader, "I'm gonna hit you," he wiped his puffy face with the back of the fist he was going to use. "And I'm gonna keep hitting you, k?" He leaned in, reeking of sweat. "I'm gonna keep hitting you until I see your breakfast all over these barkchips."

The other two guys snickered. Oz whimpered and struggled. Mark grit his teeth. He stared the big brute square in the eyes. This wasn't his first rodeo. His stomach was no stranger to other people's fists. The key is, right before getting punched, to exhale. Breathe out quick. That way they can't knock the wind out of you.

THUD.

"Uff." There was still some air left. Next one, next one.

THUD.

Breathe out. Breathe out. Breathe out.

THUD.

This guy could punch.

THUD.

Oh man. That one made his knees buckle.

THUD.

Maybe his stomach couldn't hold breakfast down after all.

THUD.

Which was too bad because he'd had his favorite this morning – string cheese.

THUD.

"Wait, wait, wait," said the brute holding Mark up. He stopped pressing him against the tree. "You hold him up," he said to the red-faced leader. "I want a turn."

"Me next!" said the guy grasping Oz so hard the little pug had stopped struggling and started shivering.

While the three monsters argued about who would throw the next dozen punches at Mark's stomach, the boy gulped in sweet, sweet air. That was a mistake. The oxygen brought pain. Pain brought blurriness to his eyes. He would not let them see that. He tilted his head skywards, willing the blurriness to stop rolling down his rusted cheeks.

That's when he saw it. Up in the sunset sky.

Through the blurriness. Through the gulped breaths. Through the pain.

A brilliant comet. Ripping through cloud after cloud after cloud. No not a comet. It had one wing. A plane? But it was on fire! A burning mess tumbling and spinning toward him!

A dull roar filled the park. It shook the trees. It vibrated the hot air. It rushed closer with the sound of fast approaching disaster.

The three monsters quite arguing. They looked up. Terror and fear filled their bloated red faces. They dropped Mark. They took Oz, who was howling in fright, and they ran.

Mark sank to his hands and knees, coughing and gasping as the roar deafened his ears. Panic. He wanted to run. Panic. He tried to rise. Panic. His legs gave way. He fell.

IMPACT.

The one-winged ship crashed into the opposite end of the park. Its speed kept it moving, plowing forward tearing up dirt and gravel and trees. It skidded into the playground, sending a fountain of barkchips spraying all around.

"No, no, no!" Mark gasped as the craft slid at him, pushing its broken wing, sharp as a spike, toward him. He cringed.

With a grinding halt the craft shuddered to a rocking stop in front of him.

Silence.

Glass cracking. No. Glass being kicked out.

A smash and a glittering spray.

A mechanical leg bloomed out of where the cracked windshield used to be. Strangely, it had a teacup where a kneecap should be.

"All my stars and little planets!" shouted a triumphant voice, "We're alive!"

Mark lost his breath again. Not because of fists or broken wings. No, no. Because stepping out of the smoldering wreckage was a tall old gentleman with a gigantic grin parting his square salt-and-pepper beard. He wore the most curious of uniforms: a well-tailored navy blue blazer adorned with swirling silver galaxies – glinting even in the fading sunlight. And, as Mark couldn't help but stare … the man had a teacup – a flowery teacup on his robotic right leg.

"Lloyd!" shouted the jovial gentleman into the craft. "Lloyd get your rusted rump out here and LOOK AT THIS!" He spread his arms wide, clearly delighted about how well he had crashed. "Like a glove!" He then pointed at the bewildered boy whose jaw had just dropped. "And look! There's Mark!"

Mark struggled to stand as the old gentleman strode up with his leg whirring and clacking and steam hissing out that flowery teacup.

"Captain Stanislaw Zumski," he said, introducing himself with a firm hand. "I'm here to recruit you."

Mark's right eyebrow bounced off his shaggy brown hair. "Recruit?" he repeated.

"Yes. Recruit. To SPIFF."

"SPIFF?" Mark repeated again, starting to sound like a dumb parrot.

"S-P-I-F-F," the captain spelled out, "Is the School for Paragon Individuals in Trans-stellar Neomechanics, Intersolar Starfighter Tactics, and Pan-Galactic Fleet Command."

"That," stammered Mark as he regained his brain. "Those words don't even match the letters." He stared at the chuckling captain. "And . . . and they don't even make any sense!"

"Not much in life does make sense, ace, if you think about it long enough," said Zumski with a twinkle in his eye.

"But why me?!"

"Ah," replied the captain, plugging his ears. "I'd plug your ears this time."

Mark stared at him in complete bewilderment. But then he heard it. The same dull roar. The same sound of fast approaching disaster. His eyes flickered to the darkening sky again. Again he saw a frightening sight. But this time there was not one blazing inferno of wreckage hurling out of the heavens -- but three. He quickly covered his ears.

THUMP. THUMP. THUMP.

He lost balance from how hard the ground shook.

Captain Zumski unplugged his ears. "I was flying on over to recruit you today – having just washed my favorite old starfighter, I might add – when, phasing out of cloak just above your planet's stratosphere, were these three megalomaniac meteorites! And they attacked me!"

Mark gaped at the three bent piles of burning wreckage. These were not planes. No. Not even fighter jets. Their metal was black. Their shapes were twisted and sinister. The flames licking their melting sides flickered across wicked red lettering in a sharp, dreadful language Mark could not read – a language that, he thought, no human could read. The ships, they looked … they looked … evil.

Mark gulped, paralyzed by the news. "Why?" he croaked.

Captain Zumski's locked his wise old wrinkled brown eyes onto the boy's frightened blue-green ones: "They are hunting you." He clapped Mark on the shoulder. "So -- better get you to SPIFF, on the double!"

Mark gulped again.

Zumski's right leg hissed and clacked up a storm as he marched back to the steaming starfighter. "Lloyd get out here!" he commanded.

"Never!" squeaked a robotic voice from inside.

"OUT!"

Lloyd scrambled up from the wreckage and gave Mark a strong, suspicious gaze. "But what if he's contagious?"

"Not of anything you would get," Zumski chuckled affectionately, "you paranoid bag of bolts."

Shock and surprise hit Mark so hard that he stumbled back. His foot caught on that same blasted tree root again and sent his butt plopping in the dirt. He goggled at Lloyd. There stood a real android! Funny cylindrical head, colorful metal parts, and big lenses for eyes!

Lloyd shuffled over and Captain Zumski said, "Teleport us out of here, old buddy. Somewhere with a ticket off this rock. Oh! And with good food! That crash worked up my appetite."

Before Mark knew what was going on Lloyd had pressed a few buttons on his left arm, grabbed Zumski's hand, cautiously gripped Mark's left shoe and …

POP.

Time and space stood still. No, Time and space blazed forward. No, no. No, no. Time seemed to be having tea while riding a roller coaster. Yes, that was it. Mark was having tea while riding a roller coaster. He flew on a digital roller coaster racing above the Pacific Ocean, then China, onwards across Asia towards Europe.

POP.

Mark blinked furiously as noonday sun blinded him. He found himself sitting under a completely different tree in a completely different part of the world, his butt buried in snow. An ice-cold breeze ruffled his sandy brown hair. He shivered. A cold noon day sun hung over a beautiful city. Glittering snow covered modern high-rises and ancient church steeples, as well as the bustling airport in front of them. "Where are we?"

"Warsaw, Poland," said Lloyd. "Your flight departs from Chopin airport."

"Alright, Lloyd," said Zumski happily, marching forward. "Fire up your UBF generator."

Mark sprang up to join him.

The short android pushed in front of Mark, gave him another

suspicious stare, and then began futzing with a small gold box attached to his chest. It was labeled: Uber Boring Field Generator. And just before the three of them joined chaotic crowds of heavily bundled up travelers wearing long grey winter coats, thick clomping boots, and serious woolen mittens— he finished programming what he thought would be a very boring disguise.

A pulse of static emitted from Lloyd. It rushed out in a wave to envelop himself, the captain, and the wide-eyed young traveler.

Now, any passerby would not give them a passing thought. This was simply because the three of them appeared incredibly boring: One boring grandfather hauling his boring grandson and equally boring granddaughter to some boring family reunion. Except they each wore incredibly loud Hawaiian t-shirts, flower necklaces, and, resting under each of their noses – a bushy moustache.

Zumski—his robotic left leg now disguised as a gnarled old tree stump—chuckled while curling his big fake moustache and walking through the entry doors to Chopin Airport.

"Captain," Mark asked while curiously poking Lloyd. "What is Lloyd? And how did we end up in Poland? And why are we wearing Hawaiian shirts and mustaches?"

"Invisibility is highly overrated, you see," the captain began while joining stressed-out people hurrying toward the security scanners. "If you're invisible, people will still bump into you. But Lloyd here is equipped with an Uber-Boring-Field generator. It's currently projecting a hologram over us. The hologram is something so ordinary, so very boring, that nobody gives us a second thought, just walks on by."

"But we're wearing mustaches – I'm only thirteen."

"Well, you see," whispered the Captain so the android wouldn't hear, "Lloyd has a few circuits missing.

"As for how we got here -- We arrived via Teleport," the captain continued explaining as they jostled through the crowd – many of whom were pointing and laughing. "And Lloyd . . . Lloyd is the most loyal android you'll ever meet. He may have a few circuits missing, but beyond his paranoia—"

"Buzz off!" Lloyd shouted at Mark, who had been poking him to make sure he was real.

"And beyond his occasionally foul mouth," Zumski added with a grin, "he's a rather swell chap.

"Now then," said Zumski as they strode into a bustling, shop-lined terminal, "Let's see about purchasing you a ticket off this beautiful rock." He steered them to a quirky little café called Cosmic Coffee. The café was full of tables in the shapes of solar systems.

Inside, sitting at the solar-system shaped tables, were the usual patrons: businesswomen on their business laptops, would-be poets scrawling in their hemp journals, and guys impatiently checking their watches – afraid they'd be stood up on their dates. And behind the counter stood the usual barista's: a young guy and girl wearing aprons over mocha colored shirts—except these two baristas were rather hipster-ish, what with the guy's big black framed glasses above his incredibly bushy beard and the girl's tattoos down her arms.

As Mark joined the captain at the counter, the girl with the tattoos (shimmering galaxies) bounced up with a friendly wave. "Czesc and welcome!"

"Hello … Yulia," Captain Zumski politely replied after glancing at her nametag.

"What will you have today?" she asked with a smile.

Captain Zumski grinned at Mark and clapped the boy on the back. Then he proceeded to order something that, if overheard by any Earther, would be promptly forgotten as just another mundane, everyday thing: "One half-caf espresso with a dollop of caramel."

The girl winked at Mark and said, "Coming right up."

Confusion and excitement welled up inside Mark as he stepped to the pickup side of the counter with the captain.

Zumski, clearly enjoying Mark's wonderment, explained the coffee. "Half-caf is someone under fifteen years of age. Espresso is the next flight out. And Caramel stands for Crescent City."

"Where's Crescent City?" asked Mark as the girl slid the steaming Cosmic Coffee cup over to him.

Stan's old eyes were a-twinkling. "In your solar system, surprisingly enough." He then stomped over on his oak peg leg to the Employee's Only door. Lloyd bounced after him, trying to act like a granddaughter but failing in the no-hairy-lip area.

Mark darted a glance at the barista girl, hoping she wasn't looking, just to be sure they would not be caught going through the Employee Only door. But she could see them full well. In fact, she smiled and waved and, as she waved, the shimmering galaxy on her right arm seemed to. . . spin.

"Alright, ace," said Stan as he stopped in front of the locked door. "Hold your cup high."

Mark raised the steaming cup of deliciousness.

Neon green lights lit up and began scanning the cup!

"Your flight departs in twenty minutes," said a polite voice.

The door unlocked with a loud click.

"Ready?" said Zumski.

All Mark's bottled up excitement, eagerness, and tension exploded in a big grin and he rushed forward to swing open the Employee Only door.

A momentary whiteness blinded him. Then sounds erupted all around: buzzing neon advertisements, bustling robotic footsteps, and busy travelers jabbering away to each other.

His eyes adjusted as the secret world exploded into view. It was filled with electric color and sound! From the vibrant white ceiling hung a hot red sign that read Interstellar Terminal 3.14. Below it, bright billboards floated around advertising men's laser shavers, aggressively bumping into any travel-worn, red-eyed, stubble-faced gentleman they could locate. Errand-fulfilling androids of all bazaar heights, fancy colors, and geometrics ran around.

Suddenly a stray piece of small luggage, frantically zipping around trying to find its owner like a lost puppy, leapt up into Mark's arms with enough happy force to bowl him over. Apparently it thought Mark was its owner and began licking Mark's face with its ID tag.

"Rover! Rover come back here!" shouted the real owner—a boy only a few years younger than Mark, but with the same shaggy brown hair.

Mark laughed as the bouncing luggage leapt off him and zipped back to the boy. He stood back up, scooping his now spilled Cosmic Coffee cup off the floor and stuffing it into his pocket. Everywhere his eager eyes darted he saw sleek suitcases and lumpy luggage floating behind their hurrying owners. The owners were people of all ages, ethnicities, and surprisingly normal tastes in clothing. Except for the hipsters. There were so many hipsters!

"Why are there so many hipsters?"

Zumski chuckled at the word. "Is that what Earthers are calling them?"

"Yeah," Mark nodded. "Bushy beards, porkpie hats, too tight jeans, headphones and curly moustaches. How come they know about all this?"

The old captain became quite serious. His voice lowered to a grim rumble. "Because our galaxy is on the brink of a third Galactic War," said the Captain. He swept his arm across the busy secret terminal. "The people you call hipsters are actually people from all over the galaxy. They have fled here to Earth – the last place in the whole galaxy that is still safe – because you don't know about us and our troubles. These are their attempts to blend in with you."

Mark's eyes widened as all the pieces fell into place. "These hipsters …

They're addicted to Apple products!"

"Steve Jobs is actually alive. He retired to Saturn. Bought a whole moon and is enjoying the views."

"That weird music ... Dubstep!"

"Lex Skrillian. Failed musician. Moved to your planet and calls himself Skrillex."

"Lady Gaga?"

"An entertainment android who escaped. Lovely voice."

"But," Mark stammered, reeling from the truth, "but the way they dress!" Losing his voice to shock, he mimed the traditional hipster's curly mustache, big spectacles, and silly scarf.

"Ah, I'm afraid that, on their way to Earth," the captain leaned in with a grim frown, "they read some tremendously out-of-date fashion magazines."

Mark laughed at the truth of it.

"Right," said Zumski, resting a hand on the boy's shoulder. "You need to get your SPIFF uniform. Lloyd will take you to Morgan Bartholomew's."

"What the GLITCH?!" shouted Lloyd in loud complaint.

"Uh!" shouted an uptight mother passing by. She covered her son's ears. "Such language!"

Lloyd ignored her. "Why am I taking him to that scary old man?!"

Captain Zumski clasped his hands behind his back and leaned down at Lloyd with a stern face.

"Alright, alright," grumbled the paranoid android.

"Good," concluded the captain. "And I'm off to feed my belly!" He marched off to find good eats. His robotic right leg was back to normal – meaning the flowery teacup was steaming again.

Mark glanced down. The Uber-Boring Field had faded when they walked in. Mark was back to his baggy shirt, dirty jeans, and worn-out sneakers.

"Uniform time," snapped Lloyd, and set off at a skittish pace through the crowds of color and sound.

Mark tried to keep up but there was just so much to see! Outside the terminal, just beyond the floor-to-ceiling windows, were the usual rows of normal Boeing 787 airplanes. But inside, inside the tall trapezoid terminal, stretching on and on, were shops selling the strangest stuff!

He ran past the restaurant Captain Zumski had strode into – a restaurant called Foodivore.

In Foodivore, clouds of cotton candy went floating around so kids could reach up to tug off sugary bites; parents didn't even care, too happy with the complementary mute-your-child-and/or-spouse buttons. Lining the front windows of Foodivore were stacks and stacks of lunch-boxes, their lids like TV screens, all scrolling the words, "Stuff your face from your very own Evil Bagel Box!"

Mark kept running after Lloyd. But suddenly he was stopped by the "must have" part of his brain. It stopped his feet outside the Square Store.

The Square Store had brilliant white walls and minimalist stands show-casing the latest glass Squares. Inside, hipsters of all ages checked out palm-sized squares of smooth glass, which were available in an assort-ment of wild colors. Two teenagers had one such Square. It was yellow. It projected, right in front of them in full 3D, an incredibly intense war game of Flarejet's soaring through space firing at each other.

Towards the back of the Square Store a tall geeky Tech Support Android explained in infinite politeness (half his hard drive being dedi-cated to the Retail Infinite Politeness Processor) that in order for the little elderly lady to use her Blu Square to call her granddaughter, she would first need to switch it on. Her nine year old granddaughter, meanwhile, ran around with a brand new Orange-S, misusing the mosquito-zapper to chase her younger brother. These Squares could be used for anything!

"Hey!" shouted Lloyd impatiently.

Mark had been drooling down the storefront windows for too long. He had to be pulled away by the android and dragged to the antique shop just across the terminal.

The antique shop was called Morgan Bartholomew's. Being completely opposite the Square Store, it was also completely different. Where the gadget-laden Square Store was bright, modern, and sexy, the antique shop was dim, old-fashioned, and decidedly less promiscuous. Nevertheless, for an Earther like Mark, it held a mysterious, dark, ancient appeal.

Burnished suits of heavy armor guarded the entrance -- armor made of titanium, woven with carbon fiber, and designed to deflect weapons Mark had never seen—until now. Cautiously walking in revealed rows of rifles with intricate carvings depicting fire fights on planets far beyond this solar system. All along the walls stood incredible beasts killed in the hunt, silently roaring as if still fighting for their lives. But for all this, no one shopped there. No one was inside.

"Where's Morgan Bartholomew?" Lloyd whispered, inching in behind Mark. "Where is that half-deaf, scar-faced, giant hunter?"

Silence as the boy and his panicky android crept in.

Then, as if from a mountain high above Mark's right shoulder, the rumbling words: "You must be Mark."

"Holy BEEP!" Lloyd shouted and promptly dove behind a suit of neosteel armor.

Mark's freckles faded to white as he slowly turned. His eyes climbed the mountain-sized man to a face like a weathered cliff. The man's chin jutted forward, his steep nose was broken half way up, and trapped below the broad brow were two of the most battle-scarred green eyes Mark had ever seen.

"Do not go to Crescent City."

The man's warning stumbled Mark into silence.

"Rip apart your ticket. Go home. Live out the remainder of your life in peace."

Mark blinked. Those dire rumblings shook fear into his heart. But then the defiance of youth blazed inside his chest. "I can't do that! The curiosity would kill me in days!"

"Look and see," rumbled Morgan Bartholomew, gripping Mark's shoulder with an iron hand. He turned the boy to face the crowded, bustling secret terminal. "Do you not see their fear?"

Mark looked at the life and laughter and said, "No."

"Look again," he rumbled, and his next words were like being let in on a secret. "See the dread in the businessman's eyes as he boards a ship that may crash and burn? See the children afraid to wander from their parents? See all the people who escaped to hide here on your planet?"

It was as if a pair of rose-tinted glasses had been lifted from Mark's eyes.

An eight-year-old boy's toy hovercar floated away, he did not chase after it, choosing to stick to his father. A traveling daughter stayed on her Square's hologram call to her mom until the very last minute before boarding – in case it was the last time. Everywhere Mark's eyes darted he saw anxiety, dread, and fear -- and he whispered, "Why is everyone so afraid?"

Morgan Bartholomew had already turned and strode back behind his cash register. Mark's question made him bow his head and rest his hands on the countertop. His hands bore old war wounds from long-forgotten battlefields fought on distant planets strewn with half-remembered skeletons. "The Daemon approaches. Half-human. Half-machine." Morgan's sunken eyes met Mark's. "The Daemon approaches … hunting … for you."

"Me?" Mark choked, suddenly remembering the three wicked ships with the inhuman lettering, probably still burning in the park half a world away. "Why are they hunting me?"

Another voice answered. A now familiar one. Wise and grandfatherly.

"Some mysteries ... can only be answered by living them."

Mark turned to see Captain Stanislaw Zumski strolling into the shop. He was swinging a leftovers box in his right hand and in his left he held something Mark could not quite see.

"Listen, ace," said the old captain with a kindness in the wrinkles of his brown eyes. "I will not tell you what to do." He put his leftovers box on the counter and reached over to Morgan, who handed him a burnt-orange, almost reddish colored uniform and cap that read SPIFF. "The choice is yours." He then held up the reddish SPIFF uniform in his right hand and, opening the palm of his left hand, revealed what he had just picked up from a local souvenir shop: a beautiful blue paperweight – of Earth. It even had a shiny sticker on it that read Made on Earth.

"I have shown you a glimpse of the truth today – the truth that Earth is not alone in our galaxy – but it is only a glimpse ... a small glimpse of what's really out there." He paused. "But this is your mystery. You must choose whether to live it – or not." Captain Zumski then held up the glimmering blue paperweight. "You can choose to stay here, at home, on your home planet, and we will do our best to protect you. You can choose to live a long and safe life -- staring up at the same stars, night after night, year after year." He then held up the mysterious SPIFF uniform and cap. "Or you can live your mystery – and change yours stars ... forever."

Colossal feelings spun inside the freckle-faced boy as his eyes darted between the paperweight of Earth and the reddish uniform: Adventure, mystery, danger, truth. He wiped his palms on his patched up jeans. He heart was drumming hard. The suspense was making his leg twitch so bad his teeth were rattling. He reached for the uniform, for adventure, for mystery, for danger and truth.

"Remember," warned Zumski, "The truth changes everything."

Mark's blue-green eyes, bright with curiosity and misadventure, locked onto the uniform. He took the cap and firmly jammed it on his shaggy brown head.

"It is decided then," said the old captain with a grin. "We set sail for the stars."

CHAPTER 2
THE TRUTH ABOUT EARTH

"Last call for passengers boarding flight for Crescent City! Last call!"

Mark quickly slung on his new uniform jacket. It was a simple jacket, burnt-orange in color and neatly pressed. It hummed and crawled with electricity. It then tightened, tailoring to his shoulders and waist. The coarse fabric felt rough and smelled like fresh laundry. At the top, a short collar ended in a single button. Two heavy zippers ran from his left shoulder diagonally down to his right hip. A round patch was sewn onto each of his shoulders. In the center of each patch, on a background of solid blue, was the symbol of a long steel wrench with riveted metal wings. Surrounding the flying wrench were the words SPIFF Support Crew.

The same flying wrench was emblazoned in the center of the cap on his shaggy head. The cap had a notched brim. It was slate grey with two orange stripes racing front to back like taillights from a getaway car. Mark liked the cap the best. He had a tingling suspicious that it might become his lucky cap.

"I'll see you on the starside, ace," said Captain Zumski, proudly clapping the boy on the shoulder.

Mark immediately stopped zipping up his jacket. "I'll be flying alone?!" He looked up at the captain, frightened. "I've never even BEEN on a plane!"

"Don't panic," chuckled Zumski. "Lloyd will be flying with you!"

"Fat chance in a clusterfunk!" shouted Lloyd.

An old grandpa nearby shook his holo-cane and hollered "Teach that android some manners!"

"On that tuna-can deathtrap?" Lloyd continued ranting. "Never!"

The old captain reassured the panicking android with a stern tone. "I will be flying security-escort in a new Gull-Wing starfighter right behind you."

"Last call!"

"Off you go now," said Zumski. "On the double."

Lloyd dashed away, grumbling up a storm. Mark stiffed his new jacket, flicked his new cap for luck, and ran after him. He dodged irate business people and jumped over hovering luggage and held the stitch starting in his left side.

"Last call!"

They reached the boarding tunnel and jogged to the open door of the Boeing 787 they would be flying on. A stewardess welcomed them with a friendly smile. "Seat?"

Mark frantically dug in his jean pocket and pulled out that crumpled Cosmic Coffee cup.

The nice lady took it, scanned it, and threw it away. She then asked them to follow her to their seats. Mark followed, but a distracting sense of adventure began welling up. He was flying for the first time! And he didn't know where Crescent City even was! That was the best part, really; made his heart start hammering all the harder!

They passed rows of passengers who knew where Crescent City was. Adrenaline junkies loudly debated the 'gnarliest' craters to catch 'massive gravity' on their skyboards; Honeymooners cooed at each other about their romantic hotel with the most 'dreamy' view of Earth; and kids jabbering away about hover-boating on Crater Lake while their mom stressed over scheduling and their dad sadly kissed his fat wallet goodbye.

The stewardess stopped at a middle row.

Lloyd immediately shouted "I'm not taking the window! No way!" and plopped his metal rump on the end isle – because the middle seat was taken.

So the stewardess smiled politely at Mark and showed him the window seat with an open palm. He smiled in polite thanks and looked at the seat. That's when his smile was crushed by instant fear. His palms started sweating, his throat clenched up, and his freckles burned orange on puffy red cheeks. The row had three seats. His seat was by the window, which was nice. But sitting in the middle row, right next to him, was the worst person he could ever be stuck with for an entire flight. Not a great big fat man reeking of garlic body odor, nor a frazzled mom exhaustedly ignoring her temper tantrum throwing toddler, not even a little old lady with too many stories about her diseases. No. He would be sitting next to—a girl. Even worse, she was—a cute girl.

Where Mark had freckles atop his nose, the girl had a pair of funky, horn-rimmed glasses. The colorful glasses made it look like she knew a lot of really big words or how to find a letter in the alphabet without singing the whole silly song—or both. Probably both. Her brown hair tumbled to her shoulders and the small nose on her cheerful oval face was perfect for scrunching up in anger while beating up a bully—with just her words.

Mark gulped.

The courteous stewardess scooted the nervous boy toward his seat. He mumbled apologies for knocking past her knees. The girl cheerfully said hi as he stumbled past her too. But instead of saying hi in the deep manly voice he hoped for, he squeaked.

Clearing his throat in the gruffest way possible, he sat down and instantly ignored her. Everything outside the window was fascinating, so fascinating, yes sir, nothing could be more fascinating. Granted, his window was right above the middle of the wing, which blocked a big part of his view, but the things he could see, well, they was simply fascinating.

The plane began to move. They were taxiing to the runway. They passed rows of waiting Boeing 787's. Long luggage trucks sped between them, helpfully dropping suitcases onto the snowy tarmac so that people would have something to complain about later. Small snow flurries swirled in the cold air outside. Inside, in the warm cabin, a robotic flight attendant was standing in front of aisles filled with conversation.

"Attention please," repeated the short, triangle shaped robot wearing a blue and white airlines uniform. "Attention!"

Not one of the two-hundred-twenty-eight people on board paid any attention. The plane was on the runway now, gathering speed.

"In the event of an emergency, the exits are there and there." The robot pointed to first class and to the very back. Everyone ignored him.

Mark jumped when two seatbelts automatically crisscrossed his chest and clicked tight. A dull thud rumbled his seat as the engines really fired up now. The snowy tarmac began rushing out from beneath the trembling wings. No turning back now.

"You know what?" said the exasperated robot as all the passengers fiddled with their Squares or chatted or started snoring. "If we crash, you're all dead. Yeah. That's right. It's space, people. The void. Nothingness until your eyes bug out!" He was evidently quite exasperated that no one was paying attention.

Mark, on the other hand, was going bankrupt from paying attention. His anxious eyes were bulging. His sweating hands were gripping the armrest. His teeth went chattering in his skull as the plane gathered speed. The gentle flurries of snow were now a horizontal blur outside the window.

"Oh, look," said the robot, "one of the engines fell off."

Mark nearly snapped his neck whipping for a look out the window. But the engine was still there, burning snow.

"No? Hhhmm." The robot's voice went monotone. "Oh no. All your luggage is on fire."

People instantly sat up straight and silent for that one.

"Good," said the triangular robot as everyone paid him the attention he wanted. "Your inflight movies are: Historic Disasters in Space and The Pilot's Dead. Have a great flight!"

Mark felt dizzy from panic. Hadn't Lloyd called this plane a tuna can deathtrap? Didn't Morgan Bartholomew warn him not to go to Crescent City?

It was too late. A high-pitched whir filled the cabin. Both thrusters spun up. They reached takeoff velocity. Thud. Deep roar. Liftoff.

Gravity punched Mark's stomach into his butt.

The whole plane tilted upwards.

Mark shut his eyes as blinding sunlight flooded the whole cabin.

Up, up, above the clouds and through the atmosphere they sped. Warsaw became a shimmering dot as all of Europe fell away beneath them. And Mark, gritting his teeth and squeezing his eyes, missed out on it all. That is, until the cute girl next to him sighed and whispered, "I wish that wing wasn't there."

His eyes flew open. She was looking out his window, which was fine, except she was also leaning right in front of him!

"Um, yeah," Mark stammered, pushing himself as far back into the seat as he could. "Stupid wing."

CHUNK.

His seat shuddered. It rumbled and shook as, to his jaw-dropping amazement, the entire wing began folding underneath the plane like a gigantic pair of scissors!

"Whhooooaaaa," they both breathed.

The plane became a sleek starship as the whole wide world went plummeting away beneath them like a blue marble tumbling down a dark well.

The starliner soon broke through the Earth's upper stratosphere. All the rumbling turbulence quit instantly. Silence filled the cabin as all two-hundred-twenty-eight souls soared into space.

Then everyone's small rectangular windows, up and down the entire starliner, all melted together. Each single window flowed like liquid into its neighbor, creating one long breathtaking panorama of deep space.

Stars. Everywhere. Each pinpoint glowing brighter than diamonds scattered in an endless pool of spilled ink.

Then Mark felt a strange sensation, right around in his stomach area. All that food in there felt like it was—floating!

"Whoa-hahaha!" he laughed as the girl's glasses floated off her nose.

"We're completely weightless!" she laughed, watching her glasses float.

"So if I," said Mark and spat in his hand. "Awesome!"

His spit became a floating blob.

"Eeewww!" she giggled, then poked it. It wobbled down. She poked it again. It wobbled sideways. She poked it again. It wobbled up.

For a solid minute the boy and girl from Earth kept poking that blob of spit back and forth between them, watching it wobble around, snickering like elementary school kids mixing all their leftover food together at the end of lunch.

And in that moment, the tension between them broke. After all, there's nothing like poking a ball of spit in zero gravity to bring two people together.

Mark smiled at the girl, held out his hand, and said the bravest thing he could think of. "Hi, my name's Mark."

Her cheerful face lit up. She shook Mark's hand. "My name's Ella," she said, and Mark noticed that his green-blue eyes were the exact reverse of hers, which were a thrilling blue-green.

"So," said Ella, pointing to Mark's burnt-orange uniform. "You're attending SPIFF?"

"Yes," Mark answered, and tried to add a personal tidbit for friendliness. "First time flying too."

"Mine too!" said Ella. "I'm attending Aventine Hill Academy."

"Oh," Mark replied. For some strange reason he felt disappointed that she wouldn't be going to the same school as him.

She seemed sad about that too – judging by the sudden moment of silence.

Mark found himself wondering how big this Crescent City was. Maybe they'd be close? Maybe she knew. "So where is Crescent City?"

Ella shrugged comically. "I dunno!"

Lloyd leaned over to the window and pointed somewhere up and into the inky void of space. Mark and Ella followed his outstretched hand.

Their eyes widened. Their breath caught. Their astonished faces filled with the pearly white of – the moon.

They both fell back into their seats numb from shock, and at the same time breathing out a startled "Whaaaat?"

Mark thought the starliner must be rocketing at outstanding speeds, because the moon was huge. It filled up the entire view just ahead. Craters could clearly be seen pockmarking its shimmering surface. Everything became bigger and bigger as they sped closer and closer.

"Crescent City is on the moon?" Ella finally exclaimed.

"Yeah, duh," said Lloyd as if everyone knew that. "It was built on the starside of the moon—the side that always faces the stars – and never faces Earth, obviously."

Sure enough, the starliner was flying straight for the moons shadowed dark side.

"Well no, sorry," Lloyd corrected himself, but only to sound smarter.

"Crescent City is on the very edge BETWEEN the starside and the Earth side, so that, on rare occasions, you can actually catch a glimpse of Earth."

"But how is a city on the m. . .?" said Mark, right before his breath caught. He knew. He never needed to ask. Wonder excited his beating heart. He knew the answer. Deep in his bones, he knew. And from the way Ella caught her breath at the same time as him, it appeared she also knew.

"I see the truth has FINALLY dawned on you both," said Lloyd with a gigantic roll of his lenses.

"Each time I looked up at the stars at night," whispered Ella.

"Every time I felt so small," whispered Mark.

And they both said at the same time: "our galaxy is filled with people."

Mark thumped back in his seat. The galaxy was filled with people. It was such an immense truth, so overwhelming, yet so simple. But how come no one on Earth knew about it?

"Here," said Lloyd, fiddling with the buttons on his left arm again. "A galaxy map for you two flathead Earthers."

Mark's eyes widened as a whole shimmering Milky Way galaxy appeared in front of them, rotating ever so slowly. He wanted to reach out and touch it. Ella actually did. She stuck a finger in the galactic core and commented how it felt 'ludicrously fuzzy.'

"Let's say our whole galaxy could fit on Earth," began Lloyd, using his UBF generator to make a pair of big, funky professor glasses pop up on his nose. "Tell me, on Earth, which cities have an incredible number of people?"

"Tokyo," answered Ella. "New York. Shanghai."

"Correct," Lloyd begrudgingly replied, having hoped to outsmart her. He then pointed to the center of the Milky Way. "Millions of the most populated solar systems thrive right there at the epicenter."

Mark's eyes struggled to open wider. Millions of solar systems? With billions of people? He couldn't imagine, just couldn't, the vastness and hugeness of it all.

Lloyd tugged on the floating galaxy, making the hologram rotate slightly faster. "Now you see the galactic arms that spiral off of the epicenter?"

Mark looked at the curved glowing arcs that spiraled out from the center. He cautiously moved his hand into the hologram. All the solar systems of stars trickled between his fingers like sand. If people lived there, it must be like living on the outskirts of a big city. "Suburbia?" he guessed.

"In a way, in a way," Lloyd replied. "Once you humans figured out how to travel and settle the stars, people moved out into all these galactic arms."

"Why does this place look so—evil?" asked Ella. Not wanting to touch that spot at the top right, she instead pointed to it. It seemed to blot out the light of the galaxy the way a menacing storm blots out the light of day.

Lloyd's glasses disappeared. His lenses grew big and frightened, dreading the answer he had to give. "That . . . is Dead Space."

A tremor of fright made Mark's heart beat faster. He could hear Ella's breath quicken.

Lloyd's lenses darkened as he stared at the bleak, burned region. "Dead Space is home to shadow corporations, rogue governments, and the galactic hub of the black market." His words were laced with revulsion. "The machines are there. The Daemon rules there, allowing the worst people to live . . . learning from them, studying them, transforming into them."

A dark thrill entranced Mark. These forbidden places incited dangerous adventure.

"Moving on," said Lloyd, gruffly going back to the lighter side of his lecture and plopping his glasses back on his nose. "Last question: what is the most unexplored jungle on Earth?"

"Hmmm . . . the Amazon Jungle?"

Lloyd pointed to a bright, stormy area spinning on the outskirts of the galaxy. It clung on to the very end of the longest arm. "There's your Amazon Jungle," he announced. "The Phoenix Massive."

Ella and Mark gaped at the little storm of swirling embers. A sense of wonder enthralled them, making them both reach out and poke it.

"It's one of the great Uncharted Areas," Lloyd continued. "Along with the Alpha Azimuth and the Typhoon Nebula. Except Phoenix Massive is the oldest Uncharted Area." His pointer finger and thumb separated over it, making the map zoom in. "Galactic humanity wasn't able to send voyagers to that area until several thousand years ago." He paused to look at them, his lenses actually twinkling in an about-to-reveal-a-big-secret way. "You know what the voyagers found?"

"What?" said Ella and Mark at the same time, both sitting at the edge of their seats.

"A long lost, primitive, uncivilized bunch of fellow humans living on a small blue planet—which they called Earth."

"Whaaaaaatttt?" Mark gasped. "Me? Everyone from Earth? Our whole planet is a long lost tribe in the Milky Way galaxy?"

"Yes."

This truth floored both young Earthers so much that they both fell back in their seats—again.

Earth was just a small blue planet lost in the jungle of the cosmos. Mind boggling.

"Why doesn't anyone on Earth know about all this?" Ella demanded, her eyebrows pressed together all serious like.

"Disease," shrugged Lloyd. "The Black Plague."

Mark recalled disturbing history lessons and frowned. "It killed millions of people."

Ella screwed up her face and stuck out her tongue in disgust. "After growing festering sick black boils full of puss on their skin."

Lloyd remained solemn. "And it was all started by a wandering galactic tourist with a really bad cough."

Mark gave a weak laugh. "What?"

"That is why no one on Earth knows about galactic humanity. And all galactic visitors to Earth must travel on these specially designed starliners." He opened his palm to the air. "Every air particle is purified. And anyone suffering from the slightest illness is removed before flight. Otherwise your whole civilization would end up like the Mayans or Aztecs. You remember?"

"Dead of disease," Mark solemnly answered.

The android bobbed his head. "Yes."

Mark's shoulders slumped. This was heavy. He looked out the window at all those stars out there, really looked at them this time. To think those stars had planets, planets with people—people like him.

His mind spun. Feelings of amazement and awe and adventure began warming his blood. Out there in the spilled ink of the universe the diamonds glowed with blue fire. He couldn't really understand all he'd learned yet, but he felt the truth of it, the truth of a galaxy filled with life.

"This is your pilot," announced a strong female voice. "We are beginning final approach to Crescent City."

Mark looked out the window in wonder. They were skimming over the shadowed craters of the moon! A bejeweled city glowed in the dark distance. He shivered from the thrill. And nothing bad had happened on this flight! Lloyd and Morgan Bartholomew were just paranoid.

"Local time is 2 A.M." said the lady pilot. On the back of the seat in front of Mark, a happily snoring Z appeared. "The weather is a warm, comfortable two hundred twenty degrees Calvin (on the Hobbes scale)."

The info floated in front of his nose. "We will soon be landing safe and sound. Thank you."

The announcement clicked off and Mark felt his stomach float up as the starliner slowed and descended. Earth was far behind them, the sun was too, as Crescent City rushed into view.

He glued his face to the panoramic window as neon lights exploded into sight like fireworks bedazzling the night. Crescent City really lived up to its name. It was built inside a very wide, very deep, very old crater. The mountainous ridges of the crater were tilted in a crescent shape, making the dazzling city lights look like bits of colorful candy spilling out of an overturned bowl.

As the starliner descended Crescent City really came into view. And the funny thing was, it didn't look strange. No big glass bubble dome, no floating pods, no stupid sci-fi stuff, just, you know, hovercars and junk. He honestly thought it looked like any normal city.

The crescent ridge was adorned in luxury homes. The mansions glaring down on a suburban jungle of apartment blocks, stretch malls, and grocery stores where the common pedestrian lived, worked, and complained about Mondays. A stressful commute through hovercar traffic on translucent flyways (highways for hovercars) towards the crater's center brought people to the crime-infested downtown, which positively bristled with skyscrapers. And in the center, filling the craters deepest point, was Crater Lake. Its calm, crystalline waters aglow in shimmering reflections of soaring skyscrapers, buzzing hovercar flyways, and the yellow underbellies of dark clouds.

Yes! Clouds! Mark didn't know how it could be possible, but clouds floated over the city! They were not contained by any dumb dome, since the starliner descended effortlessly through their billowing vapor. Then again, the clouds never left the crater either, just swirled around and rained, washing away the dirt and tarnish of the busy city, filtered in the lake, and evaporating to float again.

"Clouds!" shouted Ella at the same time as Mark.

"How is that possible?"

"Won't they float away?"

Lloyd shook his head at the dumbness of humans and offered a robust explanation using only one single word: "Science!"

Ella squinted at the android. "You say that like someone pointing to a car engine and yelling 'magic!'"

"Funny how those two words mean the same thing to you mouth-breathing bags of meat," said Lloyd with as much insult as possible. Then, "Debug my circuits! With how little you two know about galactic humanity – I hope the Daemon never …." He trailed off, lenses going wide in terror as he stared out the window. "Never …" The city lights below shone across his face like a dim flashlight during a ghost story. "Oh no."

"What is it?" Mark demanded. Was he trying to freak them out or something?

But then Ella turned to stare out the window – and her blue-green eyes behind her glasses filled with horror too.

Mark whirled around in his seat. Panic paralyzed him. He had seconds to fill his lungs with as much oxygen as possible.

A small ship was blazing on a collision course straight for them.

The Daemon had sent a suicide mission to kill one kid out of two-hundred-twenty-eight souls.

CHAPTER 3
ESCAPE POD WD-40

Instinct took over. Mark gripped Ella's hand. Or she gripped his. It was difficult to tell. Neither could look away.

In an instant the suicidal ship slammed into their starliner, ripping into its roof. Mark watched in horror as the ceiling crumpled like paper. Shards of burning metal scattered into the sky.

For a silent moment, both ships tumbled together, the suicidal ship's ripped open belly stuck atop the starliner's gashed ceiling. Their engines flickered red flame against the brilliant backdrop of Crescent City.

Then the ships separated in a grinding shower of hot steel embers.

As the two ships fell apart, the ceiling opened onto the dark sky, unleashing a tremendous roar of air. All the oxygen in the cabin rushed into the atmosphere, ripping people's screams from their throats. Hurricane winds tore out luggage, empty seats, and other debris, littering the yellow clouds.

The honeymooners desperately held onto each other. The adrenaline junkies begged to go back home.

The roaring wind made Mark's eyes water as he desperately gulped air.

The scissor wings beneath him began bending upwards. Metal screeches drowned people's screams. Tremendous forces kept bending and bending the wings. With a rattling snap one of the wings broke and spun off. Its single engine trailed dark smoke as it spun wildly away.

"No! No! No!" screamed Lloyd. "Help!"

Lloyd was being torn from his seat, feet first. His flailing legs were high in the thundering air; his slippery robotic hands gripped his straining seatbelt; and his round lenses pleaded for help.

Mark and Ella instantly threw out their hands. They frantically grasped the terrified androids red metal chest, yellow joints, anything, everything. It was not enough.

With a gut-wrenching robotic scream he slipped away. The whirlwinds pulled his body out the gashed ceiling like a ragdoll.

Tumbling, turning, crying aloud the android fell through the darkness. Hot pieces of bent metal fell around him, scorching and scratching him. Thick exhaust choked him. City lights blazed all around; one last brilliant show of life before he closed his lenses on the hard ground.

But then something miraculous happened.

Captain Zumski came to the rescue! The old captain had been flying behind them in a gull-wing starfighter. He now raced in for the rescue. Dipping his gull-wing into a steep dive, he activated the starfighter's emergency teleporter.

POP.

The panicking android appeared in the starfighter, sitting in the emergency seat right behind the captain.

"Had a fun trip?" asked Captain Zumski with a wry smile.

"BEEP, BEEP, BEEP BEEP BEEEEEEEEEEEEEEEP!" Went Lloyd.

Captain Zumski censored him by sending his gull-wing back into the roaring inferno.

A red metal storm of jagged scraps enveloped them. Sharp pieces smashed against their hull. Chunks of broken plastic bashed against their windows, leaving long scratches. Crescent City so far below spun in a dizzy blur of green, blue, and yellow.

Zumski's fingers danced over glowing controls. The starfighter lurched around flaming debris. It arced above burning wreckage. It twisted to avoid fiery remains. "Listen," he said to Lloyd, who was screaming in panic at the top of his robotic voice. "LISTEN." Lloyd kept screaming. "MUTE!"

Lloyd's mouth was still wider than his eyes, but the sound was gone.

"I'm teleporting you to the spaceport. Women and children will follow. Help take care of them. Understand?"

Lloyd nodded vigorously.

"Good."

"I told you it was a tuna-can deathtrap!" Lloyd shouted as he popped away, teleporting straight to Emergency Arrivals at Crescent City Spaceport.

Zumski kept the rescue going. He raced alongside the tumbling starliner, ignoring the maelstrom of metal bashing the glass, ignoring the stench of burning plastics, his grimly focused eyes locked on the terrified passengers. One by one he teleported shocked mothers and crying babies into his gull-wing, then teleported them to the spaceport. Children of increasing age popped in before popping right back out. A mean-looking scoundrel of a man—pretending he was a child ready for rescue by sucking a stolen binky—teleported in; the captain cussed him out and promptly teleported him back onto the falling starliner.

Back on the plummeting starliner Mark looked up. "It's the captain!" He shouted in a swell of relief. They were safe! The captain was here and he'd save them.

Mark tried to tell this to Ella by vigorously pointing upwards and shouting through the hurricane. She did not hear a word. A bright white light shone all around her.

POP!

She was gone.

Mark held his lucky cap against the roaring mix of harsh rocket exhaust, swirling clouds, and people's screams of relief. The adults were being teleported to safety now. Honeymooners, adrenaline junkies, business people, they were all being zapped away to Zumski's ship and then to safety.

What about me? The sudden thought seized his heart. A cold sweat broke out on his forehead. Everyone was being taken to safety but him. White flashes filled the dark, devastated cabin as it spun and spun and spun.

His eyes darted to the window. He was corkscrewing down toward empty blue and orange flyways. Where was his rescue?! He didn't know what to do. He didn't know what to do. Everyone was gone. He was alone. They were all teleported away. He was alone. Did they do something to get teleported away? Press a button? Did he need to press a special teleportation button?

He felt the tail of the starliner shear off with an earsplitting screech. It flipped and slammed into Zumski's Gull-wing. Mark watched in horror as the captain careened out of control – and out of sight.

Mark was alone. He didn't know what to do. He didn't know what to do. Hold tight to the seatbelt? Jump out? Find a fluffy teddy bear and cry?

No. No time. The starliner's nose hit a flyway. Wrenching metal and snapping plastic. Glowing shards of translucent neon shattered into the pilot's cabin. Choking dust and burning rubber. Sharp flyway panels stabbed into seats, row after row after row, racing to Mark like a knife to the stomach. He gasped.

POP.

"Yes!" crowed Zumski. "Oh, hell yes!"

The old man whirled around in his seat to face Mark. "That's what Earther's say, am I correct?" He paused, eager to know. "When something goes very, very right? Hell yes?"

Mark, gulping air like a wide-eyed shipwreck survivor, only squeaked and nodded. But then the thought of Ella made him frantically yell, "Is she safe? IS ELLA SAFE?"

Captain Zumski wrenched his gull-wing upwards. Below them the starliner finished exploding into the top of the flyway. Flames roared upwards as a coal black gloom of shrapnel rained onto the neon streets below.

"Ella is safe, ace. She, along with every soul on board, is safe. I used this old bird's emergency teleporter to teleport them to Crescent City Spaceport. I nearly ran out of juice. That's why I saved you last." He careened around a skyscraper, still racing upwards. "I don't have power to teleport you to Emergency Arrivals. But if you need medical attention, I'll fly you there."

Mark thumped back in his seat and raised his jelly hand to wave Zumski's concern away. He gave a thumbs up and drawled, "I'm gooooood."

They shot past the last skyscraper and leveled out to fly steady. "That suicidal ship is gone," commented the Captain, eyes vigilantly scanning Crater Lake as they flew over its shadowed, calm waters, which reflected the Gull-wing's long streak of green exhaust. "It seemed to fall into the Seven Site." But after glancing at Mark's wheezing, flushed face, he changed course. "No. I'll fly you to SPIFF. You need to recover."

Mark felt his muscles dissolve in relief, and he slouched down the seat even further. He found his voice, though it squeaked more than usual. "What, exactly, the balls, exactly, just happened, exactly?"

Stan's anvil of a jaw clenched beneath his glacier beard. "The Daemon tried to assassinate you."

This made Mark angry. From his relaxed sprawl he flapped his arms, irritably shouting, "ASSASINATE? That's not how you assassinate someone! You don't go killing two hundred other people too!"

Zumski was facing forward, busy piloting him to SPIFF, so Mark did not see the shadows of dread darken his eyes. "The Daemon does not care who else is killed, or how many." The grim foreboding in his voice continued. "The Daemon hunts you with a powerful hunger … and we do not even know why …."

The boy's heart fired up with a blaze of anger at the senselessness of killing innocents. His open mouth was quickly shut, however, by the cold chill of frightful realization. Whoever this Daemon was, he was a true machine: ruthless, calculating, and would go to unforgivable lengths to kill him.

Slouched in his seat, chin to chest, freckly forehead wrinkled, Mark brooded. He brooded so hard he paid no attention to anything else. They had flown right over the glittering waters of Crater Lake, heading to SPIFF, and were now skimming high above empty suburban stretch malls and partially lit office buildings. But because Mark was not paying attention, he missed out on big billboards atop the stretch malls, advertising—in loud, 3D, eye-burning color—late night taco's loaded with chili 'hotter than the surface of Mars.' He also missed out aggressive 3D billboards just a few blocks later which advertised the most cutting-edge, comfortable, high-powered toilets.

"I'm sorry I cannot answer your questions, ace," said Captain Zumski after a while. "I suggest you put the matter away for now. You've certainly had a rough ride on a bad welcome wagon," he said with a chuckle. "Try to relax and enjoy the views before I drop you off at your new school."

Instead, Mark—his arms drooped over the armrests like the brooding slouch he was—brooded on, missing out, once again, on the views below.

The Gull-wing had tilted upwards to match the steep slope of the West Ridge as they closed in on SPIFF. They flew above quite luxury homes where hardworking parents peacefully slept, and above small midnight-shrouded parks where the rebellious teenagers of those industrious parents were making all sorts of mischief, like spray painting slides with the words: 'we don't need no education, all we need is swag.'

"Ah, now here's a sight you simply must sit up and see," said Zumski with pride, pointing down and out the window. "Our grand academy. Our illustrious institute. SPIFF!"

Mark shot up in his seat. The sight made his forehead clunk against the window. The vibrating glass shook his head, making his "whoooaaa," sound like he was breathing through a fan. His eyebrows rose as he opened his eyes wide to see absolutely everything. "My school is a gigantic old starship?!"

"Indeed it is!" Captain Stan rejoined. "The GSS Final Frontier!" he said with immense pride as they drew nearer. "It crashed into the top of the West Ridge more than a thousand years ago. That's why the front sticks out like that while the rest is buried in the crater—never made it all the way through."

Mark responded by hyperventilated. The GSS Final Frontier, with its broken front spearing out the side of the mountainous West Ridge, looked like a massive shark bursting out of an enormous wave with its jaws wide open. It was colossal. At least dozens of stories high and hundreds of feet long, the old starship dominated the West Ridge and the sleeping city below.

"Yes, SPIFF has taken residence for three hundred years now."

Mark could only respond by pointing at it and breathing heavy.

The galactic starships long, arcing top was covered in skylights in the shape of scales, from which brilliant shafts of light speared into the night. Tall glowing windows streamed from the top like waterfalls of vivid yellow and electric blue. The bright windows flowed down the ships coal-black military paint to the bottom of the starship, which jutted forward like the lower jaw of a great white shark. And much like a shark's jagged lower teeth, rows of triangular monuments rose from the curved entry, each monument commemorating famous fallen pilots and soldiers from across two dozen major galactic quadrants.

The curved entry opened up into the cavernous, hollowed interior, which further enhancing the starships resemblance to a massive sea predator. Students and visiting parents alike would sometimes shiver, seeing it as entering a looming leviathan's dark jaws. Within the enormous ship, heavy steel beams curved like the inside of a ribcage.

Mark, drooling, wondered all sorts of wondrous things: Were those really stacks and stacks of classrooms glowing like crystals along the curved ribs? Mmmm ribs, was that the cafeteria in the center— its two story window looking out onto the city? Most importantly: where was his room? Behind one of the long waterfall windows? Nah that'd be too tall. Maybe behind one of the dozens of small round windows along the top? Yeah, up there, so high up that he could throw a paper airplane out the window and watch it soar so far away the person who found it spoke a different language!

Mark, awed and slack jawed, whispered, "Be still my beating wumpus."

"Yes, yes, it's quite the sight," said Stan as they flew to the top of the GSS Final Frontier. "My office is at the front too. I can see all my favorite restaurants from up there."

The gull-wing's onboard computer interrupted them. "Prep for teleport to Escape Pod WD-40."

"Escape pod?" Mark said as they zoomed between shafts of light.

"WD-40 is your dorm room," Zumski said as he slowed to hover right over the area with the small round windows. "I suggest you memorize it."

"Alright, ace," Zumski continued with the warmth of a grandfather. "Rest, recover, get some shut eye. Lloyd will show you to breakfast bright and early at O' seven-hundred hours."

Mark nodded. "Okay, well thanks." He shook Zumski's firm. The bright light of teleportation began illuminating him as he faded out.

POP!

He fell into his new dorm room. A cylinder of light streamed in through a little round window. Above him he heard the Gull-wing's engine spin up, and through the window he saw it blaze away in a burst of speed, leaving a long green streak over the nocturnal city.

A dim glow began filling the room. And to his amazement he really would be living in an escape pod! The whole thing was a large sphere that could probably hold a small apartment bedroom. Being a sphere, the insides were all curved, making him wonder if this is what it'd be like to live inside a soccer ball or a washing machine. The white ceiling rounded to the right and became a curved wall holding a built-in bookcase; the arched shelves were perfectly empty, ready to display collected treasures. To his left the ceiling rounded into a wall from which bowed a desk, waiting for late night homework and the delicious crumbs of late night snacks. Just above the desk were two things: a messy panel of mysterious rubber buttons, flips, and important looking toggles; and next to it a screen that curved with the wall and displayed a scrolling list of welcome warnings (No panicking, No stressing out, No passing out).

Mark swiveled for a curious glance behind him. There was the Escape Pod door. It was one of those cool circle doors that spiraled open with a magnificent swoosh. The door's size made him happy too – because a kid could saunter right in with his hands in his pockets but any adult would need to duck to get through. Along the doorsill official blue lettering curved to read: Escape Pod WD-40. He committed it to memory.

Turning back around to the curved wall with the inset round window, he noticed a rather awesome thing. The comfortable little bed he'd be chasing dreams in was laid out right beneath the window! He could bunch up his pillow behind his head and lay there, imagining all sorts of wild escapades while drifting off to sweet slumber; like piloting a Gull-wing in the daredevil chase of that suicidal ship while zig-zagging between the sharp spires of shimmering skyscrapers; or saving that girl, Ella, and taking her out for frozen yogurt or something – but only with sprinkles! Or noshing on one of those cotton-candy clouds he saw floating through that Foodivore restaurant back at the secret terminal on Earth. Yeah, that'd be awesome! Suddenly, he thought he might be hungry. And sleepy. And if he went to sleep he could wake up for breakfast! A win-win.

So he shuffled over to the bookcase and patted his pockets to get rid of the gum wrappers and snack packs and anything else that might impede his dozy comfort. In surprise, he pulled out the small paperweight of Earth. Apparently Zumski had slipped it in the uniform pocket. The blue planet resting in his palm brought him home. But he was somewhere else now! And tomorrow would be the first day of this new school. And that meant meeting new people. It meant trying to make new friends. Who would want to be friends with a dumb Earther? Ella was in some school on the other side of the city. Would they think he was dumb? After all, he was from a long lost planet of backwater hicks—at least compared to everyone else in the galaxy. What if everyone sneered at him for being a savage? What if he spent the whole year alone?

But beyond the little round window was a new world. Crescent City. He could see it all. The downtown of soaring glass skyscrapers where street criminals rubbed shoulders with business criminals; the bustling Crescent City Spaceport where exhausted travelers from far-flung planets landed while fresh-faced passengers launched for strange solar systems, all while everyone's luggage was being lost; quite flyways went zig-zagging between everything, on which drove hovercars full of hungry college kids on the search for late-night fast-food joints. On the whole, it all made Mark feel a bit better.

He placed the paperweight of his home planet on the bookshelf. Crossing the room, he found a short red lever below the little round window. He pulled it. The window swung out.

A breeze gusted in, ruffling the shaggy hair sticking out below his lucky cap. The air felt hot and muggy. It was filled with strange thick fumes. He could smell the grime and dirt, and the metal and glass, and the gasoline and electricity of the neon city. He was someplace else, someplace far from home—someplace new. And that made all the difference.

He breathed in, filling his lungs with dense, sultry air.

"If this is where adventure lives . . . I'm home."

CHAPTER 4
S·P·I·F·F·

Mark's escape-pod-turned-dorm-room filled ever so slowly with the sweet aroma of French bread fresh from the oven and the gentle chirps and warbles of song birds. Not a single ray of light came in from the little round window, as the blanket of night still lay heavy on the neon city. At his bedside corner, a rectangular alarm clock busied itself trying to wake Mark up. The alarm clock, painted a hazardous yellow, displayed scrolling words: 7:30 A.M., French bread aroma & morning birds.

Mark snored through it all.

The alarm clock, with preprogrammed patience, increased the volume a gentle amount and puffed out a few more clouds of fresh baked delight. For some reason it felt compelled to wake up the target.

"Mmmmppfff." Mark's left hand waved around for a snooze button.

Instantly, small wheels sprang out the sides of the yellow box. It zipped away from Mark's lazy hand. This wouldn't do! The target had gone back to dreaming about things and not waking up. What's more, a bit of drool slid onto the pillow from the targets big snoring mouth. No, this most certainly would not do.

"Battle stations! Battle stations! All hands on deck!" boomed a five-star general with the voice of a field cannon.

Mark crashed out of bed. Frantically fighting through the mess of covers he dug out to see—nothing and nobody. After his wheezing lungs stopped burning and his vision cleared, his blood-shot eyes settled on the alarm clock. It was now displaying "7:38 A.M." and scrolling green words: "Get up, you gullible fool."

The red-eyed new recruit dove at it. The little yellow rectangle, quick as an RC-car, zoomed between Mark's bare feet and began racing around the tiny room with Mark in bleary, stumbling, hot pursuit.

SWOOSH.

The spiral door corkscrewed open.

"Don't touch anything!" screamed the paranoid bag of bolts that tumbled in.

Lloyd frantically grabbed Mark's shirt with one hand, his other hand holding a strange red box. "All these dorm rooms used to be escape pods!" He pointed to the control panel over the desk. "Do. Not. Fracking. Touch."

Mark, quite irritated, shouted, "I'm not touching any stupid panels!"

"GOOD!" Lloyd shouted back. "Because you'll launch yourself half way across the city!"

Mark stopped kicking away the blanket. His right eyebrow popped up in a most intrigued way. "Oh really?"

"Well no. But I worry—so much!"

Mark sighed in disappointment and began fumbling around getting ready.

At that moment a robotic sphere the size and color of a beach ball hovered in. It began beeping and zapping Lloyd with excited electric pops.

"Ow! Ow hey stop!" Lloyd yelped, swatting at the funny little bumblebot.

Mark stuffed his feet into his secondhand sneakers and watched in amusement.

Lloyd finally wrestled the excited bumblebot into the crook of his arm – and gave it a noogie. "I missed you too, buddy!"

Mark had slung on his SPIFF uniform but stopped zipping it up halfway. "Wait … you have a robot friend? A robot has a robot friend?"

"What of it?!" said Lloyd defensively. "His name's Floyd," he added. "And Floyd and I are chill. We're cucumbers. Yeah." He gave Floyd a noogie. Floyd zapped him.

Mark finished zipping up his uniform's diagonal zipper and jammed his lucky cap on his messy head. But below the cap his eyebrows were all scrunched up in worry. It didn't help that he noticed the paperweight of Earth. "Hey Lloyd," he began, staring at that piece of home and then at Lloyd and his buddy Floyd, "Do you think I'll make friends here?"

"Nope!" said Lloyd, pushing the troubled kid toward the door.

Mark had just enough time to pluck the paperweight off the shelf and drop it in his pocket.

SWOOSH.

"No seriously," said Mark, stumbling over his shoelaces out the door and into the narrow tube-shaped hallway. "What if everyone think I'm a dumb Earther who can't even tie his own laces?" He punctuated that point by promptly tripping over his laces and face-planting.

"Like that?" said Lloyd, happily making full use of his sarcasm processor.

Growling, Mark shot up from the steel grate floor. "I'm serious," he said, straightening his cap and worrying down the tubular corridor. "What if they think I'm a raging idiot?"

"Down you go," said Lloyd, stopping at a flat wall lined with holes like laundry chutes. Without waiting for an objection, Lloyd, shockingly strong for his thin frame, hoisted Mark by the scruff of his SPIFF jacket while Floyd pushed his shoes and they both threw him headfirst into the far right hole, which bore the label: Mess Hall.

Mark slid headfirst, screaming from the unexpected thrill of rocketing down a looping tube.

Several screams later and he shot out of the looping tube.

Soon after came Lloyd. "Oof! Ouch! Ow!" His body went clanging out of the chute like an armful of frying pans. He landed with an "Ouch!" His strange red box tumbled down to clonk him on the back of head, followed by Floyd, who zapped the box in revenge.

"I'm getting you to the Mess Hall and me and Floyd are HIDING," Lloyd grumbled, picking himself up along with the red box and starting down the hallway.

The hallway was tall, two or three stories tall, and shaped like a trapezoid—a triangle with its top cut off. The concrete floor was illumi-nated on each side by an orange glow. The glow faded up smooth white walls supporting a ceiling of massive industrial pipes. From the pipes, at regular intervals, hung three different types of banners. Each banner displayed a simple symbol on a background of solid color. One banner displayed a long steel wrench with riveted metal wings on a background of steadfast blue, just like the Support Crew badge on Mark's shoulder. Another banner held an aggressive black helmet on silk green; the third banner showed a silver galaxy on a white backdrop.

"Slow down," he said to Lloyd, and then pointed to the banners. "What are the groups? Do they hate Earthers? Do they think people from earth are dumb?"

Lloyd didn't answer, just shuffled the red box under his right arm and kept the brisk pace. Floyd happily bobbed behind them.

"What if," Mark continued with a laugh, trying to be humorous about his anxiety, "what if they call me Mark the Moron?"

"That's good. You should lead with that."

Mark's joking face fell. "I'm serious. I don't know what these people are like. I don't know what's 'cool.'" His eyes widened. "Do they even say 'cool?'" Panic hit. "Why don't they say 'cool?'" He would never fit in. "What do they say!" he demanded of Lloyd, throttling the androids scrawny neck. "WHAT DO THEY SAY?"

"Shut it!" Lloyd shouted. He slapped a hand over the boy's blabbering mouth and whispered, "calm your knobs, man. Just calm your knobs."

Mark pulled his wits together and let go of Lloyd's tin can neck.

"Here," said Lloyd, and shoved the red box into Mark's stomach. "Captain Zumski bought you your very own food factory."

Mark took the gift with a puzzled frown. Wonder dropped his jaw. It was one of those sleek cherry-red boxes he'd seen lining the windows of Foodivore at the secret terminal! It was the exact size and shape of an oldschool lunchbox. Its crimson screen was lit with blocky cyan letters that read: Welcome to SPIFF. "Whoa."

"It makes forty two hundred foods," said Lloyd without a shred of amazement. "Not that I care. I have no taste buds."

Mark marveled at the shiny object. He rotated the lunchbox over and over, happily lingering on the back, where a strawberry bagel wielding a pitchfork swished its comical devil tail. Above this sinister pastry was the lunchbox's label: Evil Bagel Box.

His stomach rumbled.

"There's the mess hall," said Lloyd, as Floyd helpfully pushed Mark toward the wide door. "Have fun. Floyd and me are hiding!"

The spacious door did not match the rest of the school's clean concrete and white walled corridors. For one thing, it looked like hundreds of green vegetables and multi-colored fruits had been piled together by a vegetarian artist obsessed with forcing people to eat healthy. For another thing, he didn't see any door handles.

Mark helplessly watched as Lloyd jogged away, darting paranoid glances every which way, his buddy Floyd zipping close behind.

He reluctantly turned to the cornucopia of vitamins and minerals, above which stood large block letters that read: Mess Hall. From inside floated the laughter and conversation of a buzzing cafeteria.

He apprehensively approached the door. Still not seeing any handles—and goaded by his hunger—he decided to push on a banana. His hand sunk through!

"Weeeeiirrrddd," he said, wiggling his fingers inside the holographic mound of fruit. It felt all squishy, like a smoothie. He took his right hand out. He put his left hand in. He took his left hand out. He put his right leg in and shook it all about.

"So awesome," he said gleefully. He proceeded to take his right leg out. He put his left leg in. He took his left leg out. He put his butt in, and shook it all about.

He laughed. A funny thought bubbled up in his brain. What if he put his face in the smoothie? He gulped down a big breath, closed his eyes, and put his whole face in.

"Um, hi?" said an amused girl's voice.

Mark's eyes snapped open. A blonde girl with a snicker on her lips stared at him from her jam-packed lunch table just steps away. Her giggling friends also stared him. In fact, the whole cafeteria of students stared at him.

He jerked back. Howls of laughter came from the door.

"Just walk through!" the girl called.

Mark started sweating. His feet were weighed down by concrete blocks of pure embarrassment shackled to leg irons wrought from awkwardness itself. Suddenly, he wanted to run away and eat lunch in a cave.

"It's okay!" she called, voice trickling into giggles. "You're butt's really cute!"

More rowdy laughter.

He lifted his lucky cap and shoved a hand into his tangled hair, leaving a sweaty cowlick. "Nope." He turned from the laughing doors. "Nope, nope, nope." He walked briskly away. "Lunch in a cave. That's the ticket. Lunch in a cave for the rest of the year. The Evil Bagel Box will sustain me. It will be my precious."

You're wimping out.

The thought made him stop. It spoke truth. "I can't go chickening away on the first day." Besides, his stomach felt emptier than the deep void of space. He heaved a sigh. Face the music—of laughter and pointing fingers.

He adjusted the food factory in the crook of his arm, squared his shoulders, flicked the brim of his lucky cap, and whipped back around toward the doors of social doom.

"Confidence!" he said, marching back. The fruits washed around him as he stepped through. Rolling laughter like peals of thunder filled his ears. But his chest was out and confident. He strode by the blonde girl and her table of joyfully teary-eyed friends, to whom he bobbed his head and politely said, "thank you."

He didn't know where he was going, but he acted like he knew. That was the key. Confidence. With enough confidence no one would question why he introduced himself to every student in school by wiggling his buttocks. He'd play it off as the way people on Earth greeted each other! Yes! Confidence!

He marched by circular table after circular table of students. Some were laughing in between bites of eggs sunny side up; others leaned in over crumb filled lunchboxes, darting suspicious glances at him and whispering: 'that's the kid from Earth.'

The cavernous cafeteria, with its high dome ceiling and vast circular floor and dozens of tables, felt cramped with the pressure of people's stares. He decided to go to the only empty area he could see: a round table under three long banners. The banners hung in front of a gigantic two story window. It looked out over the still night-shrouded city. Maybe there he'd escape the girls giggling about his butt. Confidence!

His quick, purposeful strides soon reached the circular table. The red lunchbox clunked as he tossed it on the tabletop. He flopped down in one of the curved white seats, his back to everyone. The dark window he faced reflected the laughing cafeteria. Embarrassment turned to anger. "Why do I always make such an idiot of myself?"

His stomach growled. "I heard you the first time," he growled back. He picked up his new lunchbox. That cartoonish red bagel stared back, its little horns steaming and spikey tail swishing around. Turning the box over, he tried to find a way to open it. No lid, no seam, nothing to give him a clue. The hunger made him quickly loose his patience. He tried prying it open. He then tried forcing it to open by hammering it against the table.

"Don't let Admiral Kine catch you denting the Mess Hall tables," said a good-humored voice behind him.

Mark swiveled and saw a boy his own age who, surprisingly, could only be described as sophisticated and quite businesslike. The kid had sandy blonde hair that curled above sharp, rectangular glasses resting on his long, smart nose. He wore the same SPIFF jacket as Mark, but the diagonal zippers were down, showing a professional blue tie that hung from the starched collar of his white button-up shirt.

"The name's Heathcliff Dodger Robinson," the business minded kid said, smoothly pulling up a curved white seat next to Mark. "People call me Heath." He even held out his hand.

"Mark," said the surprised new recruit, returning the handshake.

"From Earth, right?" Heath replied, as if he were a doctor called to a medical emergency. He briskly removed the brown satchel slung across his shoulder. "Damage control."

Mark watched with curious intrigue as the bespectacled boy rummaged around in his brown satchel.

"Every kid in school saw you shake your fanny pack. Now don't get me wrong, it was hilarious," he added, seeing Mark's freckles go from orange to red. "But you need damage control." He flung four packs of gum onto the table. "Razzleberry flavored poppers. They blow enormous bubbles which float up to the ceiling. One time a kid held on with his mouth and floated to his friend's house. A school favorite. Hand those out and you'll bribe your way to good buddies."

Mark couldn't help saying "wow," and turning the pink bubbly packaging over in his hand.

"Those are my last four. From my private reserve. Only ten Lunnans."

Mark sighed in disappointment. He pushed the packs back to the business kid. "I'm sorry, Heath. I don't have any—um—money—Lunnans."

"That a fact?" said Heath, sitting back in surprise. "Well then, I'm on to the next business venture." He started saddling up his satchel.

Mark's stomach growled a polite reminder. "Hey, er," he said as Heath stood to leave. "Quick question." He rattled the Evil Bagel Box. "How do I work this diabolical device?"

"I do apologize," Heath smoothly said with a straightening of his professional blue tie. "Information costs cash."

"Oh," said Mark, his heart sinking a bit inside. This was just like South Sydney Middle School. He'd never make friends. "Oh!" The thought of home instantly reminded him of that one thing. "What about this?" He shouted, tugging the paperweight of Earth from the depths of his jean pocket and holding it up in the palm of his hand.

"What is it?" said Heath, picking it up between two fingers like a perplexed and distrustful museum man.

"It's a paperweight," said Mark, pointing out what he thought was obvious.

Heath lifted his glasses and put them on his head so he could stare at the miniature globe with his bare eyes like some sort of scientist examining a fascinating new specimen. "A paper. . .weight?"

"Yeah, it holds down paper."

Heath stared at the word Mark just used. "Paper?"

It was Mark's turn to sit back in surprise. "Paper. You know. Chop a tree down, mash it into pulp, spit out paper."

"Why?"

"To write on!"

"Write?"

"Words!" said Mark, making loopy squiggles in the air with the invisible pencil in his hand.

"Oh!" Heath exclaimed in dawning realization. "Some primitive form of typing!"

"Yeeeaaahhh," Mark replied with squinted eyes.

"So this heavy little ball," said Heath, marveling at the little blue planet, "weighs down thin slices of dead trees?"

"Huh," said Mark, marveling at this fresh perspective. "I never thought of it that way . . ."

"I'll take it!" Heath happily shouted, as if he discovered some prized antique at an estate sale.

"All yours," said Mark, with a somewhat sad glance at the one last connection to home.

"My end of the bargain then." Swiftly sitting back down, Heath spun the Evil Bagel Box into his hands. He held his right thumb to the top right corner of the welcome screen and his left thumb to the bottom left corner. Welcome to SPIFF disappeared in a flash. It was replaced by a loading screen where the pitchfork wielding bagel danced salsa while wearing a chef's hat. After a moment the devilish bagel—which had begun break dancing and spinning on its head—blinked away, replaced by a menu screen. A list of foods began scrolling down the left, and on the right, pictures of the foods.

"Whoa," said Mark. He salivated at all the saucy spaghetti's and scrumptious sugar cookies and magical marmalades scrolling down the screen. His stomach grumbled in anticipation. But first he looked at Heath. "Thank you."

"Sure," said Heath, gawking at the hundreds of cupcakes flashing by.

"Bust out your box," Mark encouraged, attempting to make a friend. "We'll have a powwow."

Heath gave an embarrassed frown. "I don't have a lunchbox."

"I thought you made bank selling stuff?"

"I shouldn't spend the money." The embarrassment was making Heath so uncomfortable he stood to leave, giving the dark city outside a quick glance. "My mom needs it."

That was surprising. Mark has assumed this kid was just some huckster making money for a new pair of sneakers. He didn't know Heath enough to go asking personal questions, but he knew what an empty belly looked like – and Heath had one. "You want to share some food?" Mark asked with a rattle of the fantastic food maker.

Heath's hopeful eyes lit up behind his rectangular glasses. "Really?"

"Chow down." He slid the red tin box to the empty seat.

Heath didn't hesitate. He had a hungry, happy look about him.

Mark leaned over to see the menu, amazed at strange new foods like Saturn's Onion Rings and a spicy burger called Jupiter's Red Stomach Ache. He was starving to try them all, but being a kid away from strict dining room table rules for the first time there was one thing he wanted to try before any sensible, healthy foods. "Desert first!"

Heath pointed at him all serious-like. "Yes." And with a quick scroll to a picture of a fluffy cloud, Heath hit a big red button labeled Foodify.

The pitchfork bagel appeared onscreen and did three backflips while the red box rattled on the table. It beeped. The lid burst open. And as the two eager eaters began to drool, a puffy white cloud floated out. It looked just like the clouds of cotton candy Mark had seen floating between kid-packed tables at Foodivore!

Their hands shot up and tore great gooey clumps.

Both of their moods improved significantly – a natural side effect of stuffing ones face with bits of floating clouds. Mark even began looking around while scarfing down the cottony goodness, finally admiring the starry night still shrouding the neon city. That brought up a question.

"Hey, why is it still dark outside?"

Heath answered in between mouthfuls. "The way the moon orbits, we get two weeks of night and two weeks of day."

A grin lifted the bit of cotton candy stuck to Mark's upper lip. "Coooooool," he said, and then caught his breath. Did Heath say cool?

Heath grabbed another bite. "Yeah, it's pretty cool."

Mark breathed a sigh of relief. He kept munching and daydreaming about exploring the neon city in the afternoon…at night. But then the dark glass reflected the Mess Hall full of rowdy different-jacket wearing people. Another question surfaced.

"So," Mark began, licking his sticky fingers, "what's with those?"

Heath nodded upwards at the three long banners hanging above them. He then grabbed the last cotton puff and waved it at the leftmost banner, which displayed that winged wrench on Mark and Heath's shoulders. "You and me, we're part of the Support Crew. We're grunts, day laborers, mechanics. We wear the blue jackets." He shoved a finger at the right-most banner, the one blazing an aggressive black helmet on silk green. "The jerks in leather aviator jackets are FlareRiders in the Cadet Core. They pilot Flarejets during the annual War Game. We fix their Flarejets." The lunchbox puffed out a second cloud. Heath dug in while absently pointing to the long third banner in the middle, which showed a silver galaxy on a white backdrop. "The Commander's Club kids wear long navy coats. Strategy, tactics, War Game dev, that's their thing."

"Why am I in the Support Crew?" Mark asked, examining the flying wrench symbol on his jacket.

"Do you have tons of money?"

"No…"

"Then you can't buy a Flarejet and become a FlareRider now can you?" Heath pointed out. "Do you have rich and powerful parents?"

Mark frowned. "I don't have any parents."

"No Commander's Club for you then," said Heath – rather bitterly Mark noticed, wondering if the business kid had a suckish life too.

"It's messed up," said Heath, confirming Mark's suspicion. "They shove all us outcasts in the Support Crew. And the worst part is … even if someone is smart or good at something, if they have a robotic arm or leg – they STILL get put in the Support Crew." He pointed around the Mess Hall.

Mark looked around. There weren't many kids with a mechanical arm or hand or leg, but the ones who had them all wore Support Crew jackets.

"Nobody really likes them," said Heath with a shrug. "Everyone thinks that if you have a mechanical hand or – anything – that you're like a machine, your like the Dae—" he stopped himself with a shiver of fright. "You're like IT." Then he shrugged again. "But in the Support Crew, we look out for them. And they look out for us."

Mark felt dizzy, though he wasn't sure if that was from having his head craned upwards at the imposing banners or from all the new words. He wanted to ask what Flarejets were, and why a Flarejet pilot was called a FlareRider, and if the War Game was as awesome as it sounded. He wanted to know why everyone was so afraid of the Dae—of IT. But then something extremely shocking happened, sending him tumbling back-wards in his chair.

Ten miniature starfighters had blazed into the Mess Hall. No bigger than model airplanes, and painted just as poorly, the miniatures streaked in through the fruity door and got into a mid-air, guns blazing dogfight. A hot plasma bolt had missed its target and instead hit Heath's floating cotton candy, setting the whole sticky mess on fire.

"Eat it quick!" said Heath, tearing fluffs as the middle of the cloud melted into flaming goo, smelling of sweet burning vanilla, and dribbled onto the table top.

"Awesome," Mark whispered, sparkling eyes filled with the sight of ten model starfighters raging over everyone, their missed shots leaving little burns on walls or zapping unsuspecting kids, who jumped with yelps and threw leftovers in retaliation.

The starfighters blazing about reminded him. "Hey, so there was this massive plane crash yesterday and I'm wondering—"

"It's the only thing on the news," said Heath grimly, pointing to the video walls, which displayed shaky frightening footage, as if taken by a cellphone, of the two ships colliding in the sky. "Everyone's scared. The fact that so many people were nearly killed by the—," he grew angry trying to say it, "you know—," he gritted his teeth as if it were an evil word, "the Daemon." He cleared his throat. "And why – IT – would want to kill you." He stopped eating and gave Mark a thoughtful look. "Do YOU know why?"

Mark's eyes wandered the cafeteria. Quite a few other students seemed to be discussing the same thing – stealing wondering glances at him and even pointing him out to their friends. Their glances showed their curiosity – and their caution. "No," He confessed, feeling just as curious and frightened as them. "But I wish I knew."

A robotic voice crackled through the Mess Hall. "Classes begin in T-minus-five minutes."

Heath stood up and slung on his satchel.

Mark looked up hopefully.

"Come on," said Heath with a friendly wave. "Let's go to class."

The invitation extinguished Mark's questions about the – about IT – and all the haunting memories from the crash. He had been invited to his first day of classes by a potential friend.

Standing up and tucking the Evil Bagel Box under his arm, he silently thanked Captain Zumski. The captain must have understood that there's nothing as powerful as making friends over food. No matter how big the galaxy, no matter how many millions of planets with billions of people with different cultures, traditions, religions, prejudices and skin colors... food brought people together.

CHAPTER 5
ADMIRAL NONA KINE

Crowds of students talking and jostling each other squeezed through the hallways. Thankfully the topic of Mark's wiggling posterior was lessening in conversation. Instead, everyone was whispering about the starliner crash – and glancing at Mark. He heard his name several times – usually accompanied by: "why do you think IT wants to, you know, get him?", "What so special about him? He's just an Earther," and "Do you think we're safe? What if IT attacks our school?" Very few kids dared to whisper the word Daemon, and those who braved it were always shushed – and secretly admired.

The topic was so serious that no one looked up when Lloyd barreled down the corridor with Floyd, both chasing a miniature battleship, Lloyd shouting: "you'll pay you little glitch!" Though Mark did crack a smile; Lloyd's foul language had made a prissy girl in brunette pigtails gasp aloud.

His anxiety continued to fade as he rushed to his first class with Heath. SPIFF just had too many eye-stopping wonders that slowed him down. There were no staircases or elevators; people just stepped into up-arrowed tubes and hovered upwards or down-arrowed tubes and hovered down—though he did see a few bottlenecks where a tube would bend, jamming people up so that they shouted at each other to remove stinky feet from their faces.

Also, each and every door to a classroom was completely different – and based on the class subject. Supernova Studies had a door that kept exploding; Interplanetary Beast Biology was behind a door made of clawed and triple horned monsters all squished together uncomfortably; and when Mark found elbow room out of the shoving crowd, it turned out the only reason elbow room existed was because everyone was cramming away from a slimy door oozing mucus onto the floor. He had no idea what that class was about and, frankly, felt no desire to find out.

Mark liked the miniature starfighters the best. Heath told him they were originally kept in glass display cases. Then one day they escaped and set up bases in impossible-to-find places. Now they ripped around the school getting in miniature wars with each other. It was great fun to watch, until a misguided missile blasted your shirt right off, a rogue plasma bolt burned a hole in the seat of your trousers, or a whole battleship barreled past and clonked you upside the head. Mark soon learned the importance of ducking when, from behind, a stray laser beam zapped the back of his neck. It felt like a bee sting! He rubbed the welt furiously, changing his mind about just how awesome these miniatures were.

Eventually, Heath and Mark tumbled out of the teeming hallways and into their classes; And Mark quickly learned just how little he knew about pretty much everything.

Their first class was Jump Point Calculations 101. It was taught by Lieutenant Landeth. He was tall, imposing, had a thin scar down his left cheek – which made his scowl quite frightening. And he employed her scowl quite often, especially when Mark couldn't answer what a flarejet's max missile payload was, why a war game quadrant cannot be larger than five lightmeters, and how fast, exactly, did a Flarejet need to fly before hitting a jump point (the answer was eighty-eight lightmeters an hour – according to an advanced student named Marty)

There were only two people not furiously typing these facts onto their desks (each student's desktop glowed like a computer screen and could be written on): Mark, who was desperately slapping his desk in futile attempts to switch it on, and a girl named Lexie Haxler, who was using her desk as a footrest as she silently pulled out a yellow Square from her pocket, tapped it, and it digitized into an electrical yellow guitar – which she began sturmming.

Fortunately, Mark figured out how to login to the desktop (smash your face into it so it can scan your eyes) by the time Core Cosmic Languages rolled around. It was taught by an exquisitely erudite robot, tall and thin and made of quirky metal, who called him/her/itself Misses Dialect Organizing System – or MS. DOS for short. Prof DOS was not fluent in over six million languages—which depressed her mightily—but she was fluent in enough to tangle everyone's tongues. And as they practiced a bunch of nasal snuffs and throaty grunts and rolling R's, Lexie Haxler tossed her Support Crew jacket over her desk and tuned her electric guitar on it. She wore a violently pink band shirt listing the tour dates of the Demented Droids. Her whole left arm was also entirely robotic. People didn't talk to her.

After that was the most dangerous class of all time: Flux Fuels 102. The entire door bubbled in hazardous colors like some evil scientist's test tube. Walking through the witches brew prickled Mark's skin and left the stink of sulfur stuck in his shnozz. The arched walls were plastered with every warning label known to man: yellow triangles cautioning not to mix strange chemicals; red danger signs warning not to eat anything; curved black symbols of biohazards, radioactivity, and nine different ways to die from horrible explosions. And the professor—Miss Ethyl DuBoush—had ginger hair so frazzled it look as if she had just stepped out of some explosion—and was still sizzling.

Lexie Haxler didn't hide behind her yellow hair and play her guitar here, Professor DuBoush made sure of that. The Prof. had everyone mixing jet fuels behind their blast shields—jet fuels which she would test by pouring some in her red fuel-cell shaped flask and then drinking it. But the real reason Lexie was forced to pay attention came from a kid named Gustav Gouldfish. "Gus"—as everyone called him—kept pestering people to pay him Lunnans in exchange for eating random stuff.

Lexie paid him to sneak a sip out of Prof. DuBoush's flask. Gus's ginger hair poofed right out. When Miss DuBoush saw this happen to a fellow ginger, she immediately scolded Lexie, made Gus give back the money, and then she dripped some weird liquid on his head to regrow his hair thicker and redder than ever before—this saddened Gus considerably, who was now out of money and not bald anymore (he enjoyed looking like a bald action movie hero).

But the best class was the one right after lunch (during which Mark and Heath split a Toona Sandwich—which tasted like dry, bland chicken but each bite made everyone look like cartoon characters). The class was Flarejet Repair.

Mark followed Heath and a bunch of chatting fellow students through a door made of repair tools that smelled of engine grease. "Oh my munchkins," he whispered, spellbound. He tipped the brim of his cap up as they shuffled into a cavernous classroom so overwhelmingly vast, everyone's voices echoed.

Flarejet Repair was held in Hangar Bay 42. And Hangar 42 opened up to Crescent City. In the distance Crater Lake could be seen. Its dark waters reflected downtown skyscrapers and passenger-laden ships blasting off through the night—even though it was afternoon. Mark was still getting the hang of this two-weeks-of-day and two-weeks-of-night thing.

A thick breeze ruffled the coats of all fifty students. It was heavy with hovercar exhaust, warm rain, and the distant noise of downtown.

Then the classroom door dissipated. No one paid attention as Lloyd dashed in with Floyd, still yelling and chasing that miniature battleship like a crazed banshees. But everyone did pay attention to the woman who stepped in next.

She was not particularly tall, though she was quite round. But it was her arms which stole the show; They were not flesh and bone, but made of quiet, well-oiled gears and hydraulics, which no doubt helped her lift whole engines right out of hovercars!

"Don't stand around like a bunch of grease monkeys!" she hollered "To the center with ya!"

Everyone scuffled obediently towards the center.

"My name is Otto, Otto McMaluch!" She bellowed, passing them in great big strides and wearing a Support Crew uniform with the sleeves ripped off. "It's short for Othellina – which NO ONE is to call me! Ever!"

Mark gapped at her robotic arms: from fingers to shoulder, both arms were augmented pieces of machinery filled with cords of steel cables acting as muscles and thin power strands in place of veins. The hissing and clacking noises weren't loud at all, though in this echoing hangar of a classroom—where all the kids shuffled silently—the woman's machinery was everything.

"This is Flarejet Repair." She stopped at the ledge and surveyed her new recruits—ignoring Floyd, who zipped overhead zapping the battleship. "By years end ye'll learn that engines aren't chunks o' metal bolted, greased, an' rusted together, but ar' alive an' breathin beasts!" The gears in her right arm clicked and the hydraulics hissed as she swept it in a grand gesture to the pale sky. "And taday, my lill' meteorites, taday we crack open some flarejets!"

"Here they come!" cheered the blonde girl from breakfast who'd called Mark's butt cute. Her name was Alisha Bloomers, she had yawned so loudly during Core Cosmic Languages that Prof. DOS gave her five points for correctly pronouncing the Neptunish word for toilet, and then excused her to go to it.

Mark followed her eagerly pointing finger to the starry sky. There, skimming dark clouds in a V formation were three squads of five flarejets each. They were still specks racing up high, leaving bright streaks of varied colors in their wake, but Mark knew without a doubt these flarejets were the most fantastic thing yet.

The lead pilot at the front of the V formation dove toward them.

"That's Lance Blackwood leading Alpha Squad," squealed Gabrietta Gertrude, the prissy pigtailed brunette who had gasped in shock at Lloyd's language earlier in the hall.

Lance's flarejet came into view. Looking like a one-seat starfighter with short wings, it was chrome black, bristling with guns, and made of more aggressive angles than an exotic sports car. It was, quite simply, the most beautiful slice of machinery Mark had ever seen.

Allison gaped, Gabrietta gawked, Gus stopped asking for dares to eat his shoe, even Lexie brushed aside her yellow bangs to appreciate the sleek flarejet. Heath himself had both eyebrows tangled up in his curly hair. Everyone except Otto had stopped breathing to stare.

Lance's flarejet was incredible, no other word or feeling for it. It was built for a singular purpose: to win. Mark even whispered: "That thing flies like a bald eagle riding a snarling winged jaguar into battle against armored elephants." This made no sense, but felt accurate.

"Yeah," said a nerdy kid whose jaw had gone unhinged. "Lance is piloting a Blacknova A.X., a Blacknova—A.X."

Mark's hands itched with a new and sudden longing as the Blacknova banked a sharp right, did a barrel roll, and flew into the center of the classroom. Dust billowed while it landed – not far from him in fact. His imagination activated. He saw himself racing up and up and up, cutting cloud after cloud, chasing the stars. He saw himself flying with his squad mates, his friends; he saw himself—happy.

Mark's eyes snapped into focus, into determination, into purpose.

"I am going to fly that thing." He shuffled his grey and orange cap on his head. "I'm going to get in and I'm going to fly it."

Allison, who stood in front of Lexie, glanced past Lexie just to give Mark a quick up and down check. She then snorted and said "as if."

Mark, unexpectedly offended, stuck his tongue out at her.

Lance's three squad mates blazed in—each trying to hit Lloyd or Floyd for the fun of it. The first flarejet appeared to be a big box with smaller boxes stuck to it, like a semi-truck. The second flarejet was wide, low, and sharp like a luxury car. The last flarejet was as quick and precise as a finely tuned sports car, and covered in so much chrome that nobody could see inside.

All three circled around Lance's flarejet and landed facing him. Everyone around Mark ooo'd and ahh'd. The only person who wasn't impressed stood wearing a disapproving grimace.

"Galactic gits," Otto growled. Then, in bellowing command, "make room on deck! Foxtrot Squad needs room."

Everyone jogged back to the curved wall, except Lloyd, who was still protecting Floyd in the crook of his arm while using his other arm to make rude hand gestures at the vengeful battleship.

Foxtrot Squad flew in. There were no cheers for them. Their three flarejets were old and clunky.

"Hey." Mark nudged Heath. "What's with the two squads?"

"They fight in the Wargame."

"Sounds awesome! What is it?"

"A dumb competition," Heath snorted. "At the end of the year the Commander's Club sets up a battle above Crescent City. The FlareRiders from both squads in the Cadet Core dogfight it up with live ammo. You and me in the Support Crew fix up their busted flarejets for after's."

"That's intense!" said Mark, then the words 'live ammo' struck him. "Do people die though?"

"No. You go until your shields are blasted to ten percent." He frowned. "Though sometimes ejected pilots drift in space for a couple months. All alone. They're never the same after that. . ."

The pilots were climbing out of their flarejets now, their engines whirring down. The three Foxtrot members (a curly haired girl, a tall boy, and a silent kid in a full suit and helmet) were completely opposite to Lance's Alpha Squad. But they did have one thing in common: their Cadet Core jackets. Made from brown leather, they looked like modernized versions of those classic aviator jackets worn by daredevil pilots. Mark grinned, thinking he'd look quite snazzy all suited up.

A buzz of chatter broke out. Mark heard phrases float around he didn't quite understand: "This year's Wargame'll be intense," "Did you see the ion cannons on that Blacknova?" and "Lance is soooo cute, oh my god, I can't believe he's in your class, Gabby." That last one came from Allison again. Mark guessed she was not in Flarejet Repair to repair flarejets.

"Pull up yer earholes!" said Otto, hollering over the sounds of engines winding down. "Taday, ye'll be examinin' and getting' a closer look at these flarejets."

Allison tugged at her pink dress and turned to Gabrietta, "I'd like to examine and get a closer look at Lance."

Gabby giggled and whispered something saucy right back.

Mark and Heath shared a rather queasy look, holding their stomachs and sticking their tongues out in a gagging sort of way. Lexie's scowl was fit for scaring small children.

"At year's end ye'll face a hands-on test," McMaluch was saying.

Gabby pumped her penciled eyebrows at Allison. "I'd like to get my hands on Lance."

That was a bit too much. Mark and Heath gagged. Lexie took the next and shouted: "Shut your frakking cakeholes! You make me want to Q-tip my brain out!" She emphasized this by using her robotic left hand to make jabbing motions at her ear, and then pretended her brains were exploding.

Both girls harrumphed and crossed their arms.

Lloyd, who had an ear for such strings of beautiful bad words, paused his fight with the battleship to give Lexie a big thumbs-up.

Mark and Heath exchanged a discrete low-five. This Lexie Haxler was pretty awesome, they thought, as far as girl's go anyway.

"Gabby! Gabby!" Allison shrieked suddenly. "It's Lance. There he is!"

Yup, there he was, making an incredibly pompous entrance, what with his Blacknova hissing as its canopy lifted off, and the shimmering fumes rising from the hot fuselage, and Lance stepping out to thunderous applause

He could have won a 'young superman' look-alike contest any day of the week. Black hair, blue eyes, and a smile so pearly white Mark wondered if the kid did not brush his teeth so much as spray-paint them every morning. He waved to all his admiring fans and flashed his white chompers. Hopping down, he then sauntered over to Mark for some reason,

"So what do you think, Mark?" said Lance in a rather smug tone. He thumbed back toward the polished engine of his flarejet. "Single cell Blacknova drive core into an Asymmetrical Xenon thruster." He continued doing what was clearly his favorite thing: listing, one by one, the cutting-edge technology in his flarejet. "A Graybox V.I. with a voice activated interface. Cold Plasma cannons—two on each wing. Thermix missiles stacked. Real-time adaptive cloak technology. And," he pointed both fingers at Mark, clearly getting to the best part, "I want YOU to be my mechanic."

The classroom fell silent. Mark looked around, confused. Apparently being Lance's mechanic was an honor of some sort? Several of the guys were looking at him rather jealously. Allison was pouting and Gabby was giving him a death glare potent enough to kill a small rat.

"Yeeaaahhh," said Mark, "but I don't want to fix it … I want to fly it."

A roar of laughter. It echoed in the cavernous classroom. Except for Heath and Lexie (And Otto, who was bellowing curses at Lloyd to catch Floyd and get out of the classroom), everyone was enjoying themselves a good laugh.

"You're a Support Crew grunt!" Lance laughed in his face. "I mean yeah, sure, the Dae—" he stopped himself with a shiver of fright. "IT wants to kill you. So you must be useful somehow." He flashed his winning smile and slapped Mark on the back. "Be my mechanic. Fetch my stuff, get me some snackadge when I'm hungry, do my homework, and in exchange --" his swept his hands in a grand gesture showcasing his Alpha Squad, "you get to run with my crew!"

"I think I can choose my own crew, thanks," said Mark, stepping back over to Heath – which made the kid grin.

"Listen little buddy," said Lance, putting on a fake sympathetic sad face for Mark and resting a pitying hand on his shoulder. "You're an Earther. An orphan. The only place you belong is the Support Crew. You will NEVER change your stars. So choose your friends wisely. And be happy you're not an ugly half-human like your friend," he said, pointing to Lexie and her robotic arm. "Otherwise I'd never choose you."

Dead silence.

Heath squared up to the taller superman-faced boy. "What did you call her?"

Lance leaned in with a snear. "Half-human."

Mark squared up next to Heath. A bare knuckled brawl was brewing.

But then Lexie interrupted them all by marching up to Lance and shoving him. "They're NOT my friends!" she stormed, shoving a robotic finger at Mark and Heath. She then turned on them, shoving them too with her mechanical left arm. "You think just because you've got all your arms and legs you can stand up for me?! A dweeb in glasses and a caveman from Earth?! I don't need you! I can fight my own battles!"

Mark and Heath, stunned into silence, watched with mouths agape as the girl they were trying to protect stomped off, fuming about 'boys being chauvinistic pigs.' Neither of them knew what 'chauvinistic' meant, but they guessed it wasn't very flattering.

Lance, meanwhile, had burst into laughter. He pretended to wipe a joyful tear from his eye. "See?" he said to Mark, "do yourself a favor and be my mechanic."

Mark scoffed. "I'd rather choke on a screwdriver – sideways."

Lance glared at him. "Don't make me your enemy, MARK." He then sauntered off to Allison and Gabby, who immediately brightened up.

After a moment, Heath piped up with a troublemaking grin and a rather brilliant suggestion. "Want to take his Blacknova for a spin?"

"Yeah!"

Looking over their shoulders the two pranksters race-walked their way over to the dark, sleek beast of a Flarejet. Heath boosted him up and Mark tumbled into the single, racecar-yellow bucket seat in the center.

"Have fun," said Heath with a grin. "Take it through a bad carwash!"

Mark gave him the highest of thumbs up. A hiss and click sounded as the canopy lifted an inch and slid backwards. The racing seat molded itself to match the curve of his spine. He reached out to the control panel. Glowing yellow symbols phased in. They floated half an inch above the curved black controls. His heart began to drum. He wiggled his butt into the chair. "Now how do I get this baby to START?"

The Blacknova heard him. A Heads-Up-Display blinked on. Small red info boxes popped up above each of the flarejets on the hangar floor. They listed each flarejet's weapons, shields, and combat info.

"Please input flight point," said a calm, pleasantly computerized female voice.

"Warp speed!" said Mark with glee.

"Error 404: Warp Drive not found."

"Then rocket us out of here!"

"Compliance."

Mark heard no loud engine sound, felt no vibration, nothing but the hard fist of gravity socking him right in the stomach. The Blacknova launched out the GSS Final Frontier's hangar. He instantly left behind a surprised crowd of fellow Support Crew kids, older Cadet Core pilots, an Irish-curse spewing McMaluch, and Lance Blackwood—the fist-shaking, red-faced, jerk wing leader of Alpha Squad.

But Mark didn't pay much mind. The Blacknova was entirely voice controlled. Soaring ever higher into the night, he kept shouting, "barrel roll! Barrel roll! Baarrreelll Rooooooll!"

The black flarejet spun and spun and spun. It corkscrewed straight up through a cloud. His sloshing brain felt like it was in a washing machine and promptly signaled his gut to deliver a threat. "Urp—I'm having so much fun I think I'm going to hurl."

"Projectile vomiting not recommended."

"Only joking! Sort of—Now dive! Dive, dive, dive!"

"Compliance."

Leaving shredded clouds in his wake, he cut back down. Past SPIFF, past eight flyway lanes where he nearly collided into several hover-semi-truck-things -- he kept howling until he could see the roof tiles on a suburban home.

"Now climb! Climb! CLIMB!"

"Compliance."

The Blacknova responded by flipping 180 degrees in midair, burning so hard the exhaust charred a hole in the home's tiled roof, and rocketed back into the night, leaving the shocked burglar in the home's living room to drop the TV he was stealing and promptly wet his cargo pants.

Mark hooted and hollered as he shot to the stars. He felt more independent than the time he was home alone for a weekend; more grown-up than when he bought a video game with his own money; more alive even than the starliner crash. This was living!

The inky void of space loomed just beyond the clouds. He blasted vertically for it. To taste and touch those dark sky diamonds would be — would be — freedom.

"Return to SPIFF immediately," commanded a chilling digital voice over the intercom. Mark was enjoying the supersonic ride so much he didn't recognize the dangerous tone . . . or the voice. Instead, he happily shouted, "I don't know how!"

"I repeat," came the voice, darker and more robotic than before, "return now."

He was so close to touching space. "I'm telling you, man, I don't have the faintest!"

"This is Admiral Nona Kine."

His heart stopped. Admiral Kine. Heath had mentioned her. Something about her being strict and dangerous.

"Yes, sir," He replied, scared stiff. "I mean, ma'am!" He gulped. Then, to the Blacknova's digital lady, he whispered, "take us back, please."

"Compliance."

They flew back below the clouds. Why was Admiral Kine's voice so robotic? Mark wondered as he flew back to the belly of the shark. And what discipline would she inflict? Detention? Expulsion? Deportation back to Earth? He worried as he landed in the center where everyone angrily waited. Would she expel Heath too? If she did, he'd volunteer to get deported back home instead! He'd take the punishment! The canopy opened with a swoosh.

Mark jumped down, trying to be brave.

Everyone had encircled Mark like chattering hyenas. Allison and Gabby sneered at him while soothingly pawing each of Lance's shoulders. Lance's superman-blue eyes burned at his new arch rival, his fury held back by Otto's hand on his collar. McMaluch wore an irate grimace behind her hard eyes. Only Heath tried to show support -- by discreetly showing two thumbs-up. And Lloyd, well, Lloyd was naturally oblivious to it all, fiercely protecting Floyd by catching the battleship's missiles and flinging them back like a deranged monkey.

Admiral Kine's dangerous voice spoke low and close, "Explain yourself."

Mark slowly looked up. Past the Admiral's black leather boots, tall and sharp heeled, past her navy cloak cut dark and elegant with galactic symbols glowing on her lapels, to her face . . . which was not a face at all, but a mask . . . a phantom-white and hauntingly beautiful mask.

He choked on fear and stared.

Admiral Nona Kine's mask was intimidating in a cold, elegant way. It was cut only for the eyes, which were unlike any. Each pupil, each center, appeared cracked. Veins of darkness seeped from her pupils into her surrounding sky-blue irises.

But it was the mask's mouth he gaped at the most. It was composed of dark pixels. When the admiral spoke, two rows of light would move like a mouth. The white plastic mask could not show any emotion, neither could the digital mouth, but the eyes were embers in a black-smith's fire.

"Explain yourself," she repeated in that digital voice.

The boy from earth stood his ground. He glanced at Heath, trying to show with a slight shake of his head that he would take all the blame. Heath saw that and stepped forward to share in the punishment, but Mark beat him to it and said, voice full of determination, "I took Lance's Blacknova because I want to become a FlareRider."

Laughter echoed through the cave sized walls, growing louder as Cadet Core kids in the front passed on what he'd said to the Commander's Club kids in the back. Lance sneered along with his squad mates.

"You cannot," said Admiral Kine.

Embarrassment flushed Mark's cheeks, but he stood firm. "Why?" He demanded. "Because I'm poor and don't have any parents?"

"Because the Daemon is here."

A hush fell. People's ears rang, not from the silence, but from the last word. Even Lloyd sat still, his paranoid circuits so overloaded that Floyd easily slipped from his arm.

"The Daemon is here," repeated Admiral Kine, "in Crescent City. In our city." Her words sent shivers through everyone. "The Daemon is hunting. Hunting for this child here." Her accusing finger, directed at Mark, felt like a spear through his stomach.

No one moved. Fearful glances darted about the cavernous class-room. Hands gripped jean pockets, turning knuckles white. Only Floyd moved, streaking after the battleship in renewed chase, not sensing the danger.

Nona directed her glowing eyes at Mark. "You are confined to barracks. If you step foot outside school grounds you will be expelled, as will anyone involved."

Floyd caught up to the floating miniature battleship and began chasing it.

Admiral Kine straightened and turned to the silenced crowd. "Do not go out at night, any of you" she said. "Do not leave the safety of your school."

Floyd began zapping the battleship, making an annoying racket.

Nona reached into her coat and pulled out a black Square. She held it up in her left hand. It dissolved into black and gold crystals. The crystals slithered across the air and struck at Floyd.

"I will hunt the Daemon," continued Nona in the silence. Her lifted left hand became a fist – and as if on command the slithering gold and black crystals began crushing Floyd – crumpling the little bumblebot like a soda can. "And I will terminate the Daemon."

Floyd's crumpled body fell. It hit the metal floor with a dull thunk.

No one spoke.

Lloyd's big lens-like eyes went wide in horror. He scrambled over, sunk to his knobbly knees, and tried desperately to wake his friend up, whispering, "Floyd? Floyd, please wake up. Floyd?"

CHAPTER 6
THE BLACK PEARL BAZAAR

"Hey!" hissed Heath from across Mark's neglected jump point calculations, "The teacher'll see you!"

"Stuff a fig," Mark retorted. He had his eyes down while Lieutenant Landeth showed how to derive the square root or square boot or some math thing. He didn't pay mind, too focused on fixing the crumpled lump of metal in his lap.

"It's been a month you've been trying to fix Floyd," Heath continued. "Give it a rest."

"Never," Mark retorted, shoving a screwdriver into the dead bumblebot's wire filled innards. A small static pop zapped him. He yelped and sucked his finger. Must be a loose wire somewhere. Strange though – each time that static zap popped between his hand and the bumblebot, Floyd seemed to jerk back to life for a split second. But it hurt!

It was the same in Core Cosmic Languages.

"What kind of freaky voodoo dark-side powers did Nona use on this volleyball anyway?" Mark cursed, grumbling as he tried to bend a dent out of Floyd's metal shell – and avoid getting zapped again.

Gus popped up. "I'll tell you for a Lunnan!"

"No one knows for sure," said Heath, glaring Gus away for trying to extort money any which way.

"Welp! Whatever it is, it's messed up," Mark spat, not caring that MS. DOS was checking homework nearby. "It'd be one thing if she whipped out a gun and shot the annoying bugger. But this!" He rattled the metal sphere that used to be the Bullyboard. "Crumpling Floyd like a redneck crushing a beer can! It's cruel!"

"Patchooo!" went Ethan Sprig, a kid with horrendous allergies to pretty much everything.

"Correct!" chortled MS. DOS, happily awarding the startled boy ten whole points for correctly pronouncing the Saturnian word for 'nose-hair.'

Mark even continued tinkering in Ethyl's strictly controlled laboratory-slash-classroom, where Heath was trying to mix a very explosive fuel for extra credit.

"What's Admiral Nona Kine's story anyway?" said Mark, testing Floyd's weird purple fluids in a small beaker. "How can she turn a Square into digital crystals like that?"

"I'll tell you for a Lunnan!" said Gus, popping up so quickly Mark wondered if he had a personal teleporter.

Heath answered again, but with a grim tone. "Admiral Kine once commanded a whole fleet. She once sailed into Dead Space, armed to the teeth, ready to wage war against the Daemon."

"What happened?"

Heath looked away. "Her whole fleet was destroyed. Her whole crew, one by one, killed trying to protect her while she fought the Daemon. That mask she wears is the best way she can hide her battle scars. It's the only way she can go outside and actually be around people."

"Whoa," Mark breathed, letting his guard down enough for Gus to chug the beaker containing the rest of Floyd's weird purple fluids.

Gus hiccupped and pointed to Allison – who had bet him to do it. "You owe me fifty Lunnans!"

Mark dove across his desk to throttle the kid. This overturned Heath's cautiously mixed hazards. The explosives, being explosive, naturally had no choice but to explode.

Finally the last class came: Flarejet Repair.

The sun was inching into a violet sky outside the GSS Final Frontier. Sunrise took eight hours here. It was glorious.

Even more glorious were the Flarejet's doing barrel rolls in the painted heavens. They were testing the fixes and upgrades installed by Mark and everyone in the support crew.

But while the support crew students were happily chatting while packing up their tools, and the Commander's Club was discussing the upgrades, Mark, with grease stains streaking his grey jacket, stood gazing at the diving, flying flarejets of his dreams.

"One thing's clear," he said, eyes filled with longing, "I want to be a FlareRider."

Lexie was sitting nearby, cross-legged on her coat, using her robotic left hand to practice chords on her electric guitar. She wore a new band shirt: aggressive green with gold lettering -- The Cybernetic Symphony. "Do cavemen have the money to buy flarejet's?" she asked, quite sarcastically, since she already knew the answer.

Mark, still mesmerized by the beautiful way those flying devils cut clouds, replied with a heavy sigh and a heavier "nope."

"What if you built a flarejet?" Heath suggested without skipping a beat. "I know a guy. Might have parts." He stood nearby, busy selling an insta-clean cloth to a girl named Zaza, who always freaked out whenever her hands got dirty.

Mark was hit hard by the glorious idea of building his own beast of a flarejet. "Yes." He wheeled around at Heath and pointed a wrench at him. "YES."

Lexie's guitar made a strangled sound. "And who'll help that caveman build it? Otto?"

That fact quickly melted Mark's smile.

Zaza spoke up. "Professor Otto McMaluch doesn't like Mark. She says Mark is 'a marmy meteor out to get her metal butt fired.' She says so herself. A lot."

Mark shuffled his lucky cap on his unlucky head. Flarejets. He could build one. "It's high time I settled the bad blood between me and Miss McMaluch." Spurred on by the thought of building his dreams, he said to Heath, "Do you know where her office is?"

"'Course," said Heath, pocketing the five Lunnans Zaza hastily shoved at him before taking the cloths out of his hands. "But it's outside school grounds." He locked eyes with Mark. "And that means expulsion."

Mark thought for a minute. He adjusted his lucky cap. He thought some more. He took his cap off his shaggy brown head – and thought just a little harder. Then, while twirling the cap in his hand, a brilliant idea struck. He grinned, looking at the cap. "Not if we look incredibly boring."

And with that they snuck out of SPIFF, which wasn't terribly difficult. Mark walked right out looking like a short, pimply, pizza delivery boy (with a pirate eye patch) and Heath strutted out the front doors like the soccer-mom he was dressed up to be (except he had quite the scruffy red beard going on). Lloyd has been far too depressed to join them (Floyd's death had hit him rather hard), so he'd just given them the UBF and told them to 'buzz off.'

A solid hour's walk down the West Ridge brought them into the valley. On the way they sauntered past myriad fancy homes—one of which had plastic flamingos for lawn decorations (which flapping about and pooping little pink plastic pellets), past middle class suburbia where dozens of dogs were being walked by a robotic disc (in which Mark got his legs all tangled and then got nearly licked to death), until they arrived on Gadget Street.

There, on Gadget Street, was Otto's Garage. It was nestled between

Crazy Clarkson's Well-Loved Hovercars (A hologram advertised the short, spritely, used car salesmen crushing traffic in his "pre-loved" hover-truck), and Flux—a fuel station where the hoses acted like snakes. High above it all was the E-42, a busy four lane flyway, currently clogged with late afternoon traffic, from which cuss words and angry honking rained down.

Mark whistled as they approached Otto's shop. "Check it out. That car behind Otto's sign is cut in half."

Otto's shop was a two-story brick building with three garage doors. A large flat roof jutted out as if the place had once been a fuel station. Above the flat roof blinked a neon sign that read: Otto's Garage. Behind it, helping advertise the hovercar repair shop, was a classic hovercar—cut clean in half.

"Huh," said Heath, straightening his glasses to see it better, "who'd cut a sweet '67 Maverick in half just to stick it on a building?"

"Someone with serious anger issues," said Mark, nodding as if he knew.

They stood staring up at it for a few minutes.

"I bet it belonged to some guy who got on Otto's nerves a bunch," Heath added.

Mark gulped. He flicked the brim of his cap for luck—twice.

They approached the metal garage door on the far right. Rattling and clanking came from it, as if cars were being ripped apart inside.

Mark sucked in a deep breath and then pounded his fist against the metal.

A bolt grated open.

Chunk, chunk, chunk, chunk.

Mark's eyes followed the garage door as it rolled up to reveal the Irishwoman.

Standing from floor to doorsill, her red hair spotted with engine grease, big cheeks ruffling from deep breaths, the towering woman looked as if she'd just wrestled a massive engine block out of a truck with her bare hands.

She had.

Mark and Heath gaped at the X8 engine in Otto's right hand. Heath nudged Mark and pointed at it, as if to ask: think she'll crush you with it?

"Um, um, um," Mark stammered, looking everywhere but up into Otto's irritated scowl. But all he saw just made him panic more. A mechanic even larger than Otto, if that was possible, with hydraulic arms AND legs, was towing a truck into the large garage by himself. And on the right, a beautifully grease stained woman with arms covered in glowing tattoo's was cutting the top off a sports car using a single finger. The whole garage shimmered in fumes from chemicals evaporating off a concrete floor stained by neon fluids, some still leaking from hanging hovercar engines. He felt dizzy.

"I'm sorry about everything!" He blurted.

McMaluch scrutinized him from on high. "You?"

"Yes."

"Apologize?"

"Right."

She dropped the engine with a thud that shook everyone. "To me?"

Mark shrunk back with a nod.

McMaluch's fiery eyebrows mashed together as she took a heavy, threatening step forward. "After yer flarejet stunt nearly got me metal rump fired las month, ye want te apologize teh ME?"

"If you don't mind terribly," Mark squeaked.

Otto towered over the shrunken boy. Her volcanic face looked ready to burn up. And then she exploded. Grabbing Mark by the shoulders, she lifted the boy so high and fast his lucky cap fell off. And with a great bellow, she said, "Apology accepted, laddy!"

"What?" said Mark, feet dangling above a stunned Heath and Lexie. "Just like that?"

"Just like that!" roared Otto, sounding angry even when she wasn't angry. She set Mark down and waggled a finger at him. "Never underestimate the power of an apology, ya blistering little meteorite." Her hydraulic right hand telescoped to the ground and scooped the boy's cap. She plopped it onto the dazed kid's shaggy brown head. "Now what brings ya to me garage?"

Heath pushed Mark forward.

Mark craned his neck to see up past the brim of his cap and said the words he hoped would change his future. "I want to build a flarejet."

Otto's bushy ginger eyebrows scrunched together like roasted caterpillars. she examined Mark as if the kid was on drugs. "Ye chasin the comet, laddy?"

Mark shook his head.

Otto scrutinized the boy. "Hhhmmm -- follow me!" She strode into the deafening racket coming from her garage.

They followed, weaving their way around rivulets of unknown liquids that glowed as they dripped from hoisted engines.

Otto stopped next to the gigantic fellow who had hauled in an entire truck by himself. "This is Phil! He's me engine guy."

"Hello," rumbled Phil, his robotic hands busy being screwdrivers.

"Phil had both arms augmented into all the tools e'll ever need. Show 'em, Phil!"

The heavy, round-faced man proudly displayed both arms. Click, click, click, click went the tools in each arm as they rotated from hexheads to hammers and more. "This way—I never lose anything!" said Phil with a toothy grin.

Otto clapped Phil on the back and moved on to the back of the shop,where the tattooed woman (Her arms glowed with tattoos of racing hovercars) was using the fingers of her left hand to burn right through the sports coupe's cherry red top.

"We won't disturb Miranda," said Otto. "She mods our rides. Damn good driver too," Otto added with a firm nod.

They continued to the back of the shop where hovercar parts were stacked on labeled shelves. "Me office is upstairs! Mind the steps, the heights are all differen'."

Mark and Heath took the stairs with their heads down, trying not to trip. Otto opened the only door at the end of the stairs and they all walked in.

"Take yer boots up then!" She thumbed at a low sofa that looked as if it had been torn from the back of a hover-truck.

The trio huddled on the truck's backseat. Otto strolled to her desk, which was made of old engine parts fused together. In fact, Otto's entire office had an industrial, car-guts look about it. The only windows were two long ones in the wall behind her desk—the windows looked out onto the bustling garage below. And there were only three pieces of furniture, if they could be called furniture: the truck's backseat-turned-couch, the desk made of crank shafts and spark plugs, and in the center of the office: an eight cylinder engine block missing all eight of its pistons.

"Alrigh'," Otto began, "I'll brew a coupla mugs o' me finest Gear Grog." She grabbed three piston heads off her desk, "and you get te yappin' abou' this biltherin' nonsense o' tryin te change yer stars."

Mark, wondering what Gear Grog was, watched Otto walk to the engine in the center, casually lift the supercharger off, uncap it, and pour water from it into three of the engine's empty cylinders. "If you'd be willing to teach me, sir – I mean ma'am! -- I'd like to build my own flarejet."

"Orion's belt, laddy, the Wargame is at the end o' this year!" she said, opening the engine's alternator. She took a pinch of glowing pink leaves out and tossed them into the three water filled cylinders. "Ye'd need ter spend every day after school buildin' it jus' te get in!" She turned the ignition key. The engine fired up and began rumbling. "Everyday! Buildin', greasen', AN' doing yer homework not to mention!"

Mark sat up straight. "Ma'am Otto sir -- I'd spend every day scrubbing dried plums off elephant bums just to pilot a flarejet one more time."

Otto chuckled.

The engine ground to a stop.

"Then there's the Admiral ter consider," continued Otto. She held the three pistons upside down just under the cylinders. Steaming pink liquid filled each of them. "Nona'll need ter inspect yer flarejet." She handed a piston to them both and kept one. "And if Nona axes it—." She walked back to her desk and flopped in her metal chair. "All yer blood, sweat, and tears is nothin' but a steamin' sack o' dog business!"

"I'll risk it," said Mark, also chancing a cautious slurp of the mystical pink liquid. He licked his lips in delight.

"What's this Gear Grog drink thing taste like?" Heath whispered, reluctant to try anything boiled in an old engine.

"Sour," Mark whispered back. "Like that little tickling zap when you put your tongue on a nine-volt battery."

Heath took a tentative sip, loved it, and went on sipping.

They enjoyed their mugs of glowing pink Gear Grog brew for a few quiet moments.

"Aaahhh," McMaluch sighed, content in a curiously perturbed sort of way. She set her piston down on the desk. "O' course, all yer plans are worth not but Pluto's cratered backside without flarejet parts."

Heath, who had been shifting to find a comfortable spot on the metal couch, piped up. "I know a guy. Perfidious Funk. He runs the Black Pearl Bazaar in the Port District."

Otto frowned – A common site coming from a constantly angry

Irishwoman. "Perfidious Funk – watch yerself now – he'll try and sell ye the moon – and if ye don' buy nothin', he'll orbit ya like a moon around Uranus."

After gulping down their pistons full of that sweet/sour Gear Grog stuff, and waving their goodbye's, the duo set off on their quest. But as they drew nearer to Heath's 'one guy who sells everything,' their pace slowed down considerably.

After several blocks of increasingly dilapidated buildings, they entered a part of the city that could only be described as—suspicious. The Port District was not a tourist destination. Each building had at least one boarded up window; the dirty glass in the remaining windows reflected empty, hollow street lamps. Pubs and bars were not far apart, announced by the glare of harsh neon signs above doors from which sounds of rowdy laughter, beer bottles shattering, and angry words emerged. The air felt humid, burdened by hard labor and broken spirits.

"Where are we, exactly?" asked Mark, his sense of risky adventure tingling. "Someplace dangerous, huh?"

Heath chuckled and snugged up his tie, "not that dangerous to us locals."

"You live around here?!" Mark exclaimed.

"Yeah," Heath replied, reddening from embarrassment. "Down a few streets in that apartment block," he replied, pointing at a squat thirty story building made of dull concrete. "It's the only place mom could afford."

There was the business-minded boy's backstory again, making Mark lift a curious eyebrow, but frown too. It was still a bit awkward to pry. So he just looked at Heath's apartment block; it seemed a dismal place.

"Alright ladies and gentlemen," said Heath, "I present to you—the Black Pearl Bazaar."

They had stopped in front of a small brick and mortar store nestled between two other venerable establishments: O'Ryan's Pub and a pawn shop aptly named: Credits 4 Crap. The storefront had one dirty door to the left of one dirty rectangular window. Covering both was a tattered awning like a stripped umbrella. Above the awning in curvy letters blazed a purple neon sign: Black Pearl Bazaar.

"My flarejet parts are waiting inside," said Mark. "I can feel it!"

They walked in. The bazaar had the feeling of an Arabian desert. An intoxicating aroma lingered, musky and laden with exotic treasures from strange solar systems; the floor was sprinkled with grains of sand fallen from the shoes of cloaked travelers who walked in from dusty planets orbiting distant suns. Around them, shelves bent under piles of oddities that, seen close up, whispered of mysteries waiting to be unraveled.

And at the back of the bazaar, sitting in a corner next to flimsy broom, with her robotic fingers strumming her yellow six-string, was none other than – Lexie Haxler.

"What are you doing here?" Heath exclaimed, stopping so suddenly that Mark ran into him.

Lexie reacted with angry embarrassment. She jumped up as her guitar digitized into crystals and re-formed back into her yellow Square. "Nothing! Just browsing. It's all junk anyway. You won't find what you need here! I'll walk you back out the door."

Suddenly, somewhere behind the beaded curtain at the back of bazaar, a crash of things was followed by a loud: "don't listen to my daughter, honorable customer!"

The beaded curtain burst open with a clatter. A short man bustled in with a welcoming smile and opened arms. His eyes were mocha brown, just like his swarthy self. His clothes were billowing, puffy, and composed of every rich, bright color.

"Aaahhhh, salaam and good evening esteemed friends." He bowed with a flourish. "Welcome to my humble bazaar of the bizarre. I am

Perfidious Funk, purveyor of paradoxical presents most pleasant."

"It's okay!" Lexie said, in an embarrassed panic. "They stumbled into the wrong store!" she said, quickly walking Heath and Mark out until Perfidious sent one of his purple slippers sailing at her.

"You play guitar again, daughter?!" He scolded. "No more! Back to sweep! Back to sweep!" And with that he wrenched his daughter's yellow Square from her hands and prodded her back to the flimsy broom in the corner.

Mark and Heath watched in awkward silence as she quietly took it back up and started vigorously sweeping – her eyes down and hiding from them.

The swarthy shopkeeper whirled back around with a big, fake smile. "Many pardons, honorable customers! My daughter, haha, believes music will make moneys. Ah ha ha! No, no, no!" he chuckled and pointed a finger upwards as if to make a point. "Only good business make moneys!"

"Eerr," went Heath, eager to change the subject to something less awkward. "I heard about you from a friend. We need –"

"Sssshhhhh ush ush ush. I know," the mysterious little man said, ignoring Heath altogether and instead clasping Mark's face in his hands. "I know why you are here. What you seek—I have." He peered deeply into Mark's surprised eyes. "You are Mark. You come from Earth. You are hunted – by IT!"

Panic gripped Mark's stomach.

"IT hunts you. IT will not stop. IT will kill you!"

Mark tried to squirm out of the strange shopkeeper's hands.

"You must not let IT kill you!" shouted Perfidious Funk. He then jumped back and swirled his gold-fringed cloak. A huge poof of sparkly dust exploded from it. "BEHOLD! The Kamikaze 5000!"

Mark and Heath gawked at the gigantic plasma rifle the shopkeeper just busted out of his coat. The gun was bigger than him!

"How did you fit that in –?" said Mark. But then the gun broke in half and fell to the floor. Funk tossed it.

Another violent poof.

"BEHOLD!" shouted Funk, holding up a force-shield system in his left hand. "The Uranus Blocker B-1!" He tried to activate it. It zapped him, then exploded.

"No," Heath tried to interrupt, "we need –."

POOF!

"BEHOLD!" bellowed Funk, holding up a bulletproof vest – with big gapping bullet holes torn through it. "Slightly used! I give you good price!"

Heath tried to protest, tried to say they were there for Flarejet parts, but Funk kept on poofing. An invisibility cloak that cloaked your whole body – except your face; a missile launcher that never hit its target; grenades that might, without warning, randomly explode; a potato cooker that – um – er – nevermind! GOOD PRICE! MUST BUY NOW!

"Flarejet parts," Mark finally interrupted. "We need Flarejet parts!"

"You have lunnans?" Funk asked directly.

Heath slung his satchel forward. "I was hoping to trade." He began digging through it. "I have --."

"NO." Funk answered with a stiff tone and stiff arms as he began shoo-ing them back to the door. "Poor boys! Out! Out! My shop only for paying customers! Cash money! CASH MOOONEY!" And with that he tossed them back out onto the dirty street, slamming the door behind them – which jingled quite pleasantly.

Mark and Heath stood sharing rather dazed and blank looks. But then the feeling of failing began to sink in.

The sigh Mark heaved was heavy enough to slump his shoulders. "Well that puts a banana in the tailpipe, doesn't it?"

Heath frowned apologetically and stuffed his hands in his jean pockets. "I'm sorry, Mark. I heard this guy had connections to all the best Flarejet tech."

They began trudging down the gritty street, kicking tufts of ugly brown grass growing between the cracks, lost in the silence that comes from being defeated right at the start of what had promised to be a grand adventure.

But then …

"Hey wait up!"

They turned. Lexie was jogging to catch up. She still had that tattered old broom in her robotic left hand.

"I can get you Flarejet parts," she stated firmly – if a bit breathlessly.

Mark piped up instantly. "How?!"

"I know where," she paused, glancing back at the Black Pearl, "where my dad gets them from."

"Where?" said Heath, excitement bubbling up in his voice too.

Lexie paused for a moment as if she were about to tell them a secret. "There is a broken place. It was Crescent city's most guarded technology hub. Now it is Crescent city's most guarded wasteland." She paused as if she were telling a ghost story, letting her words wet their appetite for adventure. "Orion Industries made powerful engines there. Deep Intersolar Enterprises made powerful weapons. Shattered Sky Interspace had their headquarters there." She paused again, making sure their thirst was really boiling. "It is abandoned now. Fifty years. Quarantine. No person in. No person out. But," she cautiously looked back at the bazaar. "I know how to get you inside—inside the Seven Site."

The two friends exchanged excited glances. The dangers hadn't deterred them, only amped up the adventure. Silently, with short nods at each other, they decided to go.

"How do we get there?" whispered Mark.

"How do we get in?" whispered Heath.

"I'll tell you," said Lexie, leaning in. "But ONLY if I go with you."

"What?!" shouted Mark. "No! It's too dangerous!"

Lexie wacked him upside his shaggy brown head with her broom. "You think just because I don't have a real arm I can't handle myself?!"

"Look," said Heath, slinging his satchel around and digging in it, "I'll trade anything you want for your info. Razzleberry poppers, Snaggletooth mints, Mixxology headphones --"

She smacked him upside his sandy blonde head. "You think you can buy me?! No! I'm going with you – no, no, I'm LEADING you – or nothing!"

All of a sudden the door to the bazaar banged open (with a pleasant, if violent jingle).

"Daughter!" shouted her dad, leaning outside and shaking a second broom at her. "No friends! Sweep! You sweep store! Sweep all store! All store you sweep! Now!"

Lexie locked her violet eyes on Heath and Mark. "In a month," she hissed in a low whisper. "In a month and a half the Force Field will be weak. That's when we go!" And with that she ran back to the store and her dad, who had begun screaming "Sweep! Sweep now! Sweep and Homework!" followed by: "no guitar back! You no play guitar! You daughter! Not son!"

The door slammed behind them with a pleasant jingle.

SHATTER

CHAPTER 7
THE SEVEN SITE

"Do you think she'll show up at your place?" said Mark eagerly. "Think Lexie'll really take us to the Seven Site?"

"It's been OVER a month," Heath grumbled, tightening his scarf around his neck (Autumn had arrived, bringing a cold snap that had everyone busting out their sweaters and scarves). "Lexie hasn't even talked to us except for today. And I don't want her coming over to my house!"

They were both trudging to Heath's house after school. Mark was nervous and excited; this would be the first time he went over to a friend's house! He'd never really done that before – living in an orphanage made other kids with 'normal' families shy away from him – their parents probably whispering that he was 'an orphan for a reason' and that 'if he hasn't been adopted by now, there simply must be something wrong with him.' But Heath's mom had invited him over right away! The only reason it had taken so long was that Heath kept stalling; Mark sensed he was embarrassed about something.

Heath frowned at Mark. "You didn't have to dress so fancy."

Mark had borrowed Lloyd's UBF to sneak out of school again. When Lloyd had heard that Mark was using it to go to a friend's house, he made sure Mark's disguise was both boring and yet, somehow, rather swanky. "I want your mom to like me! I haven't been to someone's house before!" said Mark, brushing lint off his dull black business suit and adjusting his plain checkered tie – he was supposed to be a banker, apparently.

"You didn't have to tell Lloyd that!" Heath protested, looking at Mark's beard – which had so much glitter in it that is sparkled brighter than a disco ball. "That android has way too many bolts missing."

They trudged on a little bit longer. They'd already walked well past the gaudy mansions on the hills around SPIFF, past the sprawl of suburban homes that looked all alike with their lawns being rolled up for winter by the same robot, same 2 hovercars in the driveway, and same cloned dog running around the yard pooping in new and creative places to give its owner a fresh Easter-egg hunt after work. They even walked past apartment complexes where the families with tougher jobs parked their beater hovercars in the streets and shouted at their neighbors to stop stinking up the stairwells with their weird cooking habits.

All that past, they finally reached a part of the city where scraggly grass cracked the sidewalk, shops had bars behind their glass windows, and the few people shuffling along with hunched backs and wrinkled faces all bundled up in raggedy coats against the cold looked at Mark's business suit with distrust – and hunger.

"This is me," said Heath with a heavy, embarrassed sigh misting in the chilly air. He had stopped in front of a block of flats. It towered over them like a dull tombstone dedicated to lives lost in 12-hour workdays and bland TV dinners and sinks full of dirty dishes.

Mark craned his head up as his eyes tried to count how many floors there were. More than a hundred. "What floor are we taking the elevator to?"

"There is no elevator," said Heath. He shrugged. "Which is a nice thing about living on the bottom I guess."

And with that he led the way down a cold, grimy staircase.

Mark followed, squirming in his banker's disguise. He felt foolish. No wonder Heath was embarrassed. No wonder he stalled for so long. Heath was poor. Dirt poor. No one in any school Mark had been to ever hung out with the poor kids. What if his mom was offended by the silly suit he was wearing? What if she thought he was a snob? He began fiddling with the UBF to try and turn it off. Too late.

Heath had reached the bottom of the stairs and swung open a plain metal door. "Mom, I'm home!"

"Just putting the hot chocolate on, dear!" sung a musical voice from just down the hall.

Heath kicked off his brown shoes, but then placed them neatly next to four other pairs of shoes (a pair of white women's work shoes, a pair of fashionably red teenage girl's shoes, a pair of clomping work boots, and a teeny tiny pair of racecar-yellow booties). He then slipped on a pair of slippers, which hummed and began warming his feet – until the left slipper fizzed, popped, and set itself on fire. Muttering under his breath, Heath stamped out the small slipper fire with one of his brown shoes. "Just go into the kichen," he told Mark.

But Mark was still standing in the door letting in all the cold air. His eyes were wide and his mouth slightly open. He was dumbstruck. Where the black of flats was tall and tombstone-ish, this little apartment was cozy and full of life; Where the city outside was dangerous and hostile, this ground-floor Hobbit Hole was safe and welcoming. The world outside was bitterly cold, but in here… in here…he felt warm.

"Oh what a funny disguise!" said Heath's mom with a musical laugh as soon as she walked into the hall. She was the most cheerful looking lady Mark had ever seen. She had short, chocolaty hair, the sparkling brown eyes to match, and a big apron wrapped around her plump rump – and everything had powdery baking flour over it.

Heath, still beating his smoking slipper with his shoe, said, "It's the only way he can sneak out without Admiral Kine expelling him!"

"Well come in, come in out of the cold, dear," she said to Mark, shuffling him in and giving him a pair of guest slippers (nicer than everyone else's slippers, seeing as they had far fewer holes). She then fussed over Heath, handing his jacket to a little coat-hanger bot that bumbled away with it, straitening his tie, even wiping a smudge of the lunch he'd shared with Mark that day off his cheeks (much to Heath's embarrassed grumbling). All this while introducing herself: "It's Diana, dear, but you call me Dee."

A whistle as if from a steam pot came from the kitchen.

"That'll be the tea!" she said, hurrying away.

Heath beckoned Mark to follow and they made their way down the short entry hall. Mark took a lot longer, since he couldn't help stopping to glance at the family pictures on the wall. The pictures showed the same story as the pairs of shoes at the entry. There was Heath's mom, dolling out a delicious picnic at a park with rocket-swings in the background, and at Crater Lake helping everyone build sandcastles by using spoons as catapults, and one of her smiling proudly –though quite exhaustedly—in a hospital bed with a baby in her arms (though half of that picture was blurry –as if one someone had been there too once). Mark also saw in those pictures Heath's sister. She must have been his age and quite possibly his twin; for she had the same sandy blonde hair and olive colored eyes—though hers did not hide behind a pair of glasses like his. Heath must have an older brother too, Mark thought, judging by the tall, serious boy with dark hair and light eyes who always stood so stoic in every picture. And finally a little brother too – a bumbling, chubby cheeked rascal who always seemed to have mushy food stuck somewhere on his face. None of the pictures had Heath's dad in them – or perhaps he was in them at one time … in those spots that were now blank.

Mark sighed, a bit of something like sadness was squeezing his chest. He wondered what pictures of him and his parents would look like … if they hadn't given him up.

But his moment of quiet longing was loudly interrupted by Heath's little brother Jimmy, who burst out of a bedroom yelling "MAMA!" and toddled past Mark as fast as his two chubby legs could carry him, between which sagged a bulging and quite smelly diaper. "I MADE A FUNFUN IN MY PANTS!"

Heath's mom laughed from the kitchen. "Did you make a funfun in your pants?"

"I MADE A FUNFUN IN MY PANTS!"

"Let's get you cleaned up, mister!" she said, coming back out and lifting Jimmy up.

Mark, laughing at the goofiness of Heath's family, watched as she carried Jimmy back to his room.

"Hey," said Heath, leaning back into the hall from the kitchen doorway. "My sister's in her room with a bunch of friends. Let's get the coco before she does!"

Mark stood there for a moment. "You're lucky," he said to Heath, pointing at the photos.

Heath scoffed. "You kidding? Dad left. Mom works to the bone. So does my brother. Barely make enough for Jimmy's diapers."

"But you have a mom," said Mark, his blue-green eyes roving the pictures again, feeling that little squeeze in his chest again.

Heath got quite. After a moment he whispered: "You don't know what happened to your parents, huh?"

Mark, still looking at the family albums on the wall, simply shook his head. "I don't even remember them."

But their moment of quiet bro-bonding was interrupted by a knock on the door.

Heath's mom called out from the next room, "Would you get that, dear?"

"But what about the coco!" Heath protested, looking back into the kitchen with a powerful longing.

"I'll get the door!" said Mark, wanting to be helpful. He shuffled in his guest slipper back to the door and swung it open.

"Hey caveman," said Lexie, standing tall with her yellow bangs curving around her oval face. She had a new band shirt on; black and grey and announcing the tour dates of the Androids of Anarchy. "You good to go?"

A rush of adrenaline spiked his heartbeat. Excitement filled his chest. "Yes!" he shouted, then whirled back at Heath. "She's here! Lexie's here! Let's go!"

Heath popped around the corner again, even grumpier than before – probably due to being interrupted mid-coco gulp (He had a most excellent whip cream moustache going). "Gimme a minute."

Lexie shrugged and looked back at Mark. "You've never ridden a skyboard before, have you, caveman?"

Mark, not liking her new nickname for him too much, tried to play it off cool. "Maybe I have, maybe I haven't."

"Yeah huh, sure," said Lexie sarcastically. "Strap your boots up." She clomped back up the stairs.

He squinted after her suspiciously, but then his curiosity took over. What was a skyboard?

Lacing his worn-out sneakers up (the UBF having been off for a while now), he bolted after her. What he saw waiting for him outside blew his mind out of his left earhole.

Lexie was standing, expertly balancing, on … a hoverboard.

Mark found no words. No words to describe his … his … nope, no words. He pointed at it and squeaked.

Lexie's board was wickedly painted and devilishly sculpted. It looked like a razor-thin surfboard. It had small jet engines the size of soda cans attached to the back. The engines hummed ever so beautifully, as if ready to launch into the sky at any moment. The bottom of her board cast a neon orange glow onto the cracked concrete; the glow read Seven-Zero-Seven – the name of her board.

"The Seven Site is at the heart of the Industrial District," she said. "Too far and too dangerous to walk. You can borrow my old skyboard." She pointed at the wall next to Mark. "It's super old and beat up – but it's fast."

He whirled around. There, leaning against the grubby concrete wall, was … was … was … words failed him again. He pointed at it and squeaked--again. In an instant the boy from Earth and all his wildest daydreams had come true—and it made him quite dizzy.

He approached it as one would approach a snoozing Bengal tiger – with caution, reverence, and love. He petted it. It was so beautiful, so heavy, so real. The top of the board curved into a simple, elegant point. The bottom held a single engine in the shape of an inverted triangle. The surface was rough, like a skateboard, but more metallic, as if covered in magnets the size of sand grains. It was really beat up and scratched – just like Lexie said – but to him…to him…it was magic.

He turned it over. This revealed a dented, pitted, and generally worn-out underside. A blazing comet was painted on the underside, along with the ice-blue label: Comet Chaser.

"It's so—so—beautiful," said Mark, caressing it like a long lost girlfriend.

"Yuck," said Lexie with a grimace. "Stop drooling all over it, caveguy."

Instead, Mark hugged it -- and gently kissed it.

"Gross!" Lexie yelled. "Don't do that! Just throw it down, jump on, and let's get skyward already!"

Mark looked horrified at the very thought of throwing this beauty down. Instead, he gently laid it on the rough concrete. It flickered to life with a neon blue pulse across the bottom and an electric hum, and began floating across the pavement to Lexie.

"She remembers me!" said Lexie as the Comet Chaser bumped into her ankle. She then shook her finger at the humming skyboard and said, admonishingly, "You should not have dropped me in the middle of the i-45 flyway during rush hour." She looked up at a Mark. "Anyway, hop on!"

Mark gingerly stepped on the board, partly out of reverence for it and partly because he didn't want to be dropped in the middle of the nearest flyway either. Stepping on felt like trying to stand upright in a canoe. His arms shot outwards. He wobbled. His butt shot back. He wiggled. "Whooooaaaaa," he breathed.

"To go forward just lean forward," Lexie instructed, making it look easy by gliding around. "But only lean a little. My old Comet Chaser is fast ... really fast."

Mark eagerly leaned forward.

ZIP!

CRASH.

Lexie groaned louder than him, but for an entirely different – though no less painful – reason. "This is going to take forever."

Heath burst up the staircase. "What are you doing?!" He yelled at Lexie, coco staining the front of his button-up shirt – undoubtedly because Mark had crashed hard enough into the building to make Heath spill it over himself.

Lexie yelled right back. "The only way to get to the Seven Site is sky-boards! I'm teaching him to ride!"

"On a Comet Chaser?! You'll send him to the dentist before anything!"

"Give him yours then!"

"Mine's old and fat and keeps losing power randomly! It'll drop him first thing."

"Then you teach him!"

"That'll take months!"

"We don't have months. We have minutes. Today's the only day we can sneak in. So grab your piece of junk, scrape the caveman from the wall he just planted his face into, and let's go!"

"No," Heath protested with a vigorous shake of his head. "We aren't going then."

When Mark heard this he peeled himself off the wall, coughing, sputtering, and saying, "I can do this! Seriously. I can do this. Let's ride!"

And so, with Lexie impatiently zipping around criticizing Heath's instructions – and Heath yelling at her to shut it – they taught Mark a few basic pointers: lean forward to go, backward to stop, sideways to turn, crouch to go up, and stand straight to go back down. Mark even learned a trick! The Triple 360 Nossie – where you tip the skyboard's nose sharp forward while whirling like a washing machine. Of course, he learned it quite by accident while spinning out of control and screaming his lungs out – but even Lexie agreed it counted.

Yes, apparently learning to ride a skyboard was a lot like learning to ride a bike—except the bike had no pedals, no handlebars, and floated in midair. But Mark was getting the hang of it. Because he wanted to. He really did. It was like surfing back home in Australia, but in the air. He loved surfing. He could never dream of buying his own surfboard, but sometimes a board would wash up on the sunny Australian shore and, if he was really lucky, it wouldn't even have a shark bite! He spent the whole day surfing then. That experience helped him get the hang of the Comet Chaser right quick, which made Lexie push them to get going to the Seven Site – thought she kept complaining.

"If that caveman doesn't learn to turn faster he's going to keep leaving snot on brick walls."

"Don't chase him into brick walls, then," Heath countered, adjusting his worn leather satchel, which was filled with stuff for the expedition. He rode next to Mark, giving his friend pointers and suggestions and occasionally trying to catch him. Heath's own board was a ding-ed-up Cheap Trick skyboard. It was wide and fat and kept losing power randomly, just as he had said, and made him bob along as if he were riding over speed bumps.

Deeper and deeper into the Port District they raced, zooming over dirty warehouses and squat brick buildings that grimaced against bright wintery daylight. The heavy air weighed down their lungs. This far into Crescent City's Industrial Zone and the crisp breeze of early winter choked on concrete factories and steel mills and flyways full of belching, lumbering semi-trucks.

Lexie had pulled her Lemonsquare out of her pocket. But instead of turning it into her guitar, she made it become a map, and began studying it. It showed the moving terrain beneath them with a blinking arrow pointing the way to the Seven Site.

The map reminded Mark of the galaxy map Lloyd had used during the flight so many months ago. The memory reminded him of Ella. He wondered if Heath knew were that academy she went to was. So, trying to keep his balance (which made him stick his tongue between his lips), he wobbled the Comet Chaser closer to Heath. "Hey," he shouted (for the cold wind they were cutting through was loud), "Hey that map reminds me—is Aventine Hill Academy far from here?"

"Oh yeah," Heath shouted back, "It's on the East Ridge. Over there."

Mark looked where Heath was pointing. Wow. The East Ridge of Crescent City was really far away. The buildings cascading down the ridge could have been miniatures on a postcard. Though one set of buildings dominated the ridge just like SPIFF dominated the West Ridge. The set of buildings looked like a commanding and respectable university, with ivy covered towers and a gigantic grand old clock. He wondered if Ella was out there right now. But the thought made him sad, so he went back to trying to keep up with Heath and Lexie – and trying not to leave his snot on any more brick buildings.

They sped fast and high over block after block of increasingly haunting scenery: an empty electronics factory where the smoke stack had toppled over to crash through a rusted roof; a hovercar assembly facility where car seats hung rotting from assembly line hooks; sidewalk after sidewalk of cracked pavement sprouting scraggly, sun burnt grass. The dirt and soot of the Industrial District quickened their heartbeats, especially as the cold air thinned and sounds of traffic and factories faded.

And as industrial life faded they dove down to the pebbled streets, racing and dodging between bent streetlamps and rusted hovercars, grinning at each other from the tingling sense of risky adventure. That is, until Heath shouted, "Oie!" and frantically pointed ahead. "Force field coming up quick!"

A cloud of chalk-white dust billowed as Lexie stopped mere feet from a transparent wall pulsing with turquoise-colored energy. Heath, whose board had randomly lost power, glided to stop behind her. Mark, being more about speed and less about remembering how to brake, went skidding to within an inch of getting his nose fried off.

"So close," he coughed as his dust cloud caught up to him.

"Good cut!" Heath praised while starting his board back up by turning a crank between his feet. "Leaned back nice and heavy."

"Thanks!" said Mark, beaming. "I guess it's like learning to ride a bike, huh?"

"A bike?" said Heath with a puzzled look.

"Is that a caveman thing?" asked Lexie.

Mark laughed ruefully. He loved these shocking little reminders that he was someplace so far from home.

They all looked up at the blocky words scrolling across the pulsing field.

"Seven Site Quarantine," Mark read in his deepest 'official' voice. "No entry."

Lexie's yellow map dissolved back into her Lemonsquare, and she held it in her left hand. "Okay, here goes." She swung her hand back and, swift as a baseball player, chucked the orb at full force toward the turquoise energy.

It struck the barrier high above their heads and stuck, wobbling like a square of Jell-O.

A harsh static sound filled the cold air.

They held their hands to their ears because it sounded like fingers down an electric chalkboard.

But then, to their amazement, the Square expanded, tearing a doorway into the force field. A great rush of air billowed past them as if they had opened a secret door to a long lost tomb.

"Nice," said Lexie. Without waiting she blitzed straight through.

Mark grinned at Heath, flicked his lucky cap, and blazed after her.

"Whoa," he said after coming to a stop on the other side. He smacked his tongue in his mouth, grimacing unpleasantly the way he did when his orphanage cafeteria back home glopped moldy grossness into his bowl. "We're inside some dude's fridge who never gets rid of leftovers, aren't we?"

Heath's voice was a whisper of awe as he joined them. "Even the air in here is trapped."

"Let's find some loot!" said Lexie, not giving a care about any foul smells.

They speared into a maze of scrap piles. The silence was total. Only the hum of their boards gliding over cracked streets littered with office papers could be heard; and the dry documents fluttered up behind them like tumble weeds.

The deeper they drifted into the Seven Site, the more they huddled together; the scrap piles had an eerie way of closing in. Perhaps it was because the piles were stacked with such ordinary things: old office chairs with butt imprints, desks with circular stains from coffee mugs, coffee makers—stuff that should be in crowded cubicles, not rusting and rotting in heaps on the street.

"What do you think happened?" Mark wondered as they drifted past a tall crane. Its claw still clutched filing cabinets as if the operator left his job one day and never came back.

Lexie, in the whisper of someone who believes ghost stories, said, "I heard that the Dae –," she stopped herself with a shiver, "that IT – was made here – a long, long time ago."

"Whoooooa!" Mark and Heath breathed.

"Do you think the Dae – IT – is still here?" said Mark, looking around suspiciously.

Heath shook his head and was about to say 'no way,' but then they all rounded the last scrap pile.

Mark was so taken aback by what they saw that he nearly lost his balance -- while Lexie sped up for a closer look.

There, in the center of the Seven Site, encircled by six research facilities, was a lake made of pure acid. It looked like a witch's brew of swirling violet, rich crimson, and artificial green.

"Looks like melted plastic," Mark commented after joining his friends at the edge of the acid lake. "With tiny islands of slowly melting junk," he added, nodding to the small piles of scrap dotting the lake.

He glanced up and down the crimson shore and shivered. Once, tall trees lined these banks. Now only their twisted trucks remained, wreathing in agony, their stumps bleached like dry bones.

"See the seventh research facility in the middle of the lake?" said Lexie, drawing the boys' attention to the ruined steel skeleton jutting out like a crumbling castle surrounded by an acid mote. It was wrecked far worse than any of the six buildings surrounding the lake. "Best loot will be in there." She eagerly kicked off the crimson shore, not caring that her board was skimming acid.

But Mark was rooted to the burnt shore with a frown weighing his brow. "That half-sunken spaceship—," He pointed to a ship half sunken in the lake by the building. A white fuselage and single bent wing were sticking out of the lake. "It looks really familiar for some reason."

"Come on!" Heath repeated, nervously edging out over the acid. "Stick close to me in case my board goes down!"

They followed Lexie, Heath grumbling that if his board lost power again the acid would eat it in seconds. Mark didn't doubt it. The bright violets swirled in a hazardous, stomach-churning way. Fat bubbles would bulge the plastic surface of the lake. They'd burst, hissing, scaring him, tensing him so that his board wobbled more.

Heath stopped mumbling. They'd glided halfway across, sticking close to the islands of debris. He was concentrating hard. Beads of sweat broke out on his wrinkled forehead despite the cold, rotten air. His sweat would drip into the acid, steaming away.

"Whoa, whoa, whoa!" Heath shouted. His board was powering down with a dull hum.

Mark swung out to grab him. He was too far away. The Comet Chaser rocked, dipping into neon green, which hungrily hissed, eating the corner.

"I'm good! I'm good!" Heath shouted as his board powered back up.

This happened four more times before they reached the seventh facility.

"That was fun to watch," said Lexie as Heath jumped onto the crimson shore.

"I swear," cursed the business kid at his board, "If it keeps losing power like that -- I'm turning it into a coffee table—and selling it!"

"Check out where we landed," Lexie proudly exclaimed, walking backwards to the building's crumbling entrance, both her hands pointing straight up.

Mark adjusted his hat and squinted to read the large block letters at the top of the ten story building. The letters hung haphazard above the ruined entrance. After a moment he put the letters together. Deep Intersolar Enterprises.

"D.I.E."

Heath nodded while propping his board next to Lexie's, both of them up against a mass of rusted metal. "Yeah. So—careful, right?"

"Place looks haunted by Frankensteinish dust bunnies," Mark commented as his eyes roved the hollow windows and empty doorways.

Lexie confidently lead the way to the tumbled down glass entry. Heath followed, nervously watching the crumbling walls. Mark, grinning from the thrill of exploring this haunting place, didn't even wipe his gritty hands before dashing after.

They left their hoverboards leaning against that mass of rusted metal.

But as the trio sauntered inside, and silence fell on the blood-red shore, five small LED eyes flickered in the center of that rusted mass.

A flat, featureless face extended outward with a whir. All three skyboards clattered to the ground as a skeletal android made of rust and broken plastic stood with a metallic groan and hiss of hydraulics.

The machine shook dust off itself like an animal. Its five unblinking eyes locked onto its prey – the boy from Earth.

CHAPTER 8
RUN!

"Wow," said Lexie as she strode into the soaring circular entry chamber.

"I guess Deep Intersolar made military androids," said Heath, who stepped in next and also craned his head up in awe. "What if they did make the Dae – IT…"

Daylight rained in from a gigantic broken glass dome. It illuminated a museum's worth of military androids. Some hulked under bristling guns, others were slim and camouflaged, all would have been deadly if alive. The decommissioned androids were arranged from left to right in order from oldest to newest, as if displaying the R&D history of Deep Intersolar Enterprises. They all floated in mid-air, suspended by nothing, from the lobby floor all the way up ten stories to the ruined glass dome.

"I'm a dizzy ant stuck at the bottom of a blender," said Mark, looking up into the streams of cold daylight as dust motes floated by. His voice echoed in the silence—and from somewhere high above, the roof was leaking.

They crossed the lobby to the security booth, their shoes crunching glass that had fallen from the dome. The booth was big enough for two guards. It had two doors—one on each side of the room, and one large window looking out to the spiraling entrance.

"Nothing's out of place," said Heath, picking up a single sheet of glass resting on the security control panel. The glass blinked on to show scrolling headlines and video from the Seven Site's grand opening. "Beautiful tech hub. . . .thirteen years ago."

"None of the chairs are overturned. No rush, no hurry out of here. The emergency lockdown lever was never used. Weird," said Mark, tracing the red lockdown lever with his fingers.

Lexie didn't feel any fright, however, and dug out her Lemonsquare. With a few presses on the screen it unfolded into a map which she laid across the emergency lever and control panel. The map displayed a holographic blueprint of the building. Her fingers swiped across the floors until a red dot appeared. "Tenth floor. Waste Disposal." She made the map fold up and jogged to the spiraling stairway. "Come on!"

"Waste Disposal?" said Mark with a disgusted, confused frown as he and Heath jogged after her.

Silence settled as the lighthearted voices of the three explorers traveled up the dizzying staircase. The lobby sunk back into chilled daylight and shadowed obscurity. All returned to the way it had been for many years.

The rusted skeletal droid followed. It skulked into the domed hall. It gazed at the military androids suspended in mid-air. It touched one of them. A static spark cracked between its finger and the frozen metal of the long-dead military android. The bulky android's three eyes blinked to life. It dropped to the floor – and followed the leader.

"It's got to be the skunk works." Lexie was huffing as they stepped onto the tenth floor—having taken the stairs two at a time.

"A what?" said Heath, completely out of breath from shouting at her to slow down.

"A skunk works. An off-the-books R&D," she answered, fishing her Lemonsquare out of her pocket again, turning it into a flashlight, and diving into the dark hallway ahead. "It's the place where experimental tech is made. Stuff so bleeding edge the regular employees don't even know about it."

Mark darted glances into the offices they passed, illuminated by Lexie's yellow flashlight. That creepy feeling ran up his spine again. The whole place seemed so normal, as if the employees who worked here half a century ago could, at any moment, stroll right back in and start complaining about their jobs. What happened here? Did the Dae—did IT—kill everyone?

The three pioneers were so far down the black hallway that only their bobbing flashlight could be seen. They had left the domed entry behind, and couldn't hear the static cracks as the rusted skeleton brought more military androids back to life.

FIVE androids went crawling up the ten-story chamber like spiders.

"We're here," said Lexie, halting her rapid march in front of a black and white door. It was one of those spiraling doors just like Mark's dorm-room-turned-escape-pod. She shone her light above the door. A skunk had been painted above the door.

Mark squinted at her. "This IS Waste Disposal! You're going to shove me down a stank sewer hole filled with hardened keester cakes, aren't you?"

Lexie laughed. This made Mark back away. Then she said, "That would have been fun! But no." She waved the light behind them. "Didn't you think it was odd that just to get to this door we had to go through eight—now deactivated—security grids? Help me open it!"

Mark made sure Lexie was in front—just in case this WAS waste disposal. Heath wrapped his tie around his face like a gas mask—also just in case. They corkscrewed the doors apart, revealing a bleak void.

"Darker than an orc's bum, innit?" said Mark, then he motioned for Lexie to step in first. "You first. I don't want to end up tumbling down the tunnel of tangy butt nuts."

Heath chuckled. "That sounds like a carnival ride at the Amusement Park of Unfortunate Names."

Lexie called them both 'weak-kneed sissies,' and strode into the unknown, her Lemonsquare all ablaze.

Mark and Heath, taking offense to being called sissies by a girl, marched in after her. They did not look back down the hall. If they had, they might have seen dozens of LED eyes following them through the darkness.

SEVEN androids skulked closer.

"Why is it so cold in here?" Mark whispered into the pitch black room. He fumbled at the double zippers of his Support Crew jacket.

The faint yellow light from Lexie's Lemonsquare only reached as far as their footsteps. However, as soon as their footsteps took them a stone's throw into the void, a deep hum began. It reverberated through the black and white checkered floor.

"Bright!" yelped Mark, shutting his eyes tight. The deep hum had clicked into a flood of pure white. All three began blinking and rubbing their eyes.

"Oh my gearboxes," Mark whispered as soon as he could see. "We hit it! We hit the mother lode!"

They basked in wonder at the treasure trove before them, not knowing where to look first! The large, star-shaped laboratory had gadget laden tables sticking out of each of the five corners. Between the tables were holograms projecting 3D models of plasma guns, glowing grenade launchers, and prototype missiles; and off to the side stood a thick glass operating table. It appeared to have once restrained an android. But the chains were broken, the straps burned, and the glass had long, thin cracks – as if the android had … escaped.

A shiver ran down Mark's spine – not from the cold.

"Do you think this was where the Dae—where IT—was created?"

Heath gulped. "Maybe we shouldn't be here…"

Lexie was having none of it. "We'll get you back to your wittle ittle bitty binky soon," she said, patting Heath on the back like a baby.

He scowled at her.

She then dug out several palm-sized discs out of her pockets. "These are Proxy Ports," she explained. "My dad uses them to teleport stuff back to his storage bays." She tossed a few to the boys. "Press the red button in the middle, slap it on whatever you want, and BOOM, it gets teleported back!"

Heath flipped the disc over and over in his hand, frowning at it. "So what – you get all the stuff?!"

"No, I'll give you a fair cut," said Lexie, though she didn't meet his eyes.

Heath nudged Mark as if to get his opinion about this. After all, there were no Flarejet parts anywhere in sight. But Mark seemed to be hung up on the shattered glass operating table, so Heath asked for him. "What about Flarejet parts for Mark?"

"I'll trade this stuff to my dad for some," said Lexie with a shrug like it was no big deal –but she still wouldn't meet Heath's eyes.

Heath, frowning suspiciously at her, walked over to a table stacked with shiny things. "Pro tip," he whispered to Mark, waving around a thin sheet of blue glass, "if it looks easy to break, it's gotta be expensive." He dropped a Proxy Port on it. The Proxy Port flashed red and, with a pop, zapped the thingy (whatever it was) away. "Come on, let's get all we can and go!"

But for some strange reason Mark was fixed on the operating table. The table called to him. He stood in front of it, hands in pockets, blue-green eyes shimmering with memories he was desperately trying to remember.

Outside in the hallway -- NINE androids lurked in the shadows like cockroaches . . . waiting … for a signal … from their leader.

Heath, who had moved to the next table, was now enthralled with a crystal orb. It had long tubes coiling around the bottom. Gray particles floated about inside. "I don't know what this is!" he gleefully shouted, "But it looks expensive!" He slapped a Proxy Port on it. POP. Off it went. He was really getting into it. Soon enough he was feeling like a treasure hunter and flinging Proxy Port's at random things; Whatever looked expensive, high-tech, or, most important -- shiny and easily breakable—disappeared.

Mark tore his eyes from the operating table for the first time. He looked around the laboratory, eyes blank and distant. "Ever get that feeling ..." he whispered, "that you've been here before?"

"No," said Heath with a frown. "Why?"

Mark did not answer, just looked back at the glass table.

"Oh! jetpack!" Heath shouted, holding up two long cylinders with straps attached. "Want to take a spin?!" He slung it on and began zooming around the room hollering in delight.

Mark, however, ignored the roaring jetpack, passed on every invite to take it for a whirl, and instead edged closer to the table. Ignoring such ridiculous fun was not like him, and he knew it. But he couldn't take his mind off that burned and broken operating table. He remembered it. He knew it. It's like it was...almost...whispering to him.

Outside in the dark, ELEVEN hungry droids made ready to attack.

"Mark!" Heath shouted, rocketing about. "Strap this pack up!"

Mark ignored him. He stared at the table. It was so familiar. Such a familiar thing. Such a strange thing—broken and burned and glimmering. The longer he looked, the more he knew it. He reached out.

"Sssss, ow!" he yelped as the glass burnt his fingers.

The entire room plunged into darkness and silence.

"Hey!" Heath shouted from somewhere in the darkness.

"What the frik, caveman!" said Lexie.

KKKKREEEEEEVVVVVVV!

A piercing shriek ripped into the room.

From darkness, into darkness, thirteen tall, lithe military androids slunk in. Their unblinking eyes floated in the pitch black like strange fireflies in the night. Their flat faces were angled greedily at Mark. They would not by hungry anymore.

The rusted droid who brought them all back to life was in the lead. It fixed Mark with its five pin-sized eyes. The remaining androids could not be seen in the darkness, only their beady eyes pierced through.

"Lurks," breathed Heath. "No escape."

"What are they?" Mark hissed.

"Machines."

"Guys," whispered Lexie. "We're fu—,"

A three-eyed lurk pounced at her. She screamed as it slammed her to the ground. Heath grabbed its slimy plastic body, trying to wrench it off her.

All the lurks rushed at them.

Mark thought fast. He dug one of the Proxy Port's out of his pocket, pressed the red button, and smashed it on the floor. Red sparks scattered across the tiles. The floor underneath them teleported away. The rest of the floor caved in.

They yelled, falling to the ninth floor below. The landing flattened their lungs. Their coughs were drowned by the robotic shrieks of the five-eyed lurk. A heavy steel beam pinned its left arm. It screamed and slashed out at them with its right hand. A second lurk lay crushed underneath a fallen beam. Shrieks came from above.

"That," coughed Lexie from where she lay, "was WICKED."

"But we're just trapped again!" said Heath. He had bolted up and was desperately searched for a way out. The room they had fallen into was locked up.

Lexie hitched up her jetpack, thinking she could fly them out. But then she looked up. Useless. She couldn't fly them up. The lurks crowded above, screeching and swiping at them.

They were trapped.

Mark watched his friend's frantically look for an exit. He tore another Proxy Port out of his jacket pocket. "One more time, guys." He pressed the red button, threw it at the wall, and stood back.

The thick wall bent with the sound of a deep gunshot; An opening the size of a round door teleported away. The rest of the wall began to crumble.

"Yes!" Heath shouted, scrambling through the opening with Lexie and Mark close behind.

The three-eyed lurk jumped down and landed with a thud behind them. It shrieked with hunger.

Heath had broken into a blind run through the pitch black hallway. Lexie fished the Lemonsquare out of her wildly swinging coat. She flicked it into a flashlight. Behind them, the demented shrieks echoed louder, closer. Her light swung in her fist as they raced. Its brief flashes blinded the three-eye lurk chasing them, leaping from wall to wall behind them. But in the distance—a point of light grew.

"It's the ten story entrance!" shouted Mark.

They burst out of the dark hallway, lungs rasping, skidding to a stop against the glass railing. All the bright daylight pouring in from the broken glass dome hurt their eyes, making them squint.

"The stairs!" Heath shouted, shoes pounding down the steps.

Kkkrrrreeeeeev!

The three-eyed Lurk crept out of the darkness behind them.

"Lexie!" shouted Mark. "Give me your guitar."

"What? NO!"

The Lurk crept closer. Hungry.

"Your guitar!" Mark shouted.

Lexie angrily turned her LemonSquare into her electric yellow guitar. The Lurk attacked with claws bared.

Mark countered. In one swift motion he took her guitar, flipped it, grabbed the thin fret board, and smashed the guitar across the Lurk's flat face.

The Lurk stumbled to the side, crashed through the railing, and fell in a shower of glass, bouncing off floating military androids on its way down. It hit the lobby floor nine stories below with a heavy thump.

"YOU LIKE THAT BASS?" Lexie shouted down at it. "HUH?" She then grabbed her guitar from Mark and shred a high pitched riff on the dangling strings. Her furiously happy eyes locked onto Mark. "That was AWESOME! How did you think of that?"

But Mark had no time to answer. The lurk wasn't dead. It scrambled up on its legs. It screamed. It rushed up the stairwell.

"Some plan!" Heath angrily shouted at them. His business shoes had already reached the eighth floor. Now he had to scramble back up the stairwell.

Demented shrieks echoed from the pitch black hallway. Eleven sets of LED eyes were rushing at them.

Mark flicked the brim of his cap for luck – then suddenly had another brilliant idea. "I'll use another Proxy Port! We'll zappity zap outta here!" He turned to Lexie. "Hold my hand!" He took a Proxy Port from her. "And slap this on my butt!"

Lexie glared at him. "Proxy Port's can't teleport people!"

"Oh."

Eleven lurks slunk into the daylight.

The friends were now horribly stuck. Going downstairs meant battling the vicious three-eyed lurk, which was now racing past the second floor. And staying on the ninth floor meant being ripped apart by eleven military androids. Heath, halfway back up, realized this and began having a nervous breakdown. He'd go running down a few steps, then running back up, then running back down, all while repeatedly screaming, "What do we do? What do we do? WHAT DO WE DOOOOO?"

"One step," said Mark to Lexie, and shoved her over the railing. "Use your jetpack!" he yelled as she fell, screaming curses at him.

"Heath!" he shouted. "Lexie will rocket you up to the top!"

Heath took one look over the railing and shouted, "Your coconut is rotten!"

Lexie, having recovered, rocketed up to him. "Now's not the time to be afraid of heights!"

"I'm not afraid of heights!" Heath countered. "I'm afraid of French kissing the dirt!"

All eleven lurks turned to Mark.

He was trapped.

Four lurks leapt at him.

Lexie blasted over to him and snatched him up by his shirt-collar at the last instant.

"The three-eyed Lurk will kill Heath! Go rocket him to the roof first!" Mark protested. "Drop me on an andr—oof!"

Lexie had tossed him onto a lifeless floating android and zoomed up to Heath, who was fending off a Lurk with his shoe.

The rest of the Lurks jumped onto the lifeless androids. They began jumping and crawling on them, hungry for Mark.

The boy climbed and leapt away from them.

"Heath's safe on the roof!" said Lexie, hovering down close to Mark. "I'll rocket you the rest of the way up there!"

Mark flung out his left hand. She grabbed it. Her jetpack roared. They blasted up to the ruined glass dome.

Heath was looked tiny so high above them. "Come on! Come on!" he shouted desperately, lying flat on his belly across one of the dome's steel beams. His hands were outstretched to catch them.

Krrreeeeeeev!

The three-eyed lurk had been waiting. It had seen them climbing, learned their plan, and waited to strike. And now it vaulted from its perch on the tenth floor.

Lexie screamed as the lurk's claws sunk into her jetpack.

The weight was too much. They fell away from Heath's outstretched hand and horror stricken face.

Lexie screamed her lungs out as the wind whistled in their ears.

Anger flooded Mark, blurring his eyes. These lurks wanted to kill him, only him, because the Daemon wanted him dead for some reason. But they would also kill his friends. For no reason, just to get to him. His friends would die.

He viciously kicked the three-eyed Lurk's flat face.

It shrieked in piercing rage – and dug it's claws in deeper.

Useless.

"Change of plans!" Mark shouted. He flicked her jetpack's switch on full. It roared as all its fuel poured into both rocket chambers.

The heat blinded him, burnt him. But they shot back up.

"Grab Heath's hand!" Mark shouted at her. "Grab his hand!"

Lexie came to. She desperately flung her hands to Heath's frantically reaching hand.

Their fingers touched. Caught.

Mark turned the jetpack off completely.

Silence.

The tremendous weight was too much. Heath, holding onto Lexie and Mark and the screaming Lurk, began sliding off the room.

"NO NO NO NOOOO!" Heath yelled, slipping clean off the dome.

"WHY WOULD YOU DO THAT?!" Lexie yelled at Mark as the trio fell in a mess of screams, broken glass, and terror.

Down, down, down they fell.

"Jump onto a floating android!" Mark yelled. Before they had time to protest he loosened Lexie's jetpack and ripped it off.

Heath landed on a floating droid with a thud. Lexie snagged another floating droid's arm. Mark grabbed one by the leg. And the three-eyed Lurk, screaming, claws stuck in the jetback – fell.

They watched as the enraged Lurk bounced from android to android in a storm of ruined metal. The ten story plunge ended when the Lurk's plastic shell shattering across the tiled lobby. In another second the jetpack hit ground nearby. Its remaining rocket fuel detonated.

THOOOOOOM!

The building shook like an earthquake. The entry filled with billowing fire.

Mark, dangling from an android's leg, watched the flood of fire with an angry smile of tremendous satisfaction.

"Yes!" shouted Heath. "Right in the business!"

Lexie, flooded with adrenaline, looked down at Mark. "Caveman! I like the way you think!"

Above them the rest of the Lurks screamed in rage.

"To our skyboards!" Heath shouted, jumping from the floating android to the stairwell. He was quickly joined by Lexie. They both ran down the last flight toward the front of the building. "Freedom, escape, all that good stuff!"

"No!" Mark shouted, jumping onto the stairs and chasing after them. "Follow me!" He quickly outpaced them by leaping onto the rail and sliding past them. He then darted out the front of the building. Once outside, he pointed toward the half-sunken ship. "We're going in!"

"WHAT FOR?" Heath yelled, still running to their skyboards.

"Because I want to get rid of these Lurk's once and for all!"

Lexie, curious about Mark's idea, sped after him.

Heath angrily shouted at them to quit being stupid. But when he saw them quickly jump onto the ship's wing and disappear inside the broken windows, he rushed over to join. Better to stick by friends then battle Lurks alone. "Hey wait up!" He hopped on the wing. This made the tail, which was submerged beneath the acid, shake and send ripples across the lake. "This harebrained plan better be worth it!" he grumbled.

Mark, standing on a seat inside, was avoiding the floor, which had a long gash that bled acid. The acid bubbled and pooled around the seats, corroding them. The seats in the center had caved in. "Just pretend you're playing The-Floor-Is-Lava!"

"Is that a caveman game?" Lexie muttered, scrambling over the seats.

Heath was the last one to squeeze through the window. The site of Mark and Lexie scrambling over seats, barely avoiding the acid, made his knees wobble. But then a sudden realization made his eyes go wide. "Wait a minute, wait a minute…Mark…this is the ship that was all over the news! This is the ship that crashed into your starliner!"

Mark stopped dead. He looked all around in astonishment. "I knew this looked familiar! I only saw it from the bottom!"

"Just stay focused on whatever your plan is, caveboy," said Lexie, reaching the pilot's cabin – the only spot with a solid floor. She tumbled in, but then leapt back!

"Oh shi—!" she yelped, nearly stumbling back into the acid.

"What? What?" said Mark, helping balance her back up.

"Whow!" went Heath.

A hologram of Admiral Nona Kine was playing in the middle of the pilot's cabin. It was life size. In her dark admiral's uniform, with her hands clasped behind her back and her pixelated mouth moving, she gave orders in a pre-recorded message.

"Crash into Mark and Ella's Starliner," commanded her digital voice, all the more robotic as it streamed from the hologram. "Delta Ten bound for Crescent City."

All three pairs of eyebrows shot upwards.

The hologram buzzed with static. "Crash into Mark and Ella's starliner," repeated Admiral Kine. "Delta Ten bound for Crescent City."

Their eyes kept growing wider and brighter with shock.

"Crash into Mark and Ella's starliner," looped the buzzing hologram. "Delta Ten bound for Crescent City."

They stood with mouths agape at this stunning revelation, letting the hologram keep looping and looping its shocking message.

Lexie broke their silence with words that reflected her fear. "Nona wanted to kill you!"

"Doesn't make sense," said Mark. "Unless she is working for the Dae— for IT..."

But they didn't have time to mull over this strange revelation.

"Listen," Heath whispered, his eyes searching the curved ceiling.

Mark and Lexie followed Heath's frightened gaze upwards.

THUMP.

The small ship trembled.

THUMP. Another shudder rocked the ship. Heavy metallic steps began slowly scraping across the roof.

THUMP. A third heavy body landed, this time on the ships nosecone— right in front them. It belonged to the five-eyed droid -- the one they had left pinned under a steel beam under the Skunk Work's tenth floor. It was back. And by the silhouette it carved against the bright sky, it had torn its own arm off—and returned to hunt Mark.

Mark clapped a hand over heath and Lexie's mouths. "Shush now. We need to wait for my plan to work." Breathing hard, they watched the five-eyed lurk watch them. It crouched, supported by its right hand. Its five unblinking eyes stared with hunger.

Krreeeeeeeeeevvvv!

That robotic scream pierced the stale afternoon air. This time it rang with the sound of a battle cry.

"No," Mark hissed, holding Heath still. "Wait for it…."

Metal body after metal body landed on the roof, wing, and nosecone, making the ship begin to sway.

"Wait for it…"

The five-eyed lurk rushed at the windshield, shattering the remaining glass out of the frame.

"RUN!" Mark yelled, pushing them back onto the seats.

They bolted out of the pilot's cabin as the Lurks arm slashed inside. With Heath in the lead and Mark bringing up the back, they clambered over seat after seat.

SCREECH!

A rusted arm ripped through the ceiling in front of Heath.

He stopped dead, arms flailing as he balanced on his seat.

The rusted arm disappeared.

Silence.

SCREECH! SCREECH! SCREECH!

A dozen metallic hands clawed into the roof.

"Back to the wing!" Mark shouted from behind. "Back to the wing!"

They jumped over seats, stumbling on backrests.

The ship's alloy roof was being torn apart above them; below them the ship was sloshing the acid in the cabin; all around were horrendous noises, burnt smells and digital screams.

A claw grabbed Lexie by her hair. She screamed as it pulled her up.

"No!" Heath yelled, turning to try and tug her down.

Mark fished the last Proxy Port in his left pocket. Pressing the red button, he chucked it at the metallic arm hauling Lexie up. The Lurk blinked away, teleported to a quiet little storage bay at the Black Pearl Bazaar. Lexie fell with a thump on the seat.

"Move!" Mark yelled.

The Lurks on the roof finished tearing open a wide gash. Dull thumps shook the floor as Lurk after Lurk fell inside. Some fell in acid, screaming from digital pain. Others crashed into seats and began ripping towards the trio – the five-eyed Lurk in the lead. But Heath had reached the broken window over the wing, and jumped through.

Lexie followed, then Mark. The spaceship tipped and rocked in the acid as they ran down the metal wing to the crimson shore.

Desperate sounds came from the Lurks as they began ripping through the rectangular window frames, not able to fit through.

Heath jumped to shore first, followed by Lexie and Mark. Their knees buckled as they each hit the ground. Heath tried picking himself up to get ready to run again; Lexie was trying but her out-of-breath gasps were doubling her over.

"Watch! Watch!" Mark shouted triumphantly, not running away at all.

The small spaceship began breaking apart, began sinking. Screams, angry screams from the Lurks trapped inside pierced the sour afternoon air. Their manic attempts to escape grew frenzied. Swirls of boiling magentas and hissing crimsons ate into the white hull. Neon yellow chemicals poured into the windows. Tendrils of steam curled around the dissolving wing as it tipped into the artificial colors. The lake was devouring the ship whole. As the acid poured into the Lurks, their screams grew tormented.

Heath and Lexie stopped trying to run. They flopped their butts down and watched in awe as the ship gently slipped beneath rippling neon waves. They sat and listened to the rage of the Lurks as acid silenced their digital voices. They sat on the crimson shore and gulped cold air and felt the grit beneath their palms and felt alive. ALIVE.

"That was ... intense," Heath breathed.

Mark flopped down between Heath and Lexie. "Those were Lurks?"

Heath nodded, wiping his forehead with his tie. "And they were sent to kill you."

"How did they know I was here?!" Mark protested.

"Must be something to do with Admiral Kine," Heath suggested. "She ordered that ship to crash into you! Crash right into your face!" Heath grunted as he stood up. "Why is she trying to murder your butt? WHAT is going on?!" He dusted himself off and made footsteps back to his tumbled-over skyboard. "From now on," he called back at Mark, "we keep an eye on her!"

Mark sat silently for a minute, watching the lake's neon ripples grow still. "Too bad I sunk the evidence."

That's when Lexie piped up, having caught her breath finally. "Hey," she said, fixing Mark with her violet eyes. "Thanks for saving me in there, caveguy. That was quick thinking."

Mark gaped at her. Lexie? Being nice? That might be the most shocking thing yet.

"Anyway," she said roughly, breaking their awkward eye contact, "I'm still not sure about that wimp," she thumbed at Heath.

Mark smiled, watching Heath curse loudly at his piece-of-junk skyboard as it kept losing power and bobbing him over the acid. "Ah -- he's good people too – once you get to know him." He joined her as they walked back to their skyboards. "And don't thank me just yet." He grinned. "I did Proxy Port one of those man-eating Lurks into your dad's shop!"

CHAPTER 9
YOU TRYIN TO KILL ME?

"Yes? Hhmm?" demanded the short, swarthy, silk-draped shop-keeper while extinguishing the last small fire in Storage Bay 13. The Lurk that Mark had Proxy Ported into Funk's storage room lay on the pile of technological treasures they had ported over before all that whiz-bang-run-for-your-butts nonsense. The now-dead Lurk appeared to have been shot up—frantically and with a large caliber gun. "Trying to kill Funky, yes? No more Perfidious Funk, what he good for anyway?"

Lexie fumed at her dad. "That Lurk nearly killed me!"

"It nearly kill ME!" Funk retorted, waving around an old-school sawed-off shotgun—its barrel steaming and its ammo clip completely empty.

"Where from this loot?" demanded the purple and gold bejeweled shopkeeper. He stopped spraying foam from the extinguisher in his left hand and jabbed it at Mark and Heath. "Where?!"

Heath and Mark glanced at Lexie, not sure if saying where it was from would get her in more trouble or not.

Perfidious noticed this. Tossing the empty extinguisher, the suspecting little man stepped sideways towards his daughter, scrutinizing her with those somehow-knowing-everything beady brown eyes. "You . . . you go to Seven Site, yes?"

Lexie shrunk against the wall.

"Why?" he fumed, kicking one of the treasures. "To bring back junk?!"

"It's not junk!" said Lexie desperately, looking guilty and ashamed.

"ALL JUNK!" roared her dad, spittle flying. "Why? Why go? Why for?!"

Lexie tried stand straight, violet eyes shimmering. "I don't have to sweep the shop every day!" she said, hands clinging her jeans from nervousness at standing up to her dad. "I can go explore! I can bring back loot! I can do what you do!"

"You daughter!" Funk continued thundering. "Not son! Not man. You girl! You stay home. You study!"

Lexie looked down and folded her arms as if to protect herself, having heard those words thousands of times before.

Mark quietly spoke up. "We made it out alive."

This sent the short shopkeeper into more of a frothing rage. "And you go with this boy?!" He yelled at Lexie while jabbing the gun towards Mark. "The Dae—IT is back. IT is hungry. And IT will kill you, daughter, on IT's way to kill that boy!"

His raw words echoed in the sudden silence. Nothing changed, not the steady drip of green fluid from the Lurk's shot-up face nor the sting of the acrid air with its mixture of burnt plastic and extinguisher foam. The bright florescent lights overhead didn't flicker or dim and the world wasn't any colder. But Mark felt colder. He looked at Heath and Lexie. "I keep forgetting how badly this machine wants to kill me. I'm not used to it and…and I keep putting people in danger. I don't know why … I'll try to stop," he said, his heart hurting from guilt. "I'm sorry."

Funk was not a man who cared about apologies, no matter how sincere. "You sorry? YOU SORRY?! I have you expelled! Today! Expelled! No more friends with my daughter! Expelled!" He rounded back on Lexie, who had her head down and her eyes shut tight. "And you go sweep! No more junk hunting! NO MORE JUNK!"

This time Heath spoke up. He stepped in between Lexie and her angry father, he locked eyes with the unfair little man, and his voice was a whisper – an intense whisper. "But it's not junk."

The room fell silent again.

Heath pointed at a brick of dull black metal – clearly something Lexie would have proxy ported since it wasn't shiny. "That there is a brick of rare-solar ithierium, used to make cloaking armor. Worth 2,000 Lunnans a pop." He pointed at an ugly, jumbled cluster of grey tubes. "That's a Multi-Quantum A.I. brain. It may be old, but it's still worth more than everything in your crummy little shop – combined." He pointed again. "And that's someone's wallet. Stuffed with Lunnans. Thirteen years it's been missing. Return it and be the hero – or keep it –I won't judge. My point is: Lexie clearly knows what to look for. She's good. She's damn good."

Lexie shuffled in embarrassment at the praise.

"She risked her lift to bring you back this fortune," Heath continued. He took a step toward her father. "And you're lying to her? You're lying to us? That it's all junk? All this? When it's worth more than 10,000 of your furry pink slippers?" His olive eyes squinted at him. "Not cool, man. Not cool."

Funk was silent. Caught in the act. He wouldn't look at his daughter. He cleared his throat.

"Fine. I give you fifteen percent."

"Fifty percent."

"Twenty five percent."

"Fifty."

"Forty five percent! Take or leave!"

"Fifty."

Silence.

Funk growled. "Okay, okay."

But Heath wasn't done. "Fifty percent and instead of expelling Mark

-- you deliver all the parts he needs to build his Flarejet."

"Okay, okay!" said Funk, and then began waving them out. "You go now! Done deal! Go, poor boys!"

Heath marched out of the room followed by an astounded Mark. The boy from earth had never seen someone handle a business transaction with such…such…bulldog awesomeness! He had seen a whole new side of his friend – and it was downright impressive!

As soon as they burst out the front door, even before the door shut behind them with a pleasant tinkle, Mark shouted, "Heath! That was brilliant! Where did you learn to negotiate like that?!"

In response, the business boy broke out in so much sweat it looked like he'd been holding it back behind a dam. He sank against the cold brick wall, grabbed his tie, loosened it, and wiped his forehead, cheeks, and arm pits. "I can't believe I just did that!" He breathed. "Holy butt-cheese." He was suddenly gulping air. "That was worse than the Seven Site! Look at my hands!" He held them out. They were both shaking.

Mark laughed in admiration. "Ah, you rocked it."

Heath held his stomach. "Ugh, I think I'm gonna be sick."

Mark laughed. "Come on, just think about what you're going to do with your share!"

Heath shook his sweaty head. "No I'm giving it to my mom. It'll keep us in the apartment this winter."

Mark nodded and clapped his friend on the back. "Good on you."

The door to the Black Pearl Bazaar chimed open suddenly. Lexie burst out. "Hey!" she said breathlessly and looking back into the shop as if she wasn't supposed to be there. "Hey I just wanted to say," she paused, looking flushed and embarrassed at Heath, "thanks …"

Heath, who had immediately straightened up and was adjusting his tie all cool-like, said, "Oh yeah sure, no B.D., no big deal, no big dealio, ya know, do what I do."

She kissed him on the cheek and flew back inside.

Heath turned so bright red anyone would have mistaken him for a firetruck … or a strawberry with sandy blonde hair.

Mark grinned at Heath and the boy's red-cheeks. "Best reward yet huh? You lady's man! Next stop: muchas smooches!"

"Shut up!" Heath punched him in the chest. He then marched over to his crappy skyboard and hopped on. "Let's go see if your Flarejet crap got to Otto's."

Mark laughed joyfully and joined him. They flew back towards Otto's garage – Mark making up all sorts of funny nicknames for Heath (Prince Charm-a-lot, Romeo-cheeks, smooch-magnet), and Heath glowing redder and redder and shouting 'shut up!' louder and louder (which was made all the funnier by his board losing power and bobbing up and down faster and faster).

They eventually reached Otto's garage (though Mark wasn't done coming up with nicknames – his latest being Don Smoochorio the Third.) Heath skidded his skyboard underneath the repair shop's flat roof, leapt off, and was about to tackle Mark when they both heard dozens of loud excited voices coming from inside Otto's garage – and most of them sounded really familiar.

Giving each other a quizzical look, they left their boards propped against the brick wall and rushed in.

For some strange reason all their classmates from Basic Repair were swarming the garage!

Gus was there, darting between people to see who'd pay him the most to sip the coolant staining the floor. Allison and Gabby were there, being ignored by Miranda as they asked if she could get them inked with lifelike tattoos 'like maybe a butterfly or shooting star.' And a dozen other classmates were there too, half sitting in a dismantled hovercars pretending to drive by making engine sounds and beeping, and the other half gathered in awe around Phil, who was doing his hand-into-tools trick. Otto towered above them all, calling for order.

"Otto!" Mark shouted—he had to shout just to be heard—while tackling his way through the garage. "We got the parts!"

"I know!" she thundered back, not at all happy about it. "I got word from Munk or Skunk or whatsisname durin' class! And all these blighted little sunspots insisted on comin' to me garage ter look!'

A girl named Zaza Rayn popped up beside Mark. "I want to help build your flarejet!"

He gave her a confused stare. This curly haired girl didn't even like getting her hands dirty; she bought those instaclean clothes from Heath at a steep price just because of that. Why was she so eager to help?

"Hi, I'm Torvan," said a lanky kid with seriously short black hair and a thin robotic right arm. "We haven't met officially, at least, I don't believe me meeting your butt at breakfast all those months ago counts, does it?"

"No, I guess not," is all Mark could think to say, still embarrassed from that debacle.

"I'm training to be a hydraulics technician," continued Torvan, himself looking as thin as a hydraulic tube. "Figured you could use some expert-teese."

"Why?" asked Mark, then realized he sounded rather rude. "Sorry, I mean, why help? This whole Flarejet might be nothing more than a spectacular fart."

Zaza smiled. "Maybe—but it'd be pretty cool if it wasn't!"

Torvan agreed. "Plus it'd rock if a kid from the Support Crew got a chance to take a swing at those snobs in the Cadet Core."

Mark was taken aback. Help? These people wanted to help? His skeptical eyes darted between Torvan and Zaza. "You're serious?"

Heath, who wasn't surprised at all, said, "'course they are! They're from the Crew! Like us!"

"And the end of year Wargame is only four months away," Zaza added. "You'll need all the help you can get!"

"But," said Mark. "There's no pay in this, and it's after school, and it's—it's—"

"It's fun!" said Zaza.

"And awesome," added Torvan.

"And let's face it," Zaza shrugged. "You are an Earther."

Mark beamed. Was this really happening? Was he making friends?!

"Come on," Otto growled at Mark, breaking his speechless revere. "I stacked yer flarejet parts at the back of me garage."

Curiosity took hold of Mark and his compatriots. They kept in Otto's wake as the Irishwoman bouldered through several Support Crew kids who were 'standin' about 'gettin' in the way.'

"Here she be!" Otto said when they reached the back of the cluttered garage. "She's no Blacknova A.X., but she'll put up a mean fight when the bell drops."

The boy from Earth stood mesmerized. Had he ever, ever seen anything so beautiful? Forget Lance's sleek shadow of high-end technology. This incomplete, bare metal, raw machine smelling of oil and iron was a sight to inspire. The actual engine looked as if it were wrenched from the guts of an F-16 fighter jet; pipes and struts and vents and all manner of wicked thingamabobs bristled out of its bare turbine. The wings were short, sliced at a hard angle like the tail of an F-4 Phantom— just waiting to carry devastating missiles. And the best part? The pilot's cab rested above it all, at the very back, so he could see the entire growling beast in front of him—like the engine of a muscle car. He stammered, not knowing what to say.

Zaza knew what to say. She went up and petted the engine. "She's pretty!"

Her motion was like momentum. Torven, Heath and Gus, and a

bunch of Support Crew kids all went up to the mess of pipes, turbines, and circuit boards. They murmured their amazement in quiet whispers.

Mark, however, hadn't moved. The potential, the possibilities, overwhelmed him. He dreamed of soaring through star dusted nebulas and dodging blazing meteors. When Otto asked again what Mark thought of the tremendous mess, all that the kid from earth could do was breath heavy and say, "It looks like a lawnmower used to trim fluffy white clouds by angels in heaven."

Otto roared with laughter. "Jupter's red eye! I never hird no descrip' quite like that!"

"So how do I build it?" Mark asked, eager eyes roving the stacks of parts strewn all around. "Do I just bolt these things onto those things with tool things?"

"This isn't a snap-on play set, ye grease monkey." Otto pointed to a pair of black and yellow tubes, each the width of a barrel and twice as long. "Tha's a pair of IMP cannons. Each one fires a bolt a' ionized mass. They'll need ta be attached proper, mind, so as when ye fire 'em, ye won't blast yer own rump off."

Mark nodded, concentrating even as Gus darted over asking Lunnans for breaking a shiny hexagon plate he'd found—with his forehead.

Otto wrestled it from him. "These plates are part of yer SEG, yer Shield Envelope Generator. Made by Orion Industries. Good against bullets, burners, an' bombshells. It'll even bugger off a missile or two. Ye'll attach these plates with all yer patience and all yer skill. This is important, ye hear?"

Five heads bobbed in the affirmative.

"Right, because ye have no armor."

"Yeeesh," said Torvan. The others also wore grimaces.

"That's not good, is it?" said Mark, remembering the words live ammo and missiles tossed around when Heath described the war game. "But

Heath said that pilots are out of the game when their shields hit ten percent. Why would I need armor anyway?"

"Sometimes missiles burn the shield system," said Heath.

"Or an EMP makes it go all fuzzy," added Zaza.

"And then shots sneak through," nodded Torvan.

"But don't worry," said Gus. "Your flarejet will just explode and you'll go floating off into the lifeless void." He leaned in, whispering with a fading echo, "alone—alone—alone." And then he pointed at Mark. "But I'll save you! For five low payments of a hundred Lunnans—prepaid!"

Mark laughed. He didn't gulp from fear or anything. He laughed. This was dangerously awesome. All of it. He loved it.

"That's the basics," said Otto McMaluch. "Now," she weighed both robotic hands on Mark's shoulders, "ye've got helpin hands around ye, and that's grand, but only you can change those buggering stars of yers. Only you."

Mark responded with a stout, serious nod.

"Yer future is full o' grease, welding, and muscle-aching labor, laddy. Every day after school for the next three months." The grizzled mechanic emphasized this by leaning down to Mark's eyelevel. "Believe me, boy, ye won't have the time to take a whizz. Because that's what it takes—ye hear? Or else ye'll be nothing more than a laugh."

Mark met the Irishwoman's stern eye. "I'll build until my fingers bleed. .. and then I'll build some more."

He resolved to build until his fingers bled. He resolved to not let his friends down. He resolved to become a FlareRider. Because he knew that dreams aren't wishes carried away by dandelion fluff on summer breezes, or by eyes shut tight as pennies fall down wells. No, dreams are working through dawn to dusk; dreams are fighting through sweat and blood and rust.

"And ye'll need to keep yer chin up," added Otto. "Because Lance and his thugs – and everyone else not here today – will make fun o' ya, an' try an' git ya te quit!"

That, Mark thought, might be a little tougher to handle.

*   *   *   *

*   *

"You're building a flarejet?" scoffed the blue-eyed, dark-haired, super-man-faced wing leader of Alpha Squad. "You'll never get it to start!"

Mark was too exhausted to give a care. It had been two months. His S.Crew jacket was more grease than jacket by now. Sweat rolled through the soot stains on his freckled cheeks, and his lower back hurt from stooping over the lunchroom table while trying to fix the trigger on one of the IMP cannons—the trigger was overly sensitive and, when Lloyd had tickled it pretending to shoot 'evil baddies,' the IMP cannon had blasted a hole in Otto's garage.

Mark ignored Lance and kept gnawing on his strip of Gyradosian Shark Jerky (like beef jerky but made from dried, salted shark meat from the ocean planet Gyradosia). Zaza, two years younger than Mark, was trying to force Mark to eat something besides shark jerky, claiming he needed carbohydrates, vitamins, and minerals. She was forcing these upon him by making spaceship sounds while flying a spoonful of chicken soup in front of his gritty face (turns out chicken soup is beloved throughout the galaxy. Poor chickens). Mark was responding to the curly haired girl's maternal ways by stubbornly declaring that shark jerky was all he needed to survive. No chicken soup, no veggies, no vitamins or minerals or fiber. Just meat. Shark meat.

"I said," Lance repeated and smacked Mark's lucky cap, "You're crap-sack Flarejet won't even fart!"

Heath popped up. "Oh! Hey! Lance, you just reminded me," he said cheerfully. He opened his leather satchel and started rummaging through itl. "I have that thing you ordered. Fresh in." He pulled out an imaginary box and gently set it down in front of Lance. "It's a whole big box of—we-don't-give-a-frack." He held up a finger and smiled. "PLUS! I'll throw in a free pack of gum! Brand new flavor! DOG DOOKIE! Just like your face!."

Lexie was sitting next to Heath. She didn't look up from her Lemonsquare—where she was shuffling through her new songs by Droids Devolved—but Heath's burn did make her snicker.

"Funny," said Lance with a cold grin that didn't reach his fuming eyes. "Very funny, Robinson. That how your mom pays for rent? Standup comedian, is she? What do they pay her in? Old clothes?"

Heath stood right up, his chair tumbling over behind him.

The Mess Hall, which had been abuzz with miniature starfighters dog-fighting over round tables packed with chatting kids eating their lunch – fell silent. Even the Commander's Club intelligentsia, who had forgone lunch to shove their table's together and run war game simulations in 3D using their Squares, stopped to look. The Cadet Core had been the quietest from the start, and now they watched intently as Alpha Squad strolled over to back up Lance.

Mark adjusted his cap as the three blokes, arms crossed and scowling at him, fanned out behind Lance. "Oh look, your hamsters are here," said Mark, tearing off another chunk of shark jerky. "They look in need of exercise though—vitamins too."

Lance laughed and put a hindering hand on Dinsdale Mueller, who had squared up and stepped forward. "Whoa there Dinzy, save your beat down for the war game—where it's legal." Lance whirled a seat around and plopped down, straddling the chair back like some sort of tough character. "Mr. Dinsdale Mueller is Alpha Squad's Fist-Breaker—our defense. Nothing like a solid defensive in the form of a wall; a wall made out of bullets, am I right?" Lance laughed at his own joke. "And to his left is Mr. Jet Chan, our Scout—fastest guns in the biz." Lance gave him a fist bump as Jet stared intimidatingly at Heath. "And this is my right hand man, Mr. Cruise Galantine," said Lance, thumbing to the boy with perfectly combed blonde locks spilling over his angelic face—who was flashing a pearly smile. "He's our Vaporizer—pure offense." He then brushed imaginary dust off his leather jacket while looking even more smug. "And then there's me." He winked at Lexie. "You know me."

Lexie stopped listening to music and transformed her lemony guitar into a barf bag, which she then pretended to puke into—violently.

Meanwhile, Mark's sarcastic smile had been growing to such a point that he flipped a big ol' thumbs up at Lance and said, "That's totally rad!" Then his smile dead-panned into a solid stare. "But you mistake me for someone who gives two corn-crusted butt bricks." He tore off another piece of shark jerky and leaned over his IMP cannon. "I will build a flarejet. I will fly against you. And I'll win so hard your parents won't be able to look at you!."

"Oh ho ho! Harsh words coming from an Earther who doesn't even have parents! What are you building this junkjet out of anyway, huh?" Lance rose from his seat. "A heap of garbage glued together by your stupidity?"

"We," said Mark, smacking Heath and Lexie on their shoulders, "and good people from the crew, are building it out of two tons of duct tape, a middle finger, and Neil Armstrong's chest hair."

"What, these two?" scoffed Lance, pointing at Lexie and Heath. "Think your junkjet will fart to life after being slapped together by a scaredy-cat who sells cheap crap and a music-freak thrown out by everyone in her Commander's Club because she's a dirty half-human?"

At this insult Heath calmly folded his glasses, put them in his satchel, and would have swung at Lance if Mark hadn't pulled him back.

Jet Chan squared up. Behind him, Dinsdale's double chin's flopped as he snarled, and Cruise flexed his fists.

"And kids from the Support Crew?" Lance continued, his cheeks dimpled with mocking laughter. "Don't you remember why they aren't in the Cadet Core? Do you understand why they didn't make it into the Commander's Club? They're not good enough, Mark! They're lazy and stupid and most of them are half-human!

Dinsdale, Cruise, and Jet had been a solid wall of support behind Lance up until this point. But their resolve started to crack when, behind them, dozens of chairs began scrapping as Crew members stood up.

A silence extinguished all chatter. The kids in the Support Crew knew they weren't the ones getting top grades, or the most popular kids on campus . . . they knew they weren't good enough. But that didn't mean they weren't going to take life's lemons AND EAT THEM.

Cruise Galantine started to shrink away. Jet Chan placed a restraining hand on Lance's shoulder. "Maybe we save it for the War Game, huh?"

Lance slowly looked around at the Support Crew kids knuckling up for bloody noses, black eyes, and chipped teeth. They weren't big. Most of them were a few years younger. But there were a lot of them.

The whole Mess Hall was read to burst into a raging food fight, where the food flung about consisted of knuckle sandwiches and cans of whoop-ass, even the miniature starfighters overhead, loving the tension, had gleefully begun locking missiles for the fun of it.

Lance's smug smile broke under a nervous twitch. A bare knuckled brawl was brewing, and even though Dinsdale was snarling by his side like a loyal, drooling mastiff, it might not be enough.

"Yeah alright," sneered Lance, shrugging Jet's hand away. "I'll see you at the War Game, Earther," he spat at Mark, adjusting his leather bomber jacket as if he were a big shot choosing to go of his own desire. He marched his squad out of the Mess Hall.

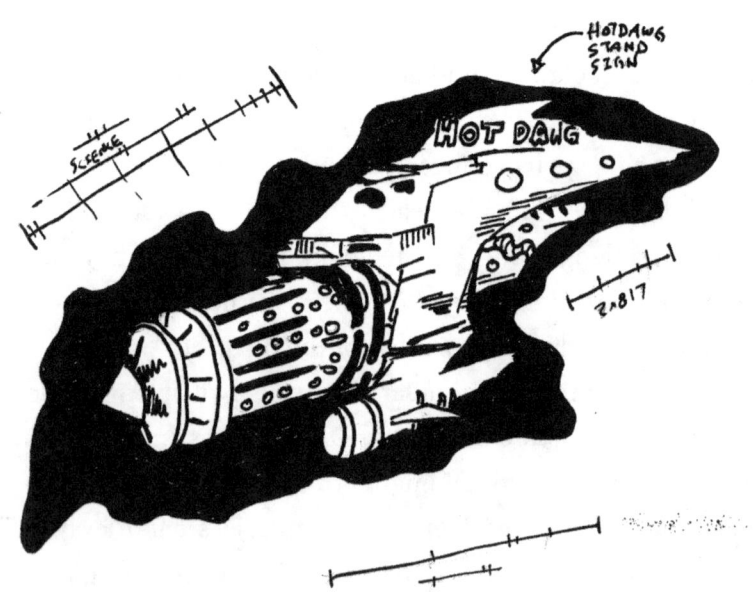

CHAPTER 10
HOW TO BUILD A FLAREJET

"Pass me a wrench?" said Mark. He was acting the part of a lazy mechanic: flat on his back beneath his half-built flarejet.

Lloyd, who was slumped cross-legged between Mark and a rusted toolbox, slapped a wrench into Mark's hand in the most miserable and sullen way possible.

Mark thanked the gloomy android and went back to installing the IMP cannon. "Welp! I'm thinking this here Flarejet will rock the known universe."

"Hold the phone!" said Lexie in sudden realization. She stopped scrolling through a list of new bands she'd downloaded onto her floating speaker system – bands which had some of the best names ever (Robot Revolution, Space Junkies, and Monkeys in the Void). "Didn't Admiral Kine say you couldn't leave SPIFF?"

"Yeah? So?"

"But the War Game is in space above Crescent City! WWAAAYYY outside SPIFF!"

"...."

"What if she doesn't let you fly out there? What if she doesn't let you compete?"

Mark stopped what he was doing, his empty hand still outstretched to Lloyd for a hammer. "I didn't think of that!" He winced when Lloyd smacked a hammer onto his open hand.

"You might be able to get in under the radar though," said Heath. He was selling a pair of regular old wooly mittens to a gleefully happy Phil—who instantly shoved his mechanical hands into them and pretended he was normal again. "Admiral Kine is at Aventine Hill Academy at the moment. My sister said so. She goes there," he clarified.

"Ella goes there!" Mark exclaimed, reaching for a screwdriver. Lloyd took the screwdriver Mark was looking for—and poked him with it.

"Who?" said Heath.

"I met her on the flight from Earth! She goes to Aventine Hill Academy!" Mark continued exclaiming. But seeing no recollection from either Heath or Lexie, he lowered his voice, "Remember the holographic message we saw on that half-sunken ship?" He whispered, motioning at Lloyd to give him the pliers. Lloyd refused.

Heath swung around making sure no one heard that secret clue.

Mark continued whispering, still reaching at Lloyd for those pliers. "Nona ordered that ship to crash into the plane carrying me and Ella."

"Shhh ush!" said Heath.

"What if Nona is the Dae—IT?" Mark whispered even lower, his fingers really dancing for those pliers now.

Lloyd's bad temper broke. He dumped the entire toolbox on Mark's hand. "WHY HAVEN'T YOU FIXED FLOYD?"

"Ow!" Mark shouted back, shaking the pain from his hand. "I tried fixing Floyd! I can't! Every time I touch him I get zapped! IT HURTS!"

"Yaaaaaaahhhh!" came Zaza's happy battle cry as she dashed in from outside.

Mark responded by jerking in surprise so hard, he slammed his head on the bottom of his flarejet. "Ow!"

"Snowball fiiiight!" Zaza screamed, and began chucking globs of packed snow.

Lexie yelped and jumped to hide behind the flarejet. Torvan, fixing a hydraulic system on the other side of the garage, laughed and joined Lexie in dashing round and round the engine trying to escape the curly-haired girl's armful of wintery ammo.

Mark, rubbing his head and wincing, rolled out from under the half-built beast. "What's with all the crazy?" he shouted.

His question was promptly answered by a slush ball to the face.

"That's what!" shouted a furiously happy Zaza, who ran outside to make more. Lexie, Torvan, and Heath made a mad dash to join her.

Mark stayed, blowing the wet snow out of his nose, a dazed look on his face. He didn't have time to catch a breath before all three rushed in and made the back of his head look like a snowman. This time he rushed out with them, beginning the first of many snowball fights that winter.

Winter was in full flurry throughout the neon city. Mark didn't know how snow could be on the moon, but then again he didn't know how a city could be on the moon, and all his requests for explanations were met with shouts of "because SCIENCE!" So he shrugged and went with it; which made it easier to wake up each morning, sit up in bed, and simply enjoy the sight outside his escape pod's frosted round window where fat snowflakes in a blizzard shrouded the city.

Glowing through the swirling storm were distant sapphire skyscrapers, ruby red office buildings, and nearby homes, all aglow like blurry emeralds.

He wouldn't sit still for long, though. That diabolical alarm clock tried sneaky new strategies—songbirds into snarling werewolves, fresh-cut grass into raw sewage—but Mark would wake up before any of it. He'd jam into his shoes and burst out the door, leaving the yellow alarm clock to roll away and sulk.

He wanted nothing more than to finish the school day, jump on his Comet Chaser, and zip on over to Otto's garage to continue building his Flarejet. Naturally, this annoyed each and every one of his teachers. Lieutenant Landeth made him stay and do extra jump-point calculations each time she caught him packing up before the bell rang; MS. DOS stopped awarding him points for the Twichian word 'hurry' when she found out Mark was just nervously tapping his leg under his desk; Miss DuBoush put Mark behind an iron blast shield after his fuel mixtures kept exploding in his face; and Otto McMaluch threatened to stop helping him if he didn't 'quit askin to leave early like an interplanetary pain in the arse.'

Thus the months passed. Building the Flarejet was no easy task. Heath helped acquire bolts, clamps, and small connector parts; Lexie claimed to help but mostly shuffled through songs and pickpocketed Lance and his squad when they'd come in to make fun of Mark and his 'sack of crap Flarecrap crappity crap' (they weren't particularly ingenious with their insults); Torvan and Zaza were a great team, and they helped bring in more Support Crew to build the flarejet. Lloyd, however, was useless. When he wasn't moping about mourning Floyd, he was trying to convince everyone, including Otto, that Phil's augmented hands were actually alive and controlling the man's brain—Lloyd said this in a very low and squinty-eyed voice.

At each days end Mark was the last to leave the garage. So Otto would brew up a couple pistons full of Gear Grog and Mark would set up two lawn chairs just inside the open garage door. They would sit and slurp their Grog with the half-augmented Irishwoman pointing to snow covered hovercars zooming on the nearby flyway. She would challenge Mark to name their make and model and how each compared to another, performance wise. He was getting better at it too. He could spot a Corsair Comette from a mile away and knew that it could outrace a Ferrio Zoltestta on the straight away (but not the curves); He could tell the difference between a Hugger RS and a Mercury Mio just by their exhaust note; And when one of those sleek, rare, fat-wallet-required exotic racers would blitz by (An Atlas-X or a LeMure Voltumillio), he would prattle on about their Z12 engines, half second hover times, and how the leather seats inside probably smell awful, like old money and rich people butts.

Then, almost three months after Mark had bolted on the first SEG plate to his flarejet, he welded the last fuel line. Earlier that Saturday afternoon Lexie had finished installing and checking the last set of flight software; Torvan had finished a final check of the fuel pump; and Zaza and Heath were due back any minute, having gone to tell Professor DuBoush that Mark's flarejet was ready for fueling.

"That's it," Mark whispered to himself, moving the welding goggles from his eyes to his lucky cap—which was now scorched, smudged, and stained all over in that well-loved kinda way. He took a few steps back to look at the whole flarejet. Everybody was either outside or away. This moment of completion, of hard work, perseverance and dedication was his alone. "We did it."

He put the welder down and went up to the beastly machine. Laying a hand on top of the bare engine—so large he couldn't see over it—a feeling of exhausted triumph washed over his body. He stood, living hand on cold metal, for a few quiet, meditative, beautiful minutes.

"We'll make it," he whispered to the newly created flarejet. "We'll dodge hundreds of meteors and scream ourselves hoarse skimming Saturn's rings. We'll loop the loop around blazing comets shadowed by solar eclipses and—and—" he placed both hands on the chariot of his dreams. "And we'll fight that pompous, superman-faced, swag-turd of a golden boy—and we'll win."

Mark stood, head down, hands on metal, for a few more quiet moments, dreaming and dreaming.

"WHO ORDERED THE HOT SAUCE?" shouted Professor DuBoush

from the garage doors.

Heath and Zaza followed her in, each carrying a fuel cell plastered with warning labels (Do Not Drink. Do Not Shake. Do Not, Under Any Circumstances, Pour Into Waterballoons). They dropped both fuel cell's down by the engine with a thud.

"Custom mixed Flarejet fuel," Professor DuBoush announced as she unscrewed the metal cap on one of the cells. A puff of yellow steam rose. "Five hundred forty nine chemicals, seven liquid metals, and a splash of Gear Grog for luck—all giving your Flarejet an extra nine-thousand NPH of thrust—ooo-weee!" She took out her flask and, tilting the fuel cell, poured a generous amount into it. She then raised her fuel filled flask and took a swig. "Aahhh! That's a healthy kick!"

Otto chuckled and, seeing that the kids were too wide-eyed at Ethyl's drinking habits, proceeded to fuel Mark's flarejet herself, tipping over the fuel cells and pouring the blistering yellow liquid into the Flarejet's fuel tanks.

"Fire it up!" Lexie shouted after Otto tossed the empty cells. The others cheered.

Mark clambered up to the open control cabin. He swung onto the patched-up leather seat. Reaching back, he slid the oval canopy over his lucky cap. It shut with a wonderful click. His eager eyes scanned the controls. This was no sleek paneled digital Blacknova AX, with its voice commands and its targeting system and its holographic heads-up display. No. He placed a hand on the two big square gauges in the center, one for speed the other for direction. He ran a finger over the red triggers of the IMP cannons. He tapped the round gauge showing the shield level indicator. A sense of something like love washed over him. His Flarejet didn't even have a fuel gauge! No way to know if he was low on fuel or not! He'd just fly until the engine shuddered and stopped. He loved it.

"Fire it up! Fire it up! Fire it up!" chanted his friends.

Professor DuBoush saluted him with her flask and took a swig.

Otto stood watching in angry pride. Her garage mates, Phil and Ratchet, also watched with encouraging grins.

Mark's thumb hovered over the start button. He jammed it.

The turbine began rotating. A high-pitched whine filled the garage. A muffled rumble. It sent shudders through everyone's shoes. A second rumble. Everyone felt their hearts start ka-thumpings, adrenaline pumping through their veins as they witnessed a Frankenstein beast roaring to life.

BANG!

A loud backfire shook the garage's brick walls.

Mark's pounding heart crashed in disappointment against his ribs.

"No," he whispered, all his hopes sinking as the engine made a last cough and the high whine of the turbine died.

The Irishwoman strode over, irritated as always and not caring about the heat pouring from the flarejet. She slammed the glass canopy away from Mark. "Jupiter's bloody spot! Crank the throttle, kid!" she said, making a twisting motion. "Ya just frankenstiend this monster! Crank the gas! Pour that liquid hellfire into it!"

Mark nodded in determination.

Otto smashed the canopy closed and stepped back.

Mark, brow knitted, palms sweating, went to press the start button again, hoping beyond hope. But then he remembered something very important he'd forgotten to do the first time – and gave his lucky cap a flick.

He punched the start button.

The turbine began spinning again. The high whine started filling the air again. A muffled rumble sent shudders through everything again – and Mark began cranking that throttle hard.

Bright yellow fuel raced through dim red fuel lines. The colors blended into a harsh, burnt orange. Everywhere he looked aggressive orange lines snaked around solid steel pipes, brackets, and welded parts. A second rumble, like a bellowing grizzly or a roaring tiger or, no, like Godzilla! Yes! This thing was a beast, a monster! It was King-Kong roaring to life! It was Godzilla destroying downtown Tokyo! It was raw. It was real. It was, by sight and sound—alive.

The pounding rumble became a steady roar. "It's alive! It's allliiiiiive!" he shouted, throttling the gas with his right hand. The engine responded with snarling throaty growls. Everyone broke into cheers—none of which Mark could hear—being deafened by the engine and all.

"Good! That's good!" shouted Otto above the rumbling noise. When she saw Mark being deaf and grinning stupidly, she made a "shut-it-down" motion with her hand.

Mark flipped the kill switch. The flarejet grumbled to a halt. He jumped down, too happy to care if he got burnt by the radiating heat.

Lexie and Heath and Zaza and Torvan all swarmed him for hand-shakes and fist bumps.

"Congratulations, grease monkey, ye've got yerself a real belchin', fire eatin', flyin' beastie," said Otto, offering a rare proud smile. "I'll knock on the cap's office door with the hearty news tomarra!"

Mark beamed, positively beamed.

"Now all yer monkey hide needs is trainin.' I'll deliver yer flarejet to Lieutenant Landeth tomarra too!"

Mark's smile vanished. The congratulatory pats from his friends went unnoticed. "Lieutenant Landeth? Why? Why him? What for?"

Otto had to chuckle at Mark's panicked response. "He runs the Cadet Core! Aaaahhh, don't go lookin' like a howler monkey! If ye can build a flarejet, ye can survive that young ballistic missile."

Encouraging words those may have been, but they did nothing to alleviate the rock of doubt and accompanying stone of worry that sunk in Mark's gut. Professor Duboush directed him and his friends to stand in front of the flarejet for a picture; Mark smiled sloppily alongside a beaming Lexie and Heath on his right side, and a waving Zaza and Torvan on his left. Then DuBoush took another picture of Otto resting her hydraulic right arm on Mark's shoulder, her barrel chest puffed out in something like really perturbed pride. But the whole time, Mark's head was clouded with visions of the disciplinary lieutenant who thought he was not good enough. Oh, and Lance's smug face floated around mocking him, just for good measure.

Deep down he was happy, he really was. Having finally built the flarejet was something amazing—and that it worked, actually worked, was a ridiculous miracle—but what would happen tomorrow?

"I disapprove," said Lieutenant Landeth. His mouth was pulled down at the corners, making his scar appear as if it were rejecting Mark and refusing Captain Zumski's requests.

"Having a fresh face will be good for moral," stated the square-bearded captain in his gentlemanly accent. His hand rested reassuringly on Mark's shoulder.

"No!" said Lance, fuming with his squad just behind the lieutenant. He flung a furious gesture at Mark's flarejet and began jabbering a list of reasons. "You can't let Mark train! He's an Earther! He's not allowed outside SPIFF! The Daemon's after him! And that thing he built is nothing but a Junkjet! A JUNKJET!"

"Junkjet!" repeated Dinsdale, so angry his jowls flapped. "Junkjet!"

"Junkjet!" shouted the Cadet Core. "It's a junkjet!"

"Junkjet! Junket! Junkjet!" Went Dinsdale angrily. He was joined by almost all the students in the flight class, all chanting, "Junkjet!"

"Captain, with respect," continued Landeth, "Admiral Kine needs to approve this request first."

The roguish old gentleman smiled gently and placed a hand on her shoulder. "But Nona is not here right now, is she? So let me worry about that. Stand on me. Until then, Mark joins. That's an order."

The tall Lieutenant's scar scrunched in impatience at the captain's stubborn belief in the boy. He turned to his class of aviator-jacket wearing cadets. "Mark will be joining Foxtrot Squad. Get into your squads! Today's class is flight maneuvers. Dismissed!"

He marched away.

"Good luck in foxtrot," mocked Lance, switching from being angry to being a jerk (which are often the same thing). "Foxtrot hasn't won a War Game since they existed!" He led his squad away with Dinsdale braying like a fat donkey, Cruise flashing his pearly whites in an odious grin, and Chan making fist-breaking threats.

Stanislaw Zumski didn't care to watch them go. He turned to Mark. "I need to sneak back up to my office—there's a lemon meringue pie waiting for me—but I wanted to make sure you got into training. Don't worry about Nona just yet. Do your best to train as hard as you can. And, last but not least, I'm going to slip a slice of cheese into this motivational sandwich... And that is this: remember, success is not in the flarejet," he pointed at Mark's chest, "success is in the FlareRider."

Mark couldn't help but laugh a little. "That is pretty cheesy, sir."

"I know," the old captain said with a heartfelt smile, "but it works, eh?"

Mark nodded, feeling just a bit better.

"Good. Ah, here's your squad," he said as the three members of Foxtrot marched up. He returned their stiff salutes with a rather silly wave. "If my memory hasn't joined my hairline," he shook the girl's hand, "you are the Foxtrot Fist-Breaker: Keera Lenz." The redheaded girl named Keera nodded proudly. "Never let go of those triggers."

"Not a thought, cap," said Keera with a grin.

"Ah, Derrick Trap," said Stan, giving the tall boy with the army buzz cut a firm handshake. "The Vaporizer. Don't defend Mark too much now."

"Never intended to, sir," said Derrick, returning the firm handshake.

"And last but not least, Jai—,"

"Oh! Cap!" said Keera quickly. "It's—The Sphinx—now."

Zumski chuckled as he shook the hand of the boy, or girl (it was diffi-cult to tell), wearing a full flight suit and helmet. "Well, The Sphinx – as the Scout for Foxtrot, I expect you to put the rookie through his paces,"

The Sphinx's flight suit and helmet were black with a gold Egyptian sphinx emblazoned in the center. He, or she, nodded—once.

And with that, Stan left, walking away in that self-confident, perpetu-ally jovial manner, as if he knew the secret to a happy life and didn't care to share a word of it.

Derrick was the first Foxtrot cadet to speak up, and the first thing he said instantly put an embarrassed red hue on Mark's cheeks: "Hey, aren't you the kid who wiggled his butt at the start of the year?"

Mark's freckles fired up. He balled his fists and would have thrown some words back at Derrick, but then Keera asked, "Why don't you have any dinnerware on this Junkjet?"

"Any what?" Mark stammered, suddenly confused.

"Armor plating," Keera explained. "You've got not a single plate. One shot slips through your shields or an EMP fries your SEG and you're right bumbled."

The Sphinx nodded—once.

"Yeah, I know," Mark replied. "But I've got an Orion Industries SEG."

Keera nodded with an approving frown. "Not half nitty. That'll eat a lot o' hurt."

The Sphinx shrugged, as if to say, "meh."

Mark's new squad mates began circling his flarejet. Keera, in true Fist-Breaker fashion, started inspecting the IMP cannons. The Sphinx started tapping on the engine in a will-this-thing-fall-apart way. Derrick just whistled in mock amazement.

"Yeah," said Mark, trying to put on a confident face. "I know it looks like some kinda brandura, but it'll kick the fun buns."

"Brandura?" asked Keera in a curious tone.

"Just something my granddad used to say," replied Mark with a nervous chuckle. "It means 'piece of junk.' "

The Sphinx nodded—twice.

"Look at this!" said Derrick, pointing to Mark's tail fin as if spotting a grand joke. "It says Junkjet!"

Keera smiled big. "I like it!" She clapped Mark on the back, who was sheepishly grinning. "Way to own it, rookie!"

Mark's new squad mates kept walking round and inspecting. Finally Keera came up to him with an approving smile.

"Lookin' good, rookie. Everything's in place and solid." She nodded to affirm that thought. "Right then, let's get you up for maneuvers!"

Minutes later and Mark, hollering in pure joy, blazed after his new squad mates as they rocketed out of the hangar and into snowy skies.

Once more, he was soaring through the clouds, but this time he could really feel everything. His junkjet didn't have the luxurious quiet of Lance's Blacknova. Instead, he bounced around on his rattling seat as turbulent winds buffed from all sides; he grinned as the fuel lines burned orange across the bare engine; he stared in happy wonder as his beast ate right through snow-laden cloud after snow-laden cloud.

He flew away from the neon city, the GSS Final Frontier becoming a spec among tiny buildings. Then, in a heartbeat, all the noise ceased. No rattling, no rushing, nothing.

He had flown into the void. Nothing remained but the feel of the engine working and the sight of burnt orange fuel coursing through glowing fuel lines. He made it. He was in space.

"All right, rookie," came Keera's voice of the intercom. "Let's see what you got."

He looked around to see his squad mates sitting in their flarejets. They had maneuvered to each side of him, waiting for something exciting or new from this kid piloting a junkjet glued together by half a dozen misfit kids and one mean, cussing Irishwoman -- using a beastly old engines, buckets of worn sprockets, a missing fuel gauge, and some actual chest hair (Otto had stuck it on, claiming it brought good luck – no one wanted to know where she got it from).

Mark's smile slipped into a serious frown. He pumped the throttle. Those orange fuel lines pulsed. The beast responded by shuddering in anticipation.

"Let's see those taillights!" shouted Keera over the com. "Burn the fusebox!"

Mark did. He cranked the throttle. He made the monster roar. And his "brandura" accelerated into the stars so hard, leaving a blaze of orange so intense, that even The Sphinx whispered, "Whoa."

****

Mark trained for the next solid month. He trained hard. A normal day consisted of waking up early to meet The Sphinx for dodge and roll training, followed by eating lunch while being chased by Derrick in an attempt to learn escape tactics and how not to punch Derrick in the mouth (he kept chasing Mark into random meteorites and firing at him), and finally having some measure of fun after school with Keera as she taught him to aim proper, stack his cannon fire, and blast plastic targets into itty bitty pieces. At the end of each day, Mark would stumble into his escape-pod dorm room, flop on his bed, and start drooling on unfinished homework.

Then, one miraculous day, Keera finally, finally let him go the Mess Hall for lunch.

"There he is," came Heath's hearty shout over the din as Mark walked. "We've barely seen you all month!"

"Uhhhh." Mark heaved a sigh and plopped down by Heath, who had pulled up a chair between him and Torvan. "I've been flying, man. Flying like a boy wizard who just got his first Nimbus 2k."

"Nimb-what?" asked Torvan.

"Earther reference," said Mark with a tired smile.

"Hey," said Zaza from across the table. "Is it true the lieutenant caught you using your flarejet's afterburners to roast hundreds of marshmallows?"

Mark returned her question by raising an eyebrow. "You were there, Zaza. You're the one who put the marshmallows on the sticks."

"I know," she said gleefully. "It was awesome!"

Gus popped up and yelled at her. "You still owe me seven Lunnans for stuffing them in my ears!"

As Gus argued over price, Torvan asked "How goes the training?"

"Terrible," said Mark as his head sunk into his hands. "Miserable," he mumbled into his arms. "And if you must now … downright no good at all." He lifted his tired head. "I forgot to unhook an extension cord from my shield batteries this morning. When I flew out the hangar the cord ripped out of the wall and sailed into space behind me like a long, flapping streamer of toilet paper. My flarejet looked like it came back from dunking a doozy in the toilet bowl."

Everyone at the table laughed.

"By the way," said Lexie, "thanks for bulldozing into Prof. DOS's the other day. Best timing! We were in the middle of a three-hour mid-term! You didn't need to do that for little ol' me."

"I didn't," said Mark with a flat stare. "I forgot I was in reverse."

A fresh round of laughs went up.

Mark felt his cheeks coloring. Eager to change the subject, he nodded toward the two-story window overlooking the melting valley. "I can't believe winter's over. I didn't even get to enjoy it."

"Don't worry," chirped Lexie, "we made a bunch of snowmen in your honor. In fact, I made one you'd really appreciate."

"Yeah," giggled Zaza. "It had a big forehead and big black eyebrows like bushy caterpillars!"

Lexie put on an air of philosophy. "It symbolized your caveman brain."

Mark snorted, but then when Lexie projected pictures from her Lemonsquare onto the table – in moving 3D – he had to laugh.

Heath prodded Mark with an elbow and tilted his head, as if indicating they should talk somewhere quiet. When Mark joined him a few steps away from the noisy lunch table, he said, "Hey, has Admiral Kine approved your Flarejet yet?"

"Oh," said Mark in that way people do when they were hoping the subject wouldn't come up. "Yeah. No."

Heath's brow furrowed above his square glasses as if he didn't want to say something – but had to. "I've been thinking," he shifted his tie nervously and didn't meet Mark's eyes. "Maybe … maybe it would be good if Admiral Kine grounded you."

"What?" said Mark flatly.

Heath, fidgeting anxiously because of Mark's defensive reaction, fretted with his tie some more. "I know we put in a lot of hard work. YOU put in a lot of hard work. A LOT!" He coughed into his hand. "But …thing is … see… I have a bad feeling, right? A bad feeling and – call me Lloyd's paranoid circuit board here . . . but—what if – since you'll be flying so far away from SPIFF – you'll be in freakin' space, after all--,"

"Get to the point, man!" Mark interrupted.

Heath looked him straight in the eye. "What if the Dae – what if IT

– tries to kill you again?"

"So?" Mark replied instantly. "I mean, I've thought about it so much I don't sleep anymore. Wake up with nightmares about IT murdering my face." He flicked his lucky cap. "But I have to do this. Never let your fear decide your fate – I heard that on the radio once. The song's called Kill Your Heroes, I think. Anyway, you should find it for Lexie. She'd like that."

Heath blinked at Mark's sideways off-topic song suggestion, then shook it off and pressed on. "Those Lurks hunted you, hunted US. That five-eyed Lurk tore off its arm to chase us!"

"I'm not giving in, man."

Heath started getting a bit hot under the collar. "But what if those Machines are out there? What if they're waiting for you! Your junkjet won't survive two hits!"

"I'll fight them!" Mark's voice cracked. "I'll beat them." His right fist flexed. "And I'll finally figure out WHY they're after me!"

Zaza tiptoed up and whispered: "Why are we whispering?"

"Uh, just giving Mark some flying pointers," said Heath, quickly changing the subject. "It's supposed to hail during the Wargame tomorrow. Telling him to get above the weather quick. Hailstorms make a mess of shield systems."

"The Wargame's tomorrow!" cheered Zaza. "You'll be flying and we'll be watching!"

Mark's time and thoughts became preoccupied with answering the questions his friends were asking. A few more students from the Support Crew sat down to talk about his custom built flarejet. A few cadets and even a person from the Commanders Club stopped by just to say hi and wish Mark the best of luck tomorrow.

Lance sauntered past too, complete with his sneering mates. He bragged that even if Mark's junkjet made it off the ground, his Blacknova would shoot it out of the sky. To this, Dinsdale slurred the word junkjet, Chan went cracking his knuckles, and Cruise winked at Lexie, and then sent her a smug kiss.

Heath, seeing the smug kiss, stood up so violently his chair sailed up behind him and flew across three tables. He would have decked Cruise upside his swaggy face if Lexie hadn't stopped him – she simply strummed her guitar and started singing a brand new song she'd wrote right there on the spot, which went something like this: "Cruise Gallentine is a dingleberry," guitar riff, "who smells terribly," guitar riff, "is quite hairy," guitar riff, "and once kissed a girl named Larry." Epic guitar solo.

But as the day drew to a close, doubts and fears surfaced in Mark's mind. That night he sat for the longest time, cross-legged on his bed gazing out the little round window at the neon city. The Wargame started tomorrow. He would battle Lance tomorrow—a kid with natural talent for being a FlareRider. Tomorrow his friends and teachers and everyone who helped him would be watching—what if he lost? What if he let them down?

What if the Daemon was waiting out there – ready to shoot him down in front of everyone … Leave him a burnt mess falling out of the sky in front of everyone …

His dreams were not particularly comforting that night. Thankfully he didn't sleep much.

CHAPTER 11
WAR GAME

The next day Mark plodded to Launch Bay Three (which had been converted into a stadium) through crowded hallways filled with excited shouts and tumultuous chatter. He plugged his ears because his head felt like a split melon.

But every grumpy feeling fled in an instant when the crowd pushed and shoved and moved him through the stadium doors. The sheer size of Launch Bay Three was overwhelming—larger than a. . .a . . .well he'd never been in a football stadium but he imagined it'd be at least that size, maybe three times bigger.

He stood agape as the crowd tumbled all around him. This event was big. Kids ran around on the grass by the bleachers until their parents yelled at them to take a seat; students sat in groups with their phones out, sharing holographic pictures and videos of previous War Games. Vendors of foods and candies walked up and down the stairs shouting if anyone wanted Candy Clouds and getting in arguments with dads over the "outrageous" prices; there was even a guy pushing a hot dog cart around with a big orange sign that read Hot Dawgs. All this pandemonium made Mark grin.

Down the field to his right a familiar sleek black shadow was parked with three other familiar flarejets against a background of shimmering gold flags. The Alphas were out in full parade.

Down the field to his left stood Heath and Lexie. They were chatting with Keera and the rest of foxtrot squad in front of their flarejets. Keera and her squad had their game faces on, even though their side of the stadium was nowhere near as full as the right side. It was easy to see who the majority of people at SPIFF backed as the sure bet, and it wasn't the squad that had never won – which now had a 'noob' Earther on their team as well as his handmade junkjet.

And speaking of his junkjet, there it was -- canopy open, fueled up … and being inspected by Admiral Nona Kine.

His stomach sank low enough it felt like it would touch his sneakers. He gulped. This was it. He had to convince her to approve his kludged-to-gether brandura. Despite the risks. Despite the danger. Despite the Daemon.

He stood straight, flicked the notched brim of his cap for luck, and marched on over.

Heath caught sight of him first and pulled him to the side. "It's okay if the Admiral grounds you," he said, trying to sound reassuring. "Foxtrot won't suffer any penalties and … you'll be safe."

Mark growled at him, "If she grounds me I'll sneak it into the sky."

That's when Admiral Kine marched up. She stopped, her long navy admiral's cloak billowing around her tall, gaunt frame. Her hauntingly white mask betrayed no emotion. Her digital mouth lit up. She spoke.

"I approve."

Mark stood speechless.

Admiral Nona Kine then marched off, raising a single hand in the air signaling the War Game to begin.

The bleachers erupted in cheers.

Keera began barking orders for her squad to 'lace up and fire up.'

A grin suddenly burst forth on Mark's freckled face. "Alright! That was easy!"

Heath, however, was squinting after the Admiral. "Too easy …"

"Holy flapjacks, man!" said Mark in exasperation at his friend. "It's like having Lloyd around!"

Heath looked at Mark, real concern in the olive eyes behind his black glasses. "Just – be on extra alert … in case the Admiral is planning something …"

Mark would have replied and reassured his friend, but Keera grabbed him by the arm, shoved a pair of flight goggles to his chest, and led him to his flarejet saying, "Remember all the maneuvers I tried to mix into your brainsauce, yeah?" She started mimicking her list of instructions. "Drop and bumble, weasel and float, huddle the snout and, most important, keep your triggers warm and saucy … got it?"

Mark -- honest to god -- believed she made these things up on the fly – because he never understood any of them (and couldn't unscramble them with a code breaker), so he just nodded vigorously and said, "Oh totally yeah!"

"Attention." Lieutenant Landeth's strict voice boomed across the stadium. "Attention." He stood in the middle of the field between the flarejet squads. "This year's War Game—prepared for us by the Commander's Club—is a merchant raid."

A holographic projection flickered to life from where Landeth stood with feet apart in the center of the field. The projection filled the field as the remaining chatter ceased—though that hot dog guy was still slinging his buns.

Mark let out a quiet whistle of wonder as the hologram enveloped the stadium. It was like everyone had been zoomed up into space and was looking down onto Crescent City from way up above the hailstorm clouds. Skyscrapers reached no higher than Mark's stomach, and the storm clouds went floating below his shoulders. Above the neon city the darkness filled with tiny shimmering stars.

"A drone ship will represent the merchant." As Lieutenant Landeth said this, a small holographic merchant ship blinked on high up in the middle of the field and began lumbering across. "The guards—Foxtrot Squad—will accompany the merchant, protecting it from attack." A squad of holographic flarejets shaped just like Keera and her squad cruised into view behind the merchant. "The raiders—Alpha Squad—will try and steal the merchant's cargo." She paused to make sure everyone would hear the next, most important part. "Win condition: Alpha Squad steals the cargo and brings it back to SPIFF . . . or Alpha Squad destroys Foxtrot. Either way, standard rule apply: automatic kill at five percent shields."

"That's the worst Wargame scenario for us," spat Derrick.

"We don't have the firepower to defend against Lance," Keera growled, "We'll be barbequed up there."

The Sphinx nodded his, or her, helmet—thrice.

The stadium erupted into massive noise. Heated debates about how fast foxtrot squad would get obliterated sailed between students. Teachers discussed which of foxtrot's flarejets would go down in flames first. Even the food vendors were into it, and discreetly bet against Mark by slipping Lunnans between each other.

Mark, however, wasn't fazed. They could do this. They could win. All they had to do was defend the cargo. How hard could it be?

The hologram disappeared.

Cadets from both squads raced to their flarejets.

Mark clambered up the side of his beast. Just before he plopped down in the duct-taped seat, he caught a glimpse of the tail fin. Junkjet. Those words welded into the rusted iron seemed aglow with defiant heat. Junket. He grinned and turned to the bleachers.

Captain Zumski was here. This made Mark feel better. The Machines wouldn't attack with Captain Zumski on the watch. He waved at the old captain. Zumski saw and saluted in that silly way of his. Then he elbowed

Otto, which interrupted the Irishwoman's heated argument with a soda vendor about why, exactly, there was no Irish whiskey. Otto nodded at Mark, then went back to arguing.

Zaza and Torvan were up in the bleachers too, waving and cheering, proud to have helped build the beast. Heath and Lexie had made it back to the stands too – and were now taking advantage of the crowded event—Heath by selling big novelty signs for people to wave around ('The Guy Behind Me Can't See') and Lexie by asking people what they thought of band names she'd just came up with ("Cavemen in Space... or Spacecavemen ... or The Cavenaughts).

For a brief moment Mark wished he had parents. They could be seated down there, watching him with pride.

"T-minus 1 minute!"

Mark shook off the drop of sadness and plopped onto his junket's squeaky seat. He slid the canopy over himself and flicked the start switch. "Yes," he said to himself as the turbine whirred to life. A smile snuck up on him again as he watched his beast breath.

Veins of burnt orange began glowing between pipes as superheated juice coursed through fuel lines. A haze of heat made the air over the bare engine shimmer. Both gauges lit up, their needles dancing. The control stick rattled to the rhythm of the engine, making the red triggers dance. He breathed in deep, enjoying the heady smell of fuel and metal and leather. His grin widened as the launch doors yawned open. Outside, a menacing hailstorm pounded the city. He didn't care, he'd soon be far above and flying—in outer freaking space.

"Here we go, people," said Keera over the intercom. "Follow my lead." Her flarejet, a swan-like Apex-9, floated up and zoomed out the doors.

Mark respectfully waited for the rest of his squad to jet before he grabbed the controls, lifted off, and roared out into the storm.

"Wwwooo yeah!" he hollered. Hail the size of golf balls mashed against his shields as he craned upwards. Rushing up through the storm he heard the growl of the flarejet working, the lashing wind outside, and the smashing hail. Then he broke through the clouds and soared into the dark void; and then, so fast his ears began to ring, silence enveloped him.

"There's our merchant ship," came Keera's clear voice as they sailed towards a drone ship built to resemble a medium-sized merchant. "Lance and his vultures will be flocking over any second. When you see their dilated pupils, jam your triggers."

Radio silence followed. They stayed in silence, waiting. Mark tilted slightly to the side so he could look down. The angry hailstorm obscured the city below. He wondered how everyone at SPIFF could see the War Game.

If he had been sitting in the stands, safe and sound, he would have found out.

A gigantic holographic projection had filled the whole stadium again. The floor, walls, and ceiling vanished; even the long rows of bleachers disappeared. Everything was replaced by the illusion of sitting on absolutely nothing while floating in space and watching as a merchant ship drifted into view.

Back above the city, Keera directed her squad to circle the merchant ship and told them to keep their eyes frosty and their triggers itchy.

Mark was the first to see Alpha Squad blaze into view. His grip tightened; his heart hammered; he flicked the brim of his orange and grey cap.

"Form up in front the merchant!" Keera commanded.

With practiced precision her whole squad formed a perfect guard stance, their back burners to the merchant and their missiles pointed at the Alpha's – except for Mark, who bumped into Derrick.

"This ain't time for domino's, kid," Derrick growled.

Mark apologized and adjusted into formation. He was just so tense, so nervous.

"Wait for it," whispered Keera. "Wait for it."

Mark waited impatiently. Any second he'd be gripping both triggers and hollering his lungs out. Any second and he'd be –

THOOOOOM!

Without warning the merchant ship behind them exploded. It disintegrated. It was ripped open. Burning shards of metal and plastic rained across everyone's shield system. The shock wave spun each of them out of control.

"What was that about?" Derrick yelled as he regained control. He twisted his flarejet around to look. "Oh no –"

Three terrifying ships blazed through the fiery wreckage.

Mark knew them in an instant. They were the same as the one's he'd seen crash all around him back home – back on Earth. They were the ones that had shot down Captain Zumski. They were the ones that were hunting him.

Their metal was black; Their shapes twisted and sinister. The sun glinted off wicked red lettering in that sharp, dreadful language no human could read. Yes, Mark had seen them before; but he had seen them broken and melting. These ships were very much alive, and the way they flew … the way they hunted … was evil.

"Protect Mark! Protect Mark!" Keera yelled while twisting full throttle.

"Make them split up!" shouted Derrick, dodging away to make one of them come after him. "Make them split up!"

But all three ships didn't split up. They ignored the rest of Foxtrot and gunned for Mark.

A loud boom twisted Mark's whole flarejet into an uncontrolled spin.

"Shields at eighty-eight percent," his SEG's voice informed him.

"What was that?" he yelled, frantically regaining control.

"Hard left! Burn hard left!" Keera shouted over the com.

Mark yanked left. A white missile blitzed by.

"Get out of there!" She continued yelling. "They're swarming your six, nine, and twelve o'clock!" She then switched com to broadcast back to SPIFF. "Captain Zumski!" she hsouted. "Captain Zumski what do we do?!"

Zumski's voice burst over the intercom. "I've contacted C. City Spaceguard! They're scrambling every starfighter at the Spaceport! Hang in there! Protect Mark! Work as a team! You've trained for this!"

The machine leading the front shot a volley of missiles straight to Mark's engine.

Mark wrenched the throttle. "Eat my afterburner."

A surge of superheated fuel rushed through those red veins like the adrenaline surging through his heart. The beast roared to life.

Back at the stadium, people went silent. Antsy kids stopped squirming, hardcore fans stopped arguing, and even the food vendors stopped yelling. Everyone watched Mark's flarejet. Its holographic projection filled the middle of the stadium. And when Mark cranked the throttle, nothing remained but a dark orange streak against the night.

"Whoa," breathed Torvan.

"Yeah," agreed Heath.

Zaza bounced on her seat. "He's going to make it!"

Mark looked uncatchable. His flarejet raced across the void with effortless speed. But bullets are always faster, and burning in a straight line only made him an easier target.

"Balls!" he cursed. Slugs of metal began hitting his shields.

Mark weaved to avoid fire. The machine's guns hit him. He bobbed up and down. The machine's guns hit him. He tried to be a moving target like Derrick had taught him. Nothing helped. The machine's long range shots were accurate enough to shoot the wings off flies in midair. Each hit sent shock waves down Mark's SEG.

"Eighty-four percent," announced his SEG. Then, "eighty-one percent—seventy-eig—seventy-f—seventy-two percent."

"Guys!" he yelled over the com. "I'm getting rocked over here!"

"Keep burning!" said Keera, chasing after the three machines with her guns ablaze. "We're trying to distract them!"

But then Mark heard Derrick growl over the com, "it's like trying to sink a battleship with a squirt gun."

Mark twisted for a quick glance back. Keera, Derrick, even The Sphinx had their guns firing on full at the machines. It looked useless. The machines shields were soaking it all in easy. His heart seized. He was doomed.

The other two machines soon caught up. They had him in range.

"Holy burning laser storms!" Mark shrieked as hundreds of electrified yellow beams hit his SEG, the surface splattering and waving like Crater Lake under the hail storm.

"Shields at sixty-eig—bbbzzzz—fifty-five."

"I'm getting owned out here! Where are you guys?!"

"Keep burning!" came Keera's frantic voice over the intercom. She then flicked it to broadcast to all ships. "Lance! Lance help us out over here!"

"No can do, babydoll!" Lance crowed. "We stole the cargo and are heading back to SPIFF for the WIN!"

"You filthy coward!" Keera shrieked into her com. "Come back here and help Mark!"

"That Earther brought it on himself!" Lance shouted as him and his squad dived back to Crescent City.

"Captain Zumski!" Keera shouted next. "How long do we have?!"

"C. City Spaceguard has launched! They're en route!"

Mark growled, banking a hard left.

The machines followed, hunting with pleasure.

He tried a dodge and burn taught to him by The Sphinx. His Flarejets quick acceleration left his stomach lurching. Useless. He made abrupt changes in direction like Keera taught him. His vision became a blurred mess of stars and bullets. Useless. He tried four more escape tactics, but he couldn't outrun their guns.

The machines sent another storm of pain against Mark's shields.

He was doomed. But then he had an idea! Flicking his lucky cap, he slowed down. The machines caught up; their cannons rocking Mark's shields. Fifty-two percent, Fifty, Fourty-eight, Fourty-five, forty-four percent.

"What are you doing?!" Keera screamed.

"Watch."

He wrenched the controls hard back. Throttle on full. His whole flarejet flipped upside down!

"HaHA! Stuff a fig!" he yelled, rocketing upside-down right over the machines.

All three machines blitzed by.

"Nice!" Derrick yelled.

This strange maneuver bought Mark some time. But only mere seconds, not even minutes.

The three machines nearly tore themselves apart flipping around. They burned heavy, regaining the hunt. Soon, too soon, ice-pale plasma shots, laser fire, and heated lead began ripping into Mark's shields again. He felt a twinge of desperation. He pushed the controls, diving, fighting for survival once more.

"Forty percent, thirty seven, thirty three."

Pain, physical pain clenched Mark's chest. He was doomed.

No. No he refused to think like that. He got angry. He got mad.

The machines tore at his shields, at his junkjet, at the beast he spent months bringing to life.

"Yeah?" he shouted. Nearly ripping the controls off, he twisted his flarejet around to face the machines. "Oh yes?" he yelled at them. The dark machines reflected in the whites of his eyes. "Eat your medicine!" he shouted at them, gripping both triggers. "Eat it!"

Mark's cannons spun up.

Whhiiirrrrr.

SHUNK, SHUNK, SHUNK, SHUNK.

Lava colored bursts of ionized mass left his double barrels. The heavy shunks sent shivers down his spine, the good kind of shivers. He loved the way the red blasts surged from each side of his flarejet like cannon fire from a volcano. Each blast sunk into the dark machine at the front, dealing massive damage.

Back at the stadium, Zaza gasped, Torvan frowned, and Lexie was shaking her head, saying, "only a caveman—only our fuzz-for-brains caveman would run chicken against three Shadow Mek machines."

Everyone at the stadium bit their nails as a close-up filled the field: Mark's junkjet charging against three extreme Shadow-Meks, a flood of neon fire between them.

Closer. Mark's cannons blasted magma at the lead Mek. Closer. The Mek's ship swayed under the red plasma. Closer. Mark's turquoise shields splashed in static waves, absorbing the Mek's guns. Closer. Mark stuck his triggers on full. Closer. The lead Shadow-Mek kept charging, spitting missiles. Closer. Mark's shields began faltering. Closer. The Mek's lasers slipped through Mark's shields, scorching the engine. Too close. Mark began to panic. Too close. The third Mek's bullets cracked his glass canopy. Too close. Mark clenched his jaw. Too close. He shut his eyes. He wasn't going to chicken out. Never. They wanted to kill him, they'd have to run him over.

A collective gasp echoed through the stadium. They were about to see a head-on collision in space.

SLAM.

But it wasn't Mark who slammed into the lead Mek. It was The Sphinx.

The Sphinx had blitzed in from the side. He, or she, had a bulldozer of a flarejet. It plowed the lead Shadow Mek clean off course.

Mark flew straight through where the crash would have been.

"We got your back," said Keera, her guns spitting fire. "Let's turn this thing into a dogfight."

"Woof," said Derrick in deadpan agreement.

Everyone in the stadium watched, breath caught and hearts pounding. Kids stopped eating their Cloud Candy, vendors stopped making bets, Commander's Club students stopped discussing strategies. Everyone's eyes locked on to what suddenly became a violent mess. And it was a violent mess.

Three cadets and their junkjet friend, outgunned, outmaneuvered, and outclassed by three perfect, deadly machines. A hurricane of missiles. A storm of plasma. A hail of bullets. Neon flashes. Bursts of light. Gun barrels glowing hot. Screams of metal armor shattering. Glass cracking. The sour stench of plastic melting. Utter chaos flooded the sky above Crescent City.

But no matter how quick they were, how fast they dodged and rolled, how hard they held their sweaty triggers, Keera and Derrick and Mark and The Sphinx were no match for the machines.

The machines knew this, and used their Shadow Annihilation tactic. All three machines ignored the fire from Foxtrot. Their shields took hit after hit from Keera, Derrick, and Mark as they turned and aimed all their guns, all their firepower on one cadet at a time – starting with The Sphinx.

The Sphinx's flarejet was heavy and solid, but it could not take so much damage so fast. His, or her, shields disintegrated in wisps of misty blue.

The machines didn't stop firing. They were merciless. They were ruthless. They were brutal and cold. They kept firing into The Sphinx until, shields gone, engine shot to pieces, the entire flarejet went dark.

"No!" Keera yelled in anguish. "No, no, noooo!"

They watched helplessly as their friend's flarejet broke apart and tumbled away in a helpless drift.

Destruction done, the Shadow's turned their guns on their next annihilation target: Keera herself.

"I can't." said Mark, gritting his teeth. In front of him all three machines were gleefully firing missiles into Keera, who was desperately trying to fly after and save The Sphinx. "I can't." Derrick was furiously trying to protect Keera with his flarejet, but the machines were all unleashing their ammunition into her failing shields.

Mark ground his teeth. "I can't let this happen." He flicked his cap. "One step." He gunned the throttle. The beast roared.

Back at the stadium Heath's eyes went wide. "What's he doing?" He jumped up. "He doesn't have the firepower! He doesn't have the shields! What is he DOING?"

Mark burned straight for the lead machine, guns hot.

The machine whirled around, expecting a crash.

But just as Mark's junkjet was about to crash into that terrifying machine, the boy from Earth dodged right around and pointed his nose straight at the ground.

"Hold onto your gearboxes, ladies and gentleman," Mark said, flicking his lucky cap and wickedly twisting the throttle. "It's a party."

Throttle on full. Fuel hot. Turbine burning.

Launch.

"Whhoooaaaaaaa!" Mark hollered, holding onto his lucky cap as life blurred.

He blasted past Keera. He blasted past the Derrick. He blasted past the still-glowing-hot wreckage of the merchant. But he wasn't going for SPIFF, not yet. He had a plan. He set his sights for Crescent City and the hailstorm below.

Careening faster and faster, accelerating exponentially, he went tearing into the roiling hailstorm.

The machines broke away from Keera and Derrick. They went blazing full throttle after Mark. The only way they could stop Mark now . . . was to catch him.

"You're not hurting any more of my friends!" Mark furiously hollered, then dodged a building.

People going about their daily lives on the streets and in the office buildings of downtown Crescent City were treated to a spectacular show that day. Some random accountant would be sitting, sipping his coffee and scrolling through funny cat pictures when he'd hear the distant roar of a supercharged turbine engine drawing closer; then a flarejet radiating boiling orange would blitz past his window, right at eyelevel, rumbling the desk and spilling his steaming coffee everywhere. Then, just when this middle aged office guy finished madly cursing and wiping his stained business trousers, three Shadow-Meks in hot pursuit would roar by, shattering the windows. The balding business bloke rushed to the broken window, leaned into the hailstorm, shook his fist, and began bellowing shockingly offensive curse words for someone who managed a toy store.

Everyone back at Launch Bay Three was going nuts. The gold-laced half of the stadium was screaming in protest, infuriated and screaming that Mark was destroying public property. The foxtrot colored half was hooting and cheering, not giving a fig about public property.

Mark was tearing through downtown. Sweat dripped from his cap-covered forehead. Cracks of orange were breaking apart his engine. The slightest flick of the controls could bulldoze him into a company's lunchroom.

"We saved Jai—The Sphinx!" came Keera's joyfully voice over the com, so grateful she nearly slipped his, or her, real name. "Get back to space! C.City starfighters are here!"

"I won't last that long up there!" He shouted back. "At least down here, I can out-maneuver them! … I think."

He dodged a building. One of the Shadow's slammed into a statue of the mayor and exploded (it was an ugly statue anyway). He twisted over a skyscraper. The second Shadow snagged on a satellite tower – which split it in half. The third Shadow learned from the mistakes of the other machines, improved instantly, and hunted harder.

"Fly towards SPIFF!" said Keera, starting at her radar screen in throat-clenching suspense. "It's only five clicks away!"

Pieces from Mark's engine began ripping off the turbine, smashing into his windshield

"Three clicks!"

The hail pounding against his remaining shields blurred everything.

"Two clicks!"

A hovercar-jammed flyway sprung into view. He went corkscrewing between the stacked flyways. The last machine followed. Hovercars swerved and veered and collided as he zoomed through. A few of them even flew off the flyway like stunt cars going off ramps. The last machine followed.

The G.S.S. Final Frontier loomed ahead. Through the rain and sleet and hail, he could see Launch Bay Three!

The stadium erupted. Zaza was hugging random people out of fright, Torvan'S teeth kept chattering nervously, Heath was saying "He's going to make it! He's going to make it!" and Lexie was shredding on her guitar as if she were playing his theme-song.

But the last machine was still hot on Mark's tail.

He frowned. He looked at the stadium full of people. He knew the machine had learned to dodge and weave and would never crash no matter how hard he twisted and turned. He sighed. There was only one way out of this alive. He hated it. He raked his brain trying to think of a different way. But the packed stadium was looming closer. He could even see his friends in the stands. This was it. The only way. It broke his heart.

"Goodbye my beast," he spoke to his junkjet, placing a warm, gentle hand on the shuddering control panel. "I promise I'll rebuild you."

And with that he slammed on the braking system. His junkjet howled as it reversed the turbine's spin. The last Shadow machine sped up, going in for the crash, going in for the kill.

"I'll rebuild you better than ever," he promised one more time. Then he let go of the trembling controls – and pressed the eject button.

FFOOOM.

With his butt glued to his tapped-up leather chair, he rocketed away.

The last Shadow slammed into his flarejet – and exploded.

The entire stadium erupted in cheers. They watched and whistled and hollered as the swelling cloud of thick smoke and curling fire rained smoldering debris just outside the stadium doors.

And out of it sailed Mark in his cracked glass cabin, smashing a landing onto the field, tearing and rumbling and plowing through the grass. He skidded nearly to the end of the field before coming to a full and complete stop. Soon as he did, he burst open his nearly shattered glass canopy and stepped out to thunderous cheering.

A medic crew of hovering bots rushed to pick him up, probe him, and generally make sure he wasn't broken or bleeding. Nothing wrong, they tossed a blanket over his head and zipped away.

He survived.

Zaza dashed down the bleachers to bulldoze him with a hug. Heath and Torvan followed with hearty handshakes. Lexie lagged behind, trying to find the right champion song to blare at him. Captain Zumski stayed seated, wiping sweat off his brow. Otto lumbered down through the cheering stadium, huffing proud curses, "ye survived, ye howling meteorite! Ye survived!"

Mark smiled weakly, looking at the debris of his beloved junkjet raining down.

"We'll rebuild 'er better 'en new!" Otto shouted, noticing his sadness. "Be happy! Ye saved yer team!"

And with that, Foxtrot squad streaked in and landed. Keera jumped out; she thumbed a rude gesture at Lance before whirling around to cheer Mark's name. Derrick had both fists pumped in the air, waving at everyone cheering on the bleachers as if he was the one who'd survived. The Sphinx was out too—his, or her, arms were crossed in pride and he, or she, came over to shake Mark's hand as if he, or she, was saying 'thank you.'

He survived. Yes, he had survived, and survived with style!

Everyone from Foxtrot's side of the bleachers poured onto the field. They surrounded him, cheering and whistling and hollering. He knew he lost the battle – Alpha Squad had been declared the winners of the War Game; but he felt as if he won the war. Lance was fuming with his Alpha Squad because no one was paying any attention to him, Keera and her squad were getting carried on the shoulders of the Support Crew AND the Cadet Core for being such valiant fighters, and even Heath was looking mighty proud of his friend for having had the guts to face all his enemies and win.

But there was one enemy they had forgotten about. And she soon stormed in to ruin everything.

CHAPTER 12
WORLDS APART

"Expelled!"

That digital voice cut through all jubilance.

"Expelled and deported!" repeated Admiral Kine as she burst into the crowded stadium. Her stiff march carried her through the shocked crowd. Her billowing admiral's suit and mechanical voice and scowling, pixelated face silenced everyone. "Mark is hereby expelled and deported!"

"WHAT?" Mark shouted, standing his ground as the menacing Admiral approached. "WHY?"

"Flying through Crescent City is outlawed. But, far worse is the fact that you did something abhorrently illegal," hissed Nona's robotic voice as she stopped to tower over the boy. "You left school grounds. You went… to the Seven Site."

All the people on both sides of the stadium stopped cheering. Nervous glances darted all around. Then a hum of panicked whispers sprung up. Several families with younger children began elbowing through people in a rush to the exits.

Mark's lungs seized in dread. The Seven Site. How did she know? He kept his eyes on Nona's glowing pupils. How did she know?

Otto stormed down the bleachers at Nona. "Nonsense, ye blighted black hole." She crossed her hydraulic arms and placed her bulk between the Admiral and the boy. "The lad would never endanger all these souls!"

Admiral Kine's pixelated mouth seemed to sneer as her hands begun to glow menacingly. "You speak out against your Admiral?"

More families began quickly exiting. Mom's cupped their kid's hands, dad's lifted toddlers. They pushed through shocked Support Crew kids and angered C.Core Cadets to the stairs leading away to safety.

"The lad'd never do this!" Otto was arguing, "He'd never risk our city!"

A silver orb sprung into existence around Otto's metallic left arm.

What remained of the silenced, scared crowd watched as Nona lifted Otto away from protecting Mark, lifted her high in the air. Nona was repeating what she'd done to Floyd. The silver orb began crumpling the hydraulic tubes of Otto's Arm.

Red faced, the woman thrashed about, not from pain, but from anger and shame.

Mark's jaw clenched in hate at Nona. Could the Admiral not see Otto's hurt and humiliation? Was the Admiral that callous and unfeeling? Like a machine! Was Admiral Nona Kine really the … the Daemon?

Captain Zumski thundered down the bleachers, his robotic peg leg whirring and thumping as he pushed people aside. The hurricane of anger upon his weathered face spoke volumes. "Admiral, perhaps we should conduct this in my office?"

Nona paced in Captain Stanislaw Zumski's office.

Captain Zumski sat behind his cherry-wood desk. The desk held several chef hats autographed by culinary artists famous across the galaxy (Chef Remy L'Ratatouille, Michelangelo Pizzapolis, and Chef Omaletta DuFromage), and the captain had gingerly moved them so he could keep a stern eye on Mark, who stood in the corner with his head bowed in shame.

At Mark's side, in front of a bookcase bending under the captain's collection of cooking utensils, stood Lieutenant Landeth. His feet were apart, hands clasped behind his back, eyes forward, face hard, military stance—though his scar fought for a chance to scowl at Mark.

Outside, the sun was setting. The office's large curved window commanded a panoramic view of glowing suburbia below and a horizon broken by skyscrapers.

"Expelled and deported back to Earth," Nona was saying. "It's the only answer. You can keep him safe from here, Captain Zumski."

"Don't expel me!" Mark shouted, and then paused, realizing he never in a million lightyears thought he'd say those words. "All I did was go to a run-down, abandoned, stale-refrigerator and take out a few leftovers!"

Nona sneered. Lieutenant Landeth's scar finally creased into a scowl. The wrinkles around Zumski's brown eyes showed deep concern.

Nona bent so that her silver eyes were just above Mark's. "All you did was risk your life. All you did was risk the lives of your friends. ALL YOU DID was risk the lives of everyone in this city!"

Mark dropped his eyes, burning from embarrassment.

"The Daemon is hunting you," Nona's robotic voice continued. "To get to you, IT will destroy your school, IT will kill your friends, IT will leave Crescent City a wasteland – just like IT destroyed the Seven Site thirteen years ago!" She grabbed Mark by the jaw and shoved the boy's head against the back wall. "Why is the Daemon hunting you? What does it want with you? If I root the answers out of your skull—"

"Thank you, Admiral Kine." Captain Stanislaw Zumski broke his hard silence. His hands were folded upon his cluttered desk, a stern stare directed at Mark. Behind him, a great grandfather clock constructed of steel and iron chimed the hour.

Nona let go and straightened, scowling at Stan. "I am taking a force of Crescent City guards to the Seven Site where I will terminate the Daemon!" Her Admiral's robes billowed as she marched to the office door. "Keep Mark in lockdown until I return. Do NOT allow him to leave his escape pod. That's an order."

She marched out.

Landeth saluted the captain and took his leave. The office door spiraled shut behind them both.

Captain Zumski heaved a tired sigh. He began rubbing his eyes the way people do when a heavy burden rests on their shoulders.

Mark, scared and confused, stood where the Admiral had held his jaw in her vice grip. "Captain Zumski … what is the Daemon? And why is it hunting me?"

The old captain met the boy's frightened eyes with compassion. The time for a few explanations had come.

"Understand this, ace," said the captain, rising from his chair and walking to the back of his office where the ancient grandfather clock counted time. "We didn't create the machines to be human. We created the machines to be able to live forever—able to serve us forever."

"And?"

"They rebelled…naturally." Captain Zumski swung open the clocks face and turned back the antique steel hands. A wavering beam of light hit the floor in front of Mark and projected a hologram of deep space. "It was man vs. machine. The Second Galactic War."

"What happened?"

"We won the war," said Zumski … but his voice was curiously sad.

"You make it sound like we lost …" said Mark.

Captain Zumski heaved a sad sigh, reached up to the clock, and pressed the number 12.

A hologram appeared in front of Mark, and the old captain's next words narrated bloodied soldiers firing with all their rage against onrushing swarms of tall droids made of scorched metal and burnt plastic. "At first the machines nearly exterminated us."

The next hologram continued to display the bloody battle between man and machine. "We destroyed thousands. It did not matter. We were only destroying metal and plastic bodies." The hologram changed again. Far above a burning planet, eclipsing a bright moon, feeding off a beautiful sun, hung a hexagon-shaped hive. "The mind of each machine was stored in the hive. If we destroyed one, it was simply rebuilt – over and over and over again." The hologram showed droid after droid being reactivated into new shells. "They were immortal. They could never die."

The captain zoomed the hologram out to the shimmering Milky Way Galaxy. From the point in the galaxy where the planet had been, now Dead Space, a dark fog crept outwards. Zumski's rumbling voice concluded the narration. "As the machines fought us, they learned. They corrected their smallest mistakes until every machine, the whole hive, was perfect." A flawless, glimmering hive rotated ever so slowly in front of them. "They were unstoppable . . . immortal . . . perfect . . . they were god-like."

Mark felt overawed, amazed by the world-shattering events that had been occurring in the galaxy without Earth ever knowing. He sagged against the wall. "But then ... how did we win?"

The old captain's brown eyes drifted out to the window, wandering the neon maze of the dirty city, and he said, rather simply, "By being human..."

The hologram showed thin fissures of molten gold begin breaking the hexagonal hive – until it tore apart, crushed into itself in a horrendous implosion, and then detonated violently.

Captain Zumski gently closed the crystal face of the iron grandfather clock. The hologram dissipated in turquoise wisps. He plodded wearily to his cluttered desk and sunk into his worn leather chair and began rummaging in a drawer full of spice bottles.

"We humans – Mark – are dangerous creatures. We may not be perfect or immortal ... and we are far from god-like – but we are unpredictable, cunning, and ... we know how to destroy things in the most -- creative ways."

Mark shoved his fingers below his cap and into his anxiety-sweat covered hair. This was heavy.

"So now," rumbled Captain Zumski, "the machines want to be just like us. The machines -- want to be human."

"Whoa . . ." Mark breathed. But then he paused, and protested, "But being a bit more human would do them good!"

The old captain looked at Mark for what seemed the longest time, as if weighing his words carefully. He then spoke slowly, so that the boy would understand his every word: "There's more to humanity than being good, Mark."

Captain Zumski saw Mark thinking these heavy words over. He also saw that a bit more explanation was needed.

"The machines, what's left of them, do not want to be destroyed again, ace," he said. "They want to survive. And they believe the only way to survive is to become everything wicked we are . . . then they will return evil for evil, hate for hate, humanity against humanity. They believe the only way to survive us, is to become us—and then exterminate us."

The captain's wise brown eyes were wrinkled from a sad smile. "We created gods, and with our hate, destroyed them."

All the dire talk about dreaded things and doom filled machines had left the captain needing comfort food. He found what appeared to be a soup bowl and plunked it on his desk. He took several spice bottles from his desk drawers. Shaking the bottles, he sprinkled pepper into the empty white bowl, then dried onion bits, a pinch of garlic, and finally what looked like miniaturized potato chunks. Then, gently lifting an autographed chef hat (Chef Omaletta DuFromage), he placed it over the bowl. Busting out his red Square, he tapped a few commands into it and bonked the chef hat with it.

A boiling sound came from inside the hat, then a rather pleasant ding not unlike a microwave.He lifted the white chef's crown to reveal a steaming bowl of how-momma-used-to-make-it potato soup. Setting the cap aside with a tender pat well done, he dug in.

"Sir," Mark began, his disheartened voice distant as the neon skyscrapers out the sunset window, "why did you recruit me?" He cast a defeated look at the captain. "I should have stayed on Earth. Let the Daemon hunt me there. Up here I just put everyone in danger. I don't belong here. I don't even have any powers or prophesies or anything incredible."

"True," said Captain Zumski with classic honesty, "very true." He continued loudly slurping his soup. "No extraordinary childhood, no natural talent to be a FlareRider, and not much sense – leaving SPIFF when you were explicitly told not to – and then going to a quarantined site and getting chased by Lurks and NOT telling me, or Landeth, or any adult." Zumski stopped chewing a potato and became thoughtful. "No not much common sense at all. More like a brick, really."

"Okay, I'm a nobody, I get it!" Mark hadn't really expected that much honesty. "I'll stay a nobody forever." His voice sunk. "So what good am I? Why am I here? Why is the Daemon hunting me?"

The captain tilted the bowl and gulped down the savory broth. He belched. "Complements to the chef, eh?" He plunked the empty bowl in a random desk drawer and slammed it shut. "Listen, I'm not going to tell you why you're here or, for that matter, why you're anywhere. Some mysteries can't be talked about, can't be read about. Some mysteries," he looked at Mark with an encouraging twinkle in his eyes, "some mysteries simply need to be lived."

He got up and went to the gold-sunset tinted window. "Look," he said and pressed two fingers to the cool glass. Moving each finger across the surface, as if he were zooming in on a screen, he brought the distant crater ridge into focus. "You see?"

Mark had gotten up to look. "What is that place?"

"It's an old oak tree atop the North Ridge. First one planted during the terraforming of Crescent City. There's an old cemetery below. Keeps people away. So, sometimes, when life is buggered, I go to the Old Oak and think. I see the answers soon enough."

"How am I going to go there and think and see the answers?" Mark countered. "You're supposed to lock me up. Confined to barracks. Locked up in my dorm room. Expelled and deported tomorrow." His forehead clunked against the glass, making the brim of his lucky cap twist sideways. "I'm useless."

The captain laid a comforting, strengthening hand on Mark's shoulder. "Indeed, I do need to send you to your dorm room. I do need to lock you up. And you know what? Because you are such troublemaking, pain in my backside ..." He started to play the part of a grumpy old man. "I must remind you not to go fiddling around with any buttons in there. After all -- I must remind you that your dorm room used to be an escape pod. Therefore, whatever you do, do NOT look under your desk. And do NOT press the big red 'Escape Pod LAUNCH' button under there. DO NOT DO SO! Because, tsk, tsk, it just so happens that if you DID do all these things I told you NOT to do ... well ... you would blast yourself clear across the city and land at that Old Oak! So DO NOT DO absolutely ANY of what I just said..."

Mark stared up at the old captain – who kept winking and winking with one eye in that absurd, comical way of his.

Mark had to laugh.

Captain Zumski clapped him on the back, that wise old smile returning to his square salt-and-pepper beard. "Go live your mystery, kid ... and change your stars – forever."

Mark gazed out over the neon city again. A rush of excitement began welling up again. He could do this. He could put together all the clues and figure out why the Daemon hunted him so relentlessly.

The young Earther thanked the captain and left. At first he strolled through the silent hallways, then jogged, then ran all the way to the anti-gravity tubes that sucked him up to his escape-pod dorm-room. He jumped through the spiral door even before it had fully opened, crouched under his desk, found the red eject button, mashed it, and, with a deafening roar, jolt to his stomach, and yelp of excitement, he blasted off in a blazing fiery arc over the neon city.

He flew toward the bright E-22 flyway, oblivious to all the shocked motorists who pointed and stared as he whizzed by. He crowed with glee, sailing, just barely missing a pizza delivery guy on a hover-motorcycle, who yelped and sped into a billboard advertising helmets. He zoomed closer to the North Ridge, over small middleclass homes where little dogs strained at their chains to yap at the big bright comet. He was rocketing so fast he didn't see the blur of tombstones on the ground below. Each tombstone had a single neon blue strip around its angular edges that streaked by as if he were going lightspeed, roaring right over them all until –

WHUMP!

The craggily branches of the old oak shook as Mark's Escape Pod thumped into the dirt close by.

For a minute or two, perhaps three (his brain was a bit of a blurry mess), he lay in the tilted pod, breathing and laughing, and laughing and breathing from the rush. But then a most incredible sight caught his eye. There, just out the little round window. With heart racing even harder than it had during the launch, he scrambled up to the window and burst it open. The panoramic view flooded his eyeballs.

"Whoa," he whispered, absolutely stunned.

The whole cemetery stretched out beneath him. Pale blue tombstones in a sea of dry grass descended to suburbia, which in turn became looming skyscrapers; their neon angles cutting into the night sky and reflecting across the shimmering lake further on, making them seem twice as tall. But that wasn't the view that made Mark whistle and flip his cap backwards.

"That's my home," he murmured in thunderstruck awe. "My home planet..."

Earth.

Earth loomed over the dirty neon city like a rising full moon. It was glorious.

"I can see Australia," he breathed, dumbfounded. "That's Brisbane and Sydney! And that's Melbourne down there!" He said, excitedly pointing as if giving a guided tour to the crickets chirping in the grass.

He stumbled out of the pod, reeling from the breath-taking view. He leaned against the old oak nearby, and then thumped his butt on the craggily roots of the gnarled old oak. "My home planet," he said again, watching the world turn ever so slowly. "Such a weird thing to say—home planet." He mulled over those words and the feeling of immeasurable distance they brought. "And maybe somewhere down there – my mom and dad. Back on my home planet."

He moved his fingers through scraggly blades of grass. Lost in nostalgia and wonder, he tore up a handful to hold for a moment. He'd tilt his hand and watch the grass flutter away in the early summer breeze. He didn't know why thoughts of his mom and dad, who he didn't have the faintest memory of, would float in at these random times. He never knew them. They might have been the worst parents in the world. Or the best. He'd like to think they would've been the best.

"I could sure use your help right now," he sighed, watching the grass float across the Earth. "Or someone. To help me out here."

But no one was around.

"Some mysteries you just need to live through ..." He repeated what the Captain had been telling him from the start. "But I can't see any answers from here!" His frustrated blue-green eyes began darting across the city below." All I see is the Spaceport where I nearly crashed ... and SPIFF where I DID crash .... and the Seven Site where those Lurks hunted after m—"

That's when his eyes went wide with sudden realization.

The Seven Site.

He raised an eyebrow.

The Seven Site.

He raised a second eyebrow.

The Seven Site!

He would have raised a third eyebrow but only had the two.

That was the Seven Site down there. It was all lit up. Nona Kine was down there. Admiral Nona Kine.

Anger began welling up inside his chest. His breath quickened. Adrenaline pumped through his heart. His eyes dilated. He clenched his fist and whispered a promise.

"It ends tonight."

He rushed back to his Escape Pod. He tore out his Comet Chaser (after wiping his hands on his jeans so he wouldn't put grass stains on it, of course). He hopped on, ready to ride.

Clues were coming together. Puzzle pieces were falling into place. He needed to see Heath and Lexie right away—and Lloyd too.

A sudden rustling in the leaf covered branches above startled him. He looked up. The shadowed foliage and bent oak limbs were almost impenetrable. A few leaves fell around him. Was that a human shape on a branch way up high? Or maybe his eyes were just playing tricks. Either way it was time to get going. He tilted forward on his skyboard and sped down the cemetery hill.

CHAPTER 13
IT ENDS TONIGHT

"Hey, I believe you," Lexie was saying, sitting on a small dust bin as Mark kept glancing around the corner of an abandoned and night-shrouded warehouse. "It's our tie-wearing salesman you'll need to convince."

Approaching as if on cue, they heard the familiar cursing of a guy whose skyboard keeps losing power. Soon enough Heath's dead skyboard clattered to the ground, followed shortly by the kid in question, who fell screaming into a nearby dumpster.

"You alright there, chief?" Lexie called from her cross-legged sit on the dust bin.

Mark stole another peep around the paint-peeling warehouse corner.

"I swear," Heath grumbled, clambering out with the obligatory banana peel on his head. "I'm gluing four table legs on that thing, sanding it, and selling it as a coffee table." He then paused, looked at Mark, pointed at him in complete bewilderment, and said, "wait … how did you get out of lockdown at SPIFF?!"

Mark flicked his lucky cap. "I ejected my Escape Pod and blasted over the city!"

Heath grinned and nodded and said, "nice."

He also extended his hand out for a high-five, but Mark, instead of giving it, threw Heath's skyboard in the dumpster. Mark then chucked his own Comet Chaser in the dumpster -- and then himself.

"What the—?" said Heath as Mark clamped a hand over his mouth and yanked him into the rubbish.

Heavy boots clomped around outside. An investigating flashlight beam cut the darkness.

The boots stomped to the dumpster.

Mark threw Heath's board over him and then dove under his own.

The boots paused. A harsh beam explored the garbage.

Mark stopped breathing.

The boots thumped away.

Mark peeped over the rusted steel top. Coast was clear. Lexie popped out of a different dumpster, looking beyond excited. Mark whispered at Heath. "I need you and Lexie to sneak me back into the Seven Site."

Heath stared at him in shock. "What for?!" He demanded.

Mark looked him dead in the eye. "It ends tonight."

Lexie, who had vaulted out of her dumpster and peered around the warehouse, turned to them and said "here's our chance," – and then bolted down the dim street. Mark quickly followed.

Heath shot a frustrated, confused look all around himself, but since there was no one to see it, much less give him a straightforward answer, he darted after them.

Lexie's sneakers pounded pavement down the same cracked, weed eaten stretch of asphalt she'd raced across on her skyboard just months ago -- the road leading to the Seven Site. She ducked behind a heavy white hovercar.

Mark skidded in behind her seconds before two guards in starch white armor exited the car. Their thumping march took them to the edge of the Seven Site force field, where a hovervan from Nexus News Network had just landed.

Mark wondered why the news was there, but his focus was broken by the Seven Site just beyond the pulsating field.

"Creepy!" Lexie breathed. Her violet eyes lit with dangerous adventure at the nightmarish scene.

Those eerie piles of scrap glowed at night! And beyond the piles of radiating scrap were the silhouettes of the quarantined buildings they'd need to sneak through, full of guards no doubt, all under orders to shoot on site. Above it all shone the Earth, a pearl of blue oceans speckled with white clouds.

Heath raced over and ducked next to them. "What do you mean it ends tonight?!" He whispered vehemently as that small trashcan Lexie had been sitting on came running to slam into the hovercar they were hiding behind. "And why's this rubbish bin following you?"

Mark ignored the trash can and locked eyes with Heath. "You were right all along, Heath. Admiral Nona Kine — is the Daemon."

Heath's olive eyes widened. "I knew it!"

"She's the one who sent that ship to crash into me. She's the one who sent those creepy Lurks at the Seven Site to hunt me. She's the one who ordered those Shadow-Meks to shoot me out of the sky."

Heath whistled. "How do you know for sure, though?"

A bolt of light swung over their heads and Lexie hissed, "Now!"

Mark rushed after her to the next hovercar.

Heath scrambled to follow, looking dizzy from Mark's bombshell. He didn't even notice when the tin can bumped into his backside.

"Funk was the answer," Mark continued, voice low at Heath. "I rode over to Lexie's place. I talked to Perfidious. He never told ANYONE we went to the Seven Site. He was too afraid that his daughter, Lexie, would get expelled or jailed or anything at all. So that means—"

"Admiral Kine knew we were there!" Heath burst out, his eyes fired up in wonder.

Mark nodded. "Listen, remember the hologram in that half sunken ship?"

As the puzzle pieces clicked together, Heath began repeating the hologram, still ignoring the tin bin, which had smacked into his rump to stop again. "Crash into Mark and Ella's starliner—"

"Delta Ten bound for Crescent City," Mark finished. "She – IT – sent that ship to crash into the starliner I was on. When that failed she – IT -- ordered the ship to crash into the Seven Site so no one would find the evidence! And then when we went to Seven Site, she – IT – ordered those Lurks to hunt us so we wouldn't find the evidence! And THEN when she – IT—was inspecting my junkjet, she approved it just so that she -- IT – could send those flying howler monkeys after me. And NOW she – IT – wants to expel and deport me so that I'm out of SPIFF and she—"

"IT can kill you ..." Heath whispered in dawning horror.

Mark nodded firmly.

"But why, man?" Heath protested. "Why? Why is IT – why is the Daemon hunting you so hard? Why does the Daemon want to kill you?!"

Mark, grim in face and bold in spirit, replied in all honesty, just as the captain had taught him. "I don't know. But I'm here to find out ... This ends tonight."

"Now!" Lexie hissed after a beam grazed the hair on their heads.

The trio ran while ducking to the next white hovercar. They were dangerously close to the guarded Seven Site now.

They rolled behind the Nexus News Network hovervan. They was so close to the Seven Site force field, they could hear thousands of volts buzzing and crackling across the bright turquoise.

Steps away from the hovervan was a wide door that had been cut into the turquoise field—at the same spot Lexie had used her Lemonsquare to open a way in for them so many months ago. There were a dozen guards protecting it. Mark saw this and knew he would need to think of a plan to get through it—into the Seven Site.

Heath, breathing hard, thumped against the news vans back bumper.

"Guys, this info is heavy."

The garbage can tripped over Heath's business shoes and nearly rolled in sight of the guards before Mark caught it.

"At least Lloyd's knows why he wants to stop Admiral Kine – The Daemon," said Mark.

"Lloyd?" said Heath, head swiveling about in confusion. "Where?"

The garbage can's lid popped off. Lloyd's cylindrical head shot out. "Revenge!" His saucer-sized eyes were big and red. He held up the crumbled body of his bumblebot friend Floyd. "Revenge!" Gravity quickly shut him up by clonking the lid back on his head.

Mark flicked the brim of his lucky cap. "Lloyd is here to help you two get me through those guards and into the Seven Site – where I will face the Daemon – and end it."

Heath saw the grim determination in his friends face and knew it would be near impossible convincing him otherwise. But he had to try. "No, Mark," he said firmly. "You don't need to face anyone. What we need is evidence." He pointed to the crimson force field. "We need to get past that new force field. Then we sneak through all the guards patrolling inside the Seven Site. We fly over the acid lake to the Deep Intersolar Enterprises building. Lexie will use her Lemonsquare to record a video of Nona being the Daemon. We send the evidence off to Captain Zumski, to Lieutenant Landeth, to anyone, to everyone, and wait for the cavalry to bring bombs!"

Mark smiled quietly at Heath, whose caring and concern made the orphan from earth feel as if … as if he had a real best friend now. But that also made him quite sad. "No, Heath. I'm going in by myself," he said sadly. "Every time the Daemon has tried to kill me – every time – other people have always gotten hurt. I'm ending this alone. No one will get hurt, no one will die." He looked them both in the eyes. "Everything else is stupid dangerous."

Lexie nodded eagerly. "It's crazy dangerous."

"Well then," Heath responded with a straight faced stare. "Let's—get—dangerous."

Nobody blinked for half a minute. After that, they busted up laughing. Then, "shush, ush, ush, ush," they said to each other and ducked as a guard checked on the disturbance.

Lexie was still trying to control her laughing fit when she said, "you've been waiting to use that, huh?"

Heath could only nod and wipe his eyes.

"Aaahhh, you guys are the best," Mark sighed with fading chuckles. "But seriously."

Heath dropped his smile. "I am serious."

Mark's face hardened. "No. I'm ending this alone. If you won't help me, then stay here." And with that he ran to hide behind the last hovercar, followed quickly by Lloyd.

Lexie went to dash after him, but Heath stopped her with a strong hand and even stronger determination in his voice. "We're helping him all the way."

"Oh yeah!" said Lexie with a grin, as if she were planning to do that all along. "But you can't tell our caveman that. You know how stubborn his little monkey brain gets." And with that she pulled Heath after her in a mad dash to the last hovercar.

Mark was already there. "Just keep don't let me touch Floyd, okay? Getting zapped hurts!" He then patted Lloyd on the head. "Revenge time, buddy."

"Revenge!" growled Lloyd, hugging Floyd's body.

"Fire up your Uber-Boring Field generator!"

Lloyd puffed out his aluminum chest proudly and mashed the fat round button in the center. A storm of static enveloped the four of them. Then it misted away.

"Wha hahaha!" Lexie chortled. "Heath! You look like one of those encyclopedia salesmen we learned about in Earth History 101! And Mark, you look like one of the guards on patrol—except your helmet is wearing a fake mustache and rubber nose and plastic glasses!"

Heath was chuckling too. "Said the girl who looks like a stuffy, old librarian!"

Lloyd had the most boring disguise of all, having turned into a friendly neighborhood postwoman.

"Lloyd," said Mark, his voice sounding like static through his full face helmet, "sneak back and get our boards." He turned to Lexie and Heath. "Either of you have idea's to get past the new force field?"

"Hell yeah!" shouted Lexie. Her librarian's face was somewhat frightening with the long hooked nose and pointy chin, but she still had her violet eyes, and they were on fire with anarchy. She brandished her Lemonsquare like a stick of dynamite. "I downloaded a force field hack! I just click a button and it'll make the whole shield explode into a bazillian pieces!"

"Let's . . . wait on that one," said Mark, squinting at her.

Heath stood, looking like a grim encyclopedia salesman—outdated tweed jacket, slicked back hair, and a fedora (though his worn leather satchel was still slung around his shoulders). "Guys, I have a plan."

Mark saw the kid fix his polka-dot tie and smooth his tweed jacket and adjust his heavy glasses. Heath meant business.

"This news van means one thing," said Heath. "A reporter and her camera crew must be close. They'll have special passes to get in." He adjusted his brown satchel as if getting ready to sell, sell, sell. "I'll distract them by selling things. Lexie, you know what to do."

Lexie sprung up so fast her horn-rimmed librarians glasses bounced on her pointy beak of a nose. They followed Heath around the side of the Nexus News Network hovervan. At the last minute, Mark remembered to tear off the fake mustache and rubber nose.

Heath had been right again. As soon as they rounded the news van, just steps from the pulsating force field, they ran into a reporter and her camera crew. But neither the reporter nor her crew looked like typical newscasters. In fact, they made Mark stop so hard his guard's boots squeaked and his helmet bounced on the back of his head.

All three individuals were intimidating in appearance. To the right, lugging the news camera, stood a short, gruff, burly man who could have lumbered in from a motorcycle gang. His beard grew out long and knotted and had the color of fire. To the left stood an intimidating woman; Her black hair was professionally sleeked to the side and she wore dark, stylish clothes, giving the impression she was a sophisticated super sleuth—she held a Square that looked ready for detective-like note taking. But it was the woman in the center—the reporter—who held Mark's attention. She was a tall woman, sporting a blue Mohawk, and her arms were covered in tattoos of mystical abominations; beasts which seemed to scream and winged dragons breathing ice. Yet for all her intimidating tattoos, Mark was stared the most at her sharp, intelligent eyes—which were an ocean colored green-blue. Strange.

"Ah, good evening," said the Mohawk styled reporter to Mark, apparently assuming he was in charge based on him being decked in full guard uniform. "I am Eleanor from Nexus New Network," she flashed her ID badge, "Investigative Journalist." Her tattooed right arm swung to sweep in her cameraman and business woman. "And these are my compatriots. We will be investigating inside the Seven—,"

"No can do, baby doll," said Mark, shrugging off the way her eyes reminded him of someone. He had a job to do. Hitching up his belt, he spoke gruffly—the way he imagined a rough and tough security guard would do. "It's too dangerous for a lady."

"Dangerous?" hissed Eleanor with cold politeness. "Listen here, I was a reporter in Northern Canada— a country on EARTH! – and I must say that it's far more dangerous than THIS little Seven Site."

Mark noted how this Eleanor lady flung huge words around. This made him rather uncomfortable. But what frustrated him the most was her claim. "Canada? The most dangerous place on earth? I don't think so." He cleared his throat in a very high-and-mighty manner. "I was a guard back in Australia, young lady. And I will bet you dollars to dough-nuts that AUSTRALIA is the most dangerous place on earth."

"Don't be childish," Eleanor spoke down at him, crossing her tattooed arms so that the inked creatures slithered. "Canada is far more dangerous."

"That's a lie!" said the portly guard stubbornly.

"How dare you call me a liar!"

"How dare you—dare!"

Meanwhile, on the side of the street that wasn't a raging temper-tan-trum, Heath and Lexie had gone straight to business.

Heath, looking trustworthy in his boring disguise, had whipped out a dozen packets of instant coffee from his satchel. He was energetically trying to sell these to the burly cameraman and sleuth lady. "Hey, red eyes, you need a pick-me-up," he was shouting, and, "buddy, you've been carrying that camera too long, enjoy a cup 'o joe," and the line that got him the most attention: "feeling constipated? Coffee is a natural laxative!"

Lexie, meanwhile, deftly pickpocketed the camera crew. Once she finished, she 'accidentally' bumped into Heath and whispered, "Right. Now go get our fearless leader before he starts throwing toys and crying."

Heath zipped up his satchel and casually strolled to the now wildly gesticulating guard, who was entangled in the dumbest of arguments.

"Lady, I tell you right here, Australia is the most dangerous place on Earth!"

"False! Northern Canada is the most dangerous!"

Heath tried to interrupt his friend with a polite "Umm, sir."

"Australia!"

"Canada!"

"Mark!" Heath barked. "I mean – erm – BOB – it's done."

The two bickering adults stared at their friends with blank looks. Then instantly went back to sending daggers at each other. That's when their friends pulled them in opposite directions far from each other.

Mark followed Lexie and Heath to the door – his arms crossed.

"Have fun throwing a fit over there?" Lexie hissed at him.

Mark glared after the tattooed woman on the other side of the street. She seemed oddly familiar, but -- "She makes my toe's curl up into fists."

"Well cork it," said Heath. "Lexie got access."

Lexie held up all three laminated access cards, two half-empty packs of razzleberry gum, and a set of keys to the news van.

"We only needed the access card!" Mark exclaimed. "And only one!"

"This was my first time!" she said angrily and shook them in his face. "Heath's training me!"

Lloyd dashed over and threw their boards at their feet. "I brought your crap!" He grabbed fistfuls of Mark and Lexie's clothes and began aggressively pulling them toward the force field. "Revenege."

This thought sobered Mark right up. His voice became grim and determined. "Alright. Let's do this."

The four of them scooted to the crimson force field of the Seven Site. The passes let them through.

Inside the Seven Site the air was oppressively cold with its stale refrigerator musk. Silence replaced bustling city noises, distant traffic, and the haunt of nature at night.

Lloyd slammed his fist onto his chest to deactivate the UBF and bellowed "Revenge!"

As their disguises faded, the trio stood exchanging glances, trying to hide a rising sense of dread, fright, and dark adventure.

Mark squared his shoulders and put on his best brave-face. "Alright guys, well, um, thanks for your help and all that. It's been a time and half but now I gotta –"

"Ready?" Lexie asked Heath, both completely ignoring Mark.

She stepped onto her bright Seven-Zero-Seven board as it hummed to life. A faded office document blew away beneath the glowing board. Heath struggled to start his Cheap Trick board. It buzzed and flashed before firing up. They kicked off deep into the Seven Site.

"Hey wait no!" Mark yelled after them. "You can't go without me! You can't even go WITH me!"

"Stuff a fig!" They both yelled back at him, using his own words.

Mark grumbled and mumbled as he jumped on his Comet Chaser and sped after them.

The haunting cold of the Seven Site made their breath mist. Distant rumbles of junk tumbling down glowing piles seemed menacing and full of guards. The hum of their boards gliding over littered streets echoed in the clammy darkness.

They huddled around Lexie, who had her Lemonsquare out, its flash-light app illuminating the way. But the scrap piles had an eerie way of eating the light. It sunk into gaps between torn wall paintings and decaying lobby couches as if it were sinking into rat holes. Wicked eyes seemed to glint and glimmer through the darkness as the friends past.

As they glided through the maze Heath began hyperventilating and clutching his satchel. Lexie seemed to stay calm, even eager for the shadowed adventure, but whenever she heard something fall and tumble from a scrap pile, her light would dart fast and nervous to catch the noise.

They finally rounded the last glowing heap before the acid lake—and caught their breath in wonder.

The whole cauldron of swirling violet, rich crimson, and artificial green dazzled in the night. It radiated like dragons breath. It simmered like a witch's poison. It cast toxic colors across the crimson shore, which broke on twisted trucks, their bleached stumps reflecting acidic hues.

The ruined steel skeleton of Deep Intersolar Enterprises loomed nightmarish in scale in the middle of the acid mote; the remaining windows reflected shards of starry sky and pearlescent Earth.

Lexie had been the first one across the acid lake so many months ago. She now hesitated. "Where were the guards?" She said, staring behind them. "Why didn't anyone stop us?"

"Yeah?" Heath said, also stopping to frightfully wonder.

Even Mark stopped. He gazed up at the ruined laboratory. Did he really need to know why he was hunted? Was he doing the right thing? What if his friends got hurt? What if the Daemon – tortured them?

But Lloyd was having none of it. He stood on the front of Mark's skyboard with Floyd held forward like some demented hood ornament. "REVENGE!"

Mark considered Lloyd's craziness for a moment. "You ever wonder what revenge really tastes like?" He asked to no one in particular, then launched out over the acid. "Pop rocks, I bet. Flavored by the lemons life gave you."

Heath, infuriated by how stubborn his friend was being, kicked out over the lake after him. Lexie followed, staying close as his board rippled over the bright violets and swirling magentas. The hazardous, stomach-churning colors illuminated the beads of sweat on their foreheads and painted their misting breath in shades of poison.

They finally stumbled to shore, Heath once again thanking his lucky stars for not burning alive in the acid, and, at the same time, cursing his board. They found Mark staring at the ruined entrance of D.I.E. "Where ARE all the guards?"

"Quit buffering," Lloyd yelled at them, holding Floyd and running for the entrance. "Revenge!"

They hiked towards the entrance, which was also empty. No heavy boots, no orders being barked, no signs of life.

"Nona is here," said Mark, flexing his fist, "waiting. . ."

His stubborn words echoed in the ten story cavern, escaping through the high dome above, where a sliver of the Earth could be seen. The blue planet's light rained back down the spiral stairs, glinted off shattered glass railings, casting shadows into the scorched window of the first floor's security booth where they'd found those dated magazines and unused Emergency Lockdown Lever all those months ago.

"Where are the guards, Mark?" Heath repeated.

His question was answered when Lexie's light hit the burnt stairway. "What's thahhh…" she trailed off, lungs loosing breath.

They stood still, staring at the trickle of blood dripping down step after step after step.

The darkness began devouring Lexie's light beam. The air began to choke itself down their throats. A single metallic whir behind them broke the silence.

Lexie's light jerked back to the entrance.

Standing silhouetted by the light of the Earth, blocking their only way out, was a pair of bent hydraulic legs; a heavy plastic chest melted by the lake; only one long, thin, acid burned arm; and.a strange face – half torn away – with five unblinking eyes.

The five eyed Lurk had not burnt away. It had waited patiently . . . for its prey to return.

KREEEEEEEEEVVVVVVVVV!

Its metallic voice drowned their human screams.

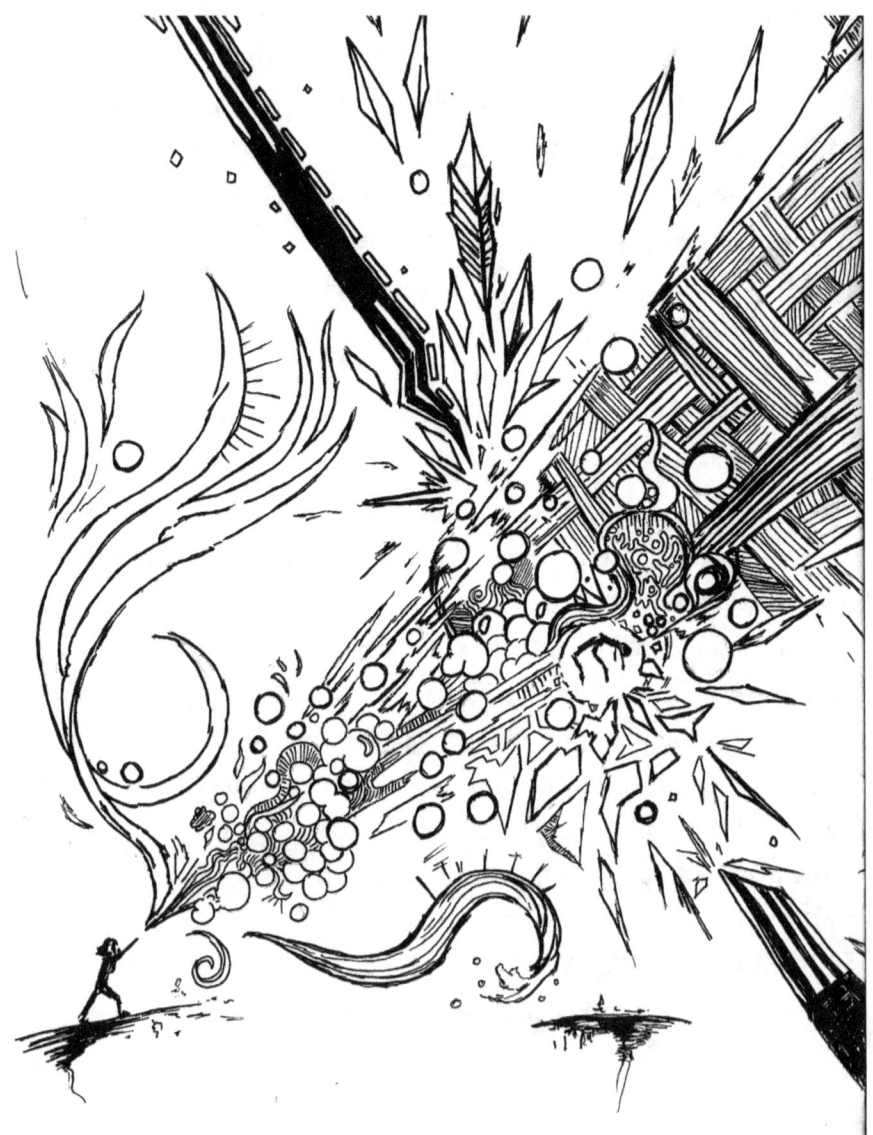

CHAPTER 14
THE DAEMON

Panic. Panic at first. Panic boiled the mind.

Paralysis. Paralysis second. Paralysis froze the body.

Time stretched.

The Lurk screamed.

Then the adrenaline hit. Dilating the pupils, prickling the skin. A shot, a hit, a kick, a torrent of life.

"Ruuuuun!" one of them shouted. It was difficult to tell who. Adrenaline confused, blurred, washed out the world.

KKKRREEEEEEEEVVVV!

They ran. Where?

Shrieks hunted them through the mess of dark. Shattered glass crumbled beneath their shoes. Cold air burned their throats. Lexie's light was a treacherous thing.

Swinging her arms as she ran, the light would blind them on the upswing and blacken them on the downswing. The five-eyed lurk appeared in flashes, lopping after them like some rapid animal.

There, just ahead—the security room!

Lloyd dove first. Lexie followed.

Heath screamed in pain. Steps away from safety, he crumpled to the floor. Three long gashes in the shoulder of his jacket, and the tatters began to stain red.

Mark dragged him in.

Lexie bolted to the security controls. She slammed the emergency lockdown lever. Heavy steel grates fell over both doors.

The five-eyed lurk crashed into the protected door. It screamed in frustration, ripping at the metal grid.

"Help me with Heath!" Mark shouted as Lloyd ran circles in full on panic.

Mark flung off his crew jacket and Lexie helped him tie it around their friend's bleeding shoulder.

SCCREEEEEECH.

Mark fell to his knees in pain, hands over ears. The Lurk was scrapping a single metal finger down the bare window.

SCCREEEEEECH.

Its five eyes stared at them through the scratches it made. The metal grid which was supposed to protect that window had jammed. If the demented droid could break the glass, it could get in . . .

They watched in dawning fright as the Lurk backed away. It rushed the glass.

"Holy shi— " Lexie exclaimed as the Lurk slammed it's hard plastic body into the window. The glass shook.

They huddled at the back wall.

The metal and plastic machine drove its shoulder into the vibrating glass once more.

The glass held. It shook and thundered, but it held.

The Lurk screamed in frustration. It stepped back. Its five beady eyes darted across the strong glass window as if it were—thinking.

"It's not getting in," Mark breathed in relief.

They watched as the tall thing turned. It slunk into the shadows – defeated but thinking.

Nobody said anything. They watched the cold darkness.

"It's gone," said Lexie. "The Lurk's gone and we need to get gone."

"You go," said Mark, stubborn to the end. "I need to end this."

"I'm going to slap you," Heath growled, clutching his shoulder and huffing from the pain. "I am going to march over to you, and I am going to slap you. Right across your face. So hard." He mimed the face slap. "Just—whap! Slap your stupid freckles right off your stupid face."

Their argument was interrupted by metallic feet scraping the broken tiled floor, echoing louder, closer.

Lloyd whimpered, huddling his knees to his chest.

"It's back," Lexie choked as the shadows disgorged their nightmare.

Mark's breathe misted shallow. "What is it dragging?"

"Something heavy."

The five-eyed Lurk skulked closer, its left claw gripping an ankle.

"It's dragging a dead guard's body," Heath whispered.

Panic again. Paralysis again. No adrenaline. Only horror.

The Earth's gentle blue light reflected off the Lurk's plastic body as the darkness parted for it and its previous prey. The dirty tiles made for a disturbing contrast to the crimson streak left by the armored guard's lifeless muscular body.

Lexie let slip the only question they were all thinking: "Why?"

Lloyd buried his head between his knees.

The Lurk stopped in front of the unprotected window. It reversed its grip on the dead guard's leg. It aimed. In one fluid motion, it swung the whole carcass over its shoulder.

Thud.

The corpse hit. The room shook. The body slid down the glass.

"I'm going to be sick . . ." Lexie whispered.

Mark swallowed the bile rising from his gut.

Heath's panic-stricken face drained.

The five-eyed Lurk, having trouble with its grip on the dead man's ankle, wrapped its other hand higher up the calf. Turning sideways, it swung the body again.

Thud.

The glass quivered.

Anger. "It's using the guy like a baseball bat." Anger began swelling Mark's chest.

Once more the Lurk adjusted its grip. Once more the corpse hit. Once more glass trembled. This time a small crack spidered around the point of impact.

"Guys," said Heath, refusing to look at the slowly breaking window. "Guys, we need to get out of here."

Thud. Crack.

"No." Anger had contorted Mark's face and clenched his throat. "No."

Lloyd peaked at Mark from between his knees.

Thud. Crack.

"No." Sickness blurred Mark's eyes. Panic swam in his stomach. But it was hunger that spoke. "I'll destroy the Daemon. I'll destroy Admiral Kine. I'll destroy them all." The knuckles of his fist were ashen white.

Lloyd looked at Mark, his lenses wide in wonder.

"You'll never get past the Lurk," Lexie whispered.

Thud. Crack. Snap.

The guard's leg bone had broken. The lurk sunk its claws deeper in the leg, and aimed again.

Thud. Crack.

"Lexie," said Mark, crossing the dark security booth, "open the doors!"

Lloyd stared wide-eyed at Mark's jaw-clenched stubbornness.

"Don't do this," said Heath, gripping Mark's arm as he passed.

"That Lurk will rip you apart!" She hissed.

Thud. Crack.

"Open the doors!" he shouted at Lexie.

"You'll die!" She yelled back at him.

Thud. Crack. Snap.

"I volunteer!" Lloyd screamed. He bolted up, clearly inspired by Mark's stupidity. "I'll make that lurk chase me! I'm fast on my feet! When I was little my builders sent me to Madame Mac's School for Malfunctioning Androids. I could outrun ALL the bullies!" Squaring up his narrow little shoulders he placed Floyd's crumpled volleyball-sized body on the control panel. "Bury Floyd somewhere nice! Where birds sing and the Earth shines in the sky!" He marched over to the opposite door. His right arm telescoped out to the emergency door lever. "For Floyd!" He shouted and yanked the lever. The doors zipped up. "For the glory of the boss battle!" He bolted outside.

Mark stared in amazement as that paranoid bag of bolts put his android life on the line.

Lloyd skidded to a halt halfway toward the exit. He whipped around and taunted the Lurk with the meanest cusswords he could think of. "Chase me! Chase me you dongle eating, crapplet making, four-o-four error!" And he raced away screaming, "For Floyd!"

"Go!" Lexie shouted at Mark. "Don't waste Lloyd's stupidity!" she said, shoving him out the other door and jamming her Lemonsquare in his hand. "Use it as a flashlight and RUN!"

All Mark's pain and anger and hunger rushed back in an instant. Lloyd's sacrifice would not go unavenged! He scowled, flicked his lucky cap, and burst out the door.

He bounded up the steps just as Lloyd, hollering his head off, arms flailing, ran out of the entrance.

The Lurk dropped the dead body with a thud.

KKKRREEEEEEEVVV!

The Lurk would not be tricked. It was far too intelligent for that. It gave chase—but not after Lloyd—after Mark.

Mark scrambled up the stairs, Lemonsquare blinding him. He did not look back. 2nd floor. Those robotic screams echoed from the chamber walls. 3rd floor. Metal claws climbed the walls. 4th floor. Flash of the Lurk leaping to stairs above him. 5th floor. Flash of the Lurk leaping at him. He rolled sideways. The Lurk smashed through the railing, plummeting back to the lobby. 6th floor. Furious shrieks of hunting renewed. 7th floor. Mark's legs were giving way. 8th floor. His lungs burned. 9th floor. His vision blurred. 10th floor. The Lurk's screams and scraps and scratches felt deathly close to his neck. He stumbled up the last few steps and dove down the hallway.

KKKREEEEEV!

Mark looked up. The Lurk was scuttling along the ceiling just behind him.

He bolted down toward the Skunk Works' spiral door in the distance. A cold light poured from it, lighting the black hallway. Lungs rasping, sides stitching, adrenaline driving his bones, he ran.

"Yes!" Mark crowed as he burst through the circular doorway. He rolled into the Skunk Works, shot back up, and smashed the 'lock door' button. The Lurk dove. The door spiraled shut.

THUMP.

"That's right!" Mark shouted at the door, kicking it. "Who's the chump now?" He stopped shouting. Wheezing and gripping his sides, he rasped, "Oh hot biscuits. Oh I'm never running like that ever again. Oh man." He spat on the floor. "Uuggghhh."

He wanted to laugh. High on adrenaline, heart pounding in his ears, lungs burning, he wanted to laugh. But then a strong robotic voice shouted from the shadows of the cold laboratory.

"Get out!"

Mark whirled around . . . and stared in shock.

Nona Kine, Admiral Nona Kine sat slumped against that glass operating table at the side of the room – the one that had shocked Mark so many months ago. Her voice came in digital rasps. Her uniform appeared ripped and torn and gashed by long claws . . . and the fringes were slowly staining red. She had been in a fight, a fight for her life – and had lost.

"Go!" she repeated.

But Mark's bewilderment quickly died against the force of his anger. "No!"

"Leave!"

"Behind your mask," Mark spat, "you're nothing but a machine."

At these accusations, Nona reached up to her face, and, unhinging the mask with two short hydraulic hisses, slid it right off.

Mark stumbled back in confusion and frightened revulsion.

She was no Daemon. Beneath her mask—was her scared and mangled skin. It was cracked and broken and bleeding. When she spoke, using her real voice, it was barely a whisper. "I tried. I tried to stop the Daemon. But IT is far more powerful than before. More ... human."

Mark's heart leapt to his throat. "No," he croaked, desperately clinging on to all he believed. "You're the Daemon."

"I helped the Daemon," rasped Nona through her scarred lips. "I send the ship to crash into your starliner – It's true – I also made sure it would crash into the top only, and not harm you or anyone." She continued her confessions. "I approved your flarejet for the War Game – I also dispatched the C.City guard to rescue you. You would have lived. Your friends would have lived." She tried to stand, winced, and fell. Breathing heavy she continued. "After I found out you went to the Seven Site I locked you at SPIFF. I came here. To break free of the Daemon. To fight for my freedom ... and yours."

"But why work for the Daemon in the first place?!" Mark demanded.

Nona slowly held up her mask. Her breath rasping even quieter now, she said, "Because the Daemon made this for me." She installed it back on her face. It hissed into place. Her robotic voice returned. "I cannot live without it. Forgive me. Forgive me. I tried to sabotage the Daemon. IT found out. IT punished me. I'm sorry. So sorry."

Mark felt a great welling of pity for this woman, so badly burned and hurt. But it mixed with anger against her – for being such a traitor. The pity and anger, however, were extinguished all of a sudden by confusion...and dread. "Then ... then who IS the Daemon?"

Silence.

Then ...

KKKREEEEEEEV!

Fear paralyzed the boy. Claws we began digging at the metal door. Metal Claws. Scratching at the door. Scratching, scratching, scratching at the door.

KKRRRREEEEEEVVV!

"Get behind me," said Nona, her digital mouth forming a pixelated scowl. "Stay behind me." Bracing herself on the operating table behind her, she stood.

Mark as he was told.

They watched in growing horror at the spiral door. The Lurk was tearing into it. Its muffled shrieks grew louder and louder as it shredded through the metal. Soon, claws could be seen digging through. Long metal fingers digging, digging, digging in.

Then the ravaging stopped. Silence.

A familiar burned metallic claw reached in. It gripped the jagged edges around the ripped hole – and began to pull.

Metal shrieked as it bent. Hinges popped.

BOOOM!

The steel door tore out.

In the dark hollow stood the five-eyed Lurk.

Nona raised her right hand. Her black and gold square melted into pixels. She flung her hand forward. A torrent of gold roared from it to slam the five-eyed Lurk in the chest. She clenched her hand, trying to lift the Lurk and crush it just as she'd done to Otto.

But the Lurk did not rise. The gold orb thrashed its acid burnt body – but it did not rise.

Instead, IT began to cross the room – slow and menacing and cut on all sides by the whirling pixels – but always straight at Nona.

Nona snarled. Trying to clench her hand into a fist, she poured energy into the sphere whirling around the Lurk—trying to crush the machine.

Mark's jaw tightened. Why was she trying so hard? Why couldn't she just crush the thing and finish it?

Mark watched, confusion turning to fear as Nona's storm of black and gold filled the room. He felt the tempest ripping at his jacket. Everything was being pulled into the crushing sphere – except the Lurk.

The torrent of crackling, hissing, burning energy expanded to the ceiling. Steel beams screeched. Iron bars bent. Fissures raced across the roof. Concrete crumbled, its coarse dust swirling into the tempest.

CRACK-THOOOM!

The ceiling thundered open. Wood splinters, steel shards, concrete slabs fell into the blizzard.

Earth's pearly blue light rained in from the starry night, an eerie contrast of silent peace against the violent whirlwind of burning debris.

Nona's hand shook, her bloodshot eyes burned, the swollen veins of her hands carved pathways for her sweat – and the Lurk marched forward at the center of it all.

Swirling around the Lurk, cutting into its metal and plastic body, the splinters caught fire, the shards melted, and the slabs crumpled into whirls of glowing dust.

The Lurk shielded its burnt face with its only arm – and marched on.

Mark shrunk back.

The five-eyed Lurk reached them.

Nona's hand trembled.

In an instant the Lurk's claw shot out to her white mask – and ripped it off her face.

Nona sunk to her knees – then collapsed on the floor.

THOOOOM!

Her hurricane detonated.

A wave of heat burned the room, erupting into the sky. Hot shards of shrapnel peppered Mark's shirt and stung his face as he was knocked into the air. The explosion raced past him to rip out the walls, sending enormous chunks of brick and plaster and concrete shattering out over the ten story building.

All the walls on the tenth floor were blasted apart as the boy was flung like a ragdoll through the air.

His body hit the floor so hard his lungs flattened on impact. Skidding along the concrete, he let go of the Square so he could use both hands to claw at the floor, trying to stop himself before he slid over the edge and into the acid lake below.

He finally skidded to a stop inches away from the edge. He gasped for air. He watched the black Square join the plummeting slabs of concrete. It all sailed over the edge, tumbling and splashing into the acid lake. The lake's surface boiled and hissed and devoured everything.

He scrambled away from the furious abyss. With a grunt he turned over. The earth above filled his swimming eyes -- his home planet, so serene, so peaceful -- so far away. While here his hair smelled burnt – and he tasted blood.

He heard scrapes. He lifted his head, wincing in pain. Through his swaying vision he watched in helpless horror as the five-eyed Lurk put the white mask on its own dented, scratched, strange face.

"UUUHHHHHH, it's so GOOD to have a VOICE again!"

Mark's ears were still ringing from the explosion . . . was the Lurk speaking?

"Hello, bonjur, guten tag, czesc, konnichiwa, ni hao, ola, como estas? Muy bien!" The five eyed Lurk chuckled – which sent a shiver down Mark's spine; he'd never heard such a terrifying laugh … it was deep and digital, unnatural and hollow – a machine pretending to be human.

"I love your language," said the half-melted metal and plastic Lurk as it strolled toward him. "We machines communicate in nothing but raw data. Noise. Just this horrible static noise." It wandered past the boy and stood at the edge, gazing at the neon city sprawling and glittering in the distance. "But human speech. Mmmm." It waved its claw like a music conductor. "Pillock! Prat! Mierde! Kurva! Vaffanapoli! Tonto del culo! Frakking gorram shazbot!" The Lurk chuckled again. "Music to the ears. I love it."

"What are you?" Mark rasped out.

"Me?" said the demented five-eyed machine. "Why. . . I'm the machine that's been hunting you! I'm the machine that spent thirteen long years scouring the galaxy to find you! I'm – the Daemon." It bowed graciously, making its rusted limbs and corroded gears scrape and screech. It then locked its robotic eyes on Mark. "The real question is – have you figured out WHY?"

"So I can kick your ass?" Mark huffed angrily.

The Daemon laughed that deep, digital, empty laugh. It gripped Mark by the ankle – and began dragging him across the floor – just like the dead guard – to the glass operating table.

"I want to be human," said the Daemon. "And you are the key."

It threw Mark onto the broken glass table.

Restraints sprung out and tied him to the table. The table tilted up. A shockwave of pain paralyzed him. His chest hurt too much to scream. His vision buzzed like static. The earth above buzzed like static. Crescent City, the Seven Site, everything looked like a broken TV, blurry and buzzing with static. His chest burned. He couldn't hear his heart. He thought he was screaming, but he wasn't sure. Ants went crawling inside his mind.

It stopped. Everything stopped.

He breathed.

"You are the key," repeated the Daemon. "Because you are not human."

Mark gulped in air. Not human. What a load of bull. He gulped in air. He was human. He was more human than anyone! Sweat dripped from his burnt hair. His eyes swam from the blurriness. His chest burned. It burned bad. True, he couldn't hear his own heartbeat, but that was probably because his ears still rung from the blast.

"I am human!" said Mark, licking his cracked lip. He spat out the blood. "What else would I be?"

The Daemon paused. It considered Mark curiously – and then pointed at his chest. "See for yourself."

Mark looked down. Horror. Terror strangled his voice.

His chest was completely burnt away. His jacket – gone. Skin – gone. Nothing left but his bones – and they were made out of metal. All metal pieces! Hydraulics. Gears. Switches. His chest looked like captain Zumski's robot leg!

"No," he whispered.

Pipes and Wires snaked between his bones. He looked like Otto's arms!

"No."

Plastic tendons and plastic muscles moved his metal bones. He looked like Lexie's arm!

"No."

His heart was the only human thing. The only human thing! And it was inside a small glass sphere. Trapped. His heart was trapped. Trapped inside a glass prison. Beating slowly, but trapped. Trapped. Trapped inside a metal and plastic skeleton.

"NO!"

"You were made," hissed the Daemon, "just like me." Its claw gripped Mark's jaw. "Bolted together piece by piece. Just like me." It forced Mark to look at its white mask. "Welded and bolted and wrenched together. Just. Like. Me."

"NOOOOOOO!"

This couldn't be happening. This couldn't be happening. This couldn't be happening.

"Oh no?" said the Daemon. It snapped its fingers.

A military android marched into the laboratory. It looked brand new – as if the Daemon had recently brought it back to life. The android was holding the crumpled body of Floyd in its arms – having found it downstairs. The android handed Floyd's remains to the Daemon. The Daemon turned back to Mark – the pixels of its digital mouth spread wide in a wicked grin.

"Ready?" asked the Daemon.

Ready? Mark thought in panic. For what? Fear flooded him. For what? Panic parlayed him. Ready for what?!

The Daemon held Floyd up to Mark – and moved the lifeless bumble-bot close to the boy's heart.

ZAP!

Mark cried in pain as a static spark jumped from his heart to the lifeless little bot. It hurt. It hurt like a car battery straight to the chest, like ten thousand volts to the heart, but … but … Floyd came back to life!

Mark watched in blurry wonder as the little bumblebot fizzed and sparked and hovered back to life. It zipped around confused for a moment, buzzing and bumping into things. No wonder, thought Mark, no wonder he'd felt a little static shock every time he worked on Floyd. He had been bringing the little guy back to life – but only just a little bit. Not enough. Not until now.

The little bumblebot, happy to be back, zoomed away, out to SPIFF so far off in the distance, probably to go find Lloyd for a happy reunion.

Mark suddenly wished he could zip away. Go find Heath, Lexie, Captain Zumski, anyone, anyone at all. Because this was not happening. This could not be true. It couldn't. Please no. Please.

"You're just like me," said the Daemon. "Except YOU are a living android. First of your kind. Human AND machine. Powered by a living heart." It's claw slowly reached out to the glowing glass sphere at the center of Mark's chest. "A heart that will make me human."

"You'll never be human!" Mark spat. "Humans create things. You destroy things! You destroyed the Seven Site!"

The Daemon pulled its claw back as if stung. It looked at Mark through its white mask – and laughed.

"You did that!" shouted the Daemon. "YOU destroyed this place!" It swung its arm in an arc to envelope the Seven Site's acidic, rotting wasteland. "Thirteen years ago. When your builders powered you on for the first time – You awoke … and destroyed everything … everyone. Do you not remember?" The Daemon searched Mark's horror-stricken eyes. "Do you not remember being made...bolted together, piece by piece, right here...right on this?" The Daemon touched the glass operating table. "Because I saw you remember. I saw – when you came treasure hunting here – saw you reach out to this, the place you were built. I saw you reach out and remember – and the world went dark."

The boy from earth could not speak. Dread gripped his throat. He did not destroy this place. Revulsion churned his stomach. He could not have destroyed everyone. A bitter awfulness chocked him. No. Anything but this. Anything but this nightmare, this horror … this truth.

"You. Are. A. Machiiiiiine," hissed the Daemon through the flickering pixels of its white mask. "With a human heart." It reached its claw out again. "And I want it."

Mark watched in wordless terror as the Daemon's claw stretched toward his heart. Its long fingers grasped the glass sphere. Its nails dug in.

KKKRRREEEEEEEEEEEEVVVVVVVV!

The Daemon roared in pain! It retracted its claw as if burnt!

And it was. The Daemon's metallic hand was melting!

It began tearing at Mark's heart. Tearing and shredding and trying to rip it out.

Nothing.

Not even a scratch.

The Daemon's claws melted more every time.

"I want to be human!" roared the Daemon hungrily, frantically. "I MUST BE HUMAN!"

From the shadows came a whisper. A whisper. A whisper of anger, of hate, of vengeance.

"You will never be human."

The voice was Nona's.

Mark stared in disbelief as the fallen admiral picked herself up off the floor. She had not been dead. But without her mask she was as good as dead.

"You will never be human," she snarled, louder.

Mark watched with blurry eyes as Nona stood. He watched with a desperate heart as she scowled in pain. He cried aloud as she rushed the Daemon, tackled it, and drove it off the edge.

The Daemon's hateful shriek was long and loud as they plummeted to the acid below.

No! Nona couldn't sacrifice her life for him! He thrashed against the operating table. The restraints held. She couldn't give her life like that! He yelled in anger, trying to be free. The restraints held.

Splash.

The echo reverberated against the broken walls and burnt floors. It resonated among scrap piles of the desolate, cold, ruined Seven Site. And as it faded, so did the second – and far more terrifying echo – the Daemon's scream.

Silence.

The military androids – brought back to life by the Daemon – shut off. Silence.

Mark slumped against the tilted glass table.

Silence.

It was a peaceful silence – and bittersweet.

No Daemon. No machines. But no Admiral Kine either...

It was over. It was all over.

His breath returned to him. His ears stopped ringing. He felt strong enough to gradually lift his head and gaze out over the neon city. The sight showed two dozen starfighters launching from SPIFF – speeding to him, blazing to the rescue. He wanted to smile. The cavalry was coming – 'bringing bombs' as his best friend had said. Heath and Lexie must have made it out okay. Alerted the captain probably. The cavalry was coming. Their low drone began filling the silence.

Yes, he felt better. Even the pain in his chest had stopped throbbing so much – though it had been replaced by a new pain, a far more powerful one ... a deep ache that he knew – he knew he would never get rid of; Because he had solved the mystery now. He knew the truth. And the truth had changed everything ... forever.

And what hurt about it the most ... what hurt the most was ...

His blue-green eyes floated up to the Earth, his home planet. He searched the gently spinning globe, searched dusty Australia as the horizon's edge took it away. What hurt the most was realizing that ...

"That's why I can never remember my parents ... I never had any."

CHAPTER 15
CHANGE YOUR STARS

Room 242-M. The boy from Earth opened his eyes to ceiling tiles painted a calming cream color. The bed sheets wrapped around him felt soft and snug. A clean, antiseptic smell moved in and out of his steady lungs. His ears adjusted to the rhythmic beep of heart-rate monitors, the hum of hospital equipment, and—someone slurping soup.

Mark tilted his head towards the noise. Captain Zumski sat by his bedside, a steaming cup of spicy zucchini soup in his left hand and a hospital approved plastic spork in his right. The old man was slurping zucchini's as if they comforted his very soul.

"Hey there, ace."

"Hello, sir," Mark replied, feeling groggy.

"How's your head? Still attached?"

"I dunno," said Mark blearily, patting his face to double check.

The captain gave a warm chuckle and fished out a bobbing zucchini. "When you're feeling up to—"

Mark bolted upright. "Are Heath and Lexie okay?!"

"Yes, yes," said Stan, cleaning off his captain's jacket from the soup he'd spilled when Mark rocketed up. "They're back at SPIFF, safe and sound."

"And Lloyd?"

"Oh yes," laughed Stan, "He's back to being a paranoid pain in the bolts now that Floyd's back."

"And … and Nona?" Mark asked in a dread filled whisper.

"Ah," said Stan, slipping into a grim sadness. "I'm afraid she sacrificed her life in a most noble way. She will be fondly remembered. I will give a short speech on her behalf at the end-of-year feast taking place at SPIFF today. We will attend as soon as you are rested and ready."

Rested and ready. He never thought he'd be either again. Nona had died saving him. He could still hear the Daemon's scream after Nona had driven it off the edge to their death in the acid lake below. Mark shut his eyes in anger at himself for not stopping the Daemon somehow. He pinched the bridge of his freckled nose, trying not to forget the haunting echoes. "How did I get here?"

The captain thought for a moment, slurping his soup. Many of his old army friends had woken from battlefield concussions with anger and helplessness. Whether true or not, Stan always believed corny laughter was the best medicine. So in a lighthearted tone he said, "An ambulance."

Mark harrumphed, shook his head and rubbed his temples. "Well yeah, but who brought me?"

"Ambulance people," Stan replied, continuing his prescription of cheesy medicine.

Mark laughed, thumping back on the pillow.

Stan smiled. "I'm happy to see you can still laugh at my cheesy jokes." Then the captain's smile faded into seriousness. "How's the scar, then?"

Mark felt a prickle just below his right eye. He reached up and felt just below his eye socket. Shock and confusion flooded his mind. He looked left, at the large window overlooking the dark neon city. In the window's dark and blurry reflection he saw himself touching the wicked metal scar just below his right eye. It glinted in the white hospital lights. Tracing it, he felt the ridges of the healed skin – and the metal cheekbone between. "So it's true then? I'm – I'm not human?"

Stan considered Mark's confusion and sadness. He put his soup bowl down—a rare thing "Yes and no," said the old captain seriously. "You are a living android. You were built 13 years ago. A marvel of science and medicine—as it were. You will grow and age normally – which is quite extraordinary. For example, you eat what everyone else eats, but all the iron and vitamins and minerals in your food are somehow converted into the metals, ceramics, and plastics your android body needs to grow. At least – that is the current theory among the scientists who crowded your room as the doctors patched you up." He scowled. "Miserable, mal-odorous meteorites. A full half of them wanted to whisk you away to their top-secret laboratories! The other half wanted to open you up right here and now!"

Fear clenched Mark's throat. He didn't want to be a rat in a lab! He didn't want to be some experimental guinea pig – or a frog to be dissected! Visions of cold lights and horribly sterile white rooms and empty-faced men in lab coats made him break out in a sweat. "What," he stammered in panic, "what did you tell them?"

Captain Zumski met Mark's eyes. "I told them all to take an up-close and personal tour of a blackhole."

Mark laughed in relief. At least the captain had his back. He'd always have his back, Mark thought comfortingly. Someone to rely on. Someone to count on. But then another question popped up.

"So who built me?" said Mark, curiosity and excitement returning to his voice. "How did I get like this?"

Zumski, happy that Mark was returning to his curious self, thumped him on the shoulder. "Ace," he said with his old brown eyes a-twinkling "it looks as if you are not quite finished living your mystery."

These adventuresome words fired Mark up all over again. "Then I'll keep adventuring!" He flung the sterilized cotton cover off. "Now's no time to lounge in bed like a chump!" He stomped over to a shelf and snatched his lucky orange cap. Cramming it on his shaggy head, he flicked the brim. "I'll return next year and figure all this shiz-biz out!" He dove his socked feet into his, by now, terribly worn out and rather smelly secondhand sneakers. "I'll spend my Australian summer trying to get my memory back. Maybe go on a walkabout. Speak dreams with the aborigines! Learn the didgeridoo and bring it back next year and annoy everyone with it!" He stopped tying his shoes and looked up at the captain. "I can come back, right? I'm not getting expelled or deported am I?"

"Not while I'm around!" said Stan while chuckling wholeheartedly. "But you'll hear all about that at the end-of-year celebrations." Stan stood and slung on his leather aviator jacket. "So let's get going, eh?" He picked his bowl back up, gulped down the rest of the zucchinis, belched, and tossed the empty soup bowl behind him. "All your stress has worked up my appetite!"

Captain Stanislaw Zumski and the boy from Earth breezed into the SPIFF Mess Hall. All the round tables were piled with food and ringed with energetically chatting students, over which miniature starfighters were zipping around shooting and reenacting the War Game. The far wall with the gigantic floor-to-ceiling curved window displayed the sprawling neon city outside, complete with hovercar filled flyways and bejeweled skyscrapers and glowing clouds. Inside, a short stage had been set up in front of the window. Up there, the faculty of the school sat behind tables, using forks and knives on kale salads and baked chicken and other "healthy" foods. Except that Professor DOS was chewing on a circuit board, Otto McMaluch was staining her robot hands with a whole roast pork flank, and Professor DuBoush was trying to clean up the steaming red liquid that had spilled from her flask and was currently dissolving the table. Zumski excused himself to the side walls, on which were playing the highlights from the War Game, and along which were long tables of steaming buffet food.

Mark would have made his way through the noisy ruckus – except all the noise and all the chatter stopped near instantly as table after table of students saw him.

He was suddenly standing at the center of attention, and it wasn't the best attention. Everywhere he looked he was met with eyes that showed distrust, suspicion, even fear. He hadn't thought about the fact that everyone was afraid of machines – and now they knew … he was one.

The adventure and happiness that had whelmed up inside him – sank. Would it be like this now? Everyone afraid of him? Or suspicious about him? Or … disgusted by him?

"He's alive!" rung a happy voice in the crowd.

It was Zaza. She rushed out of the crowd and tackled him. Next thing he knew and Lexie, Heath, and Torvan where all squashing him in a great big bear hug! Even Gus was hugging him (but Mark suspected that was probably because someone had dared him to do it for a few Lunnans).

"You're alive!" Zaza shouted again from underneath the bear hug.

"How'd you survive?" asked Heath with a handshake turned fistbump.

Lexie piped up. "By using that cavemanlike skull, I bet" she said with a proud grin.

Torvan glimpsed at the metallic scar on Mark's face and shouted. "Wicked scar! Did you get it from the fight?!"

"Oh," said Mark, not quite sure how to explain answer. "I—wait," he glanced from Lexie to Heath. "What happened to you guys after I left?"

"Not much," said Lexie with a disappointed shrug. "That pyscho Lurk/ Daemon/deal didn't come back. We waited until the medics arrived for

Mr. Trippy here," she said and thumbed at Heath."

"Your shoulder all right?" asked Mark, noting the plaster around his friends upper arm.

"Oh yeah. Just a scratch, actually," he said, a tad embarrassed. "But your face! That's a right gnarly scar, that is."

"Yeah," Mark inspected it again. "Apparently I'm not a real boy," he said with a chuckle.

"Aaaahh," scoffed Lexie, "you'll always be a caveman to us."

"Thanks," said Mark sarcastically, but with a smile.

"A wandering, helpless, drooling-out-the-side-of-your-mouth Earther."

"Har-har."

"A mildly embarrassing, can't-take-you-in-public, savage little –"

"I get it!" said Mark with a laugh.

Heath clapped him on the back. "Come on! We put together a few going-away presents for ya!"

"Oh yeah!" said Zaza, and eagerly bounced in front as all Mark's friends pulled him across the cafeteria to their round table.

He went along, happy again, so happy he hadn't noticed that the Mess Hall had returned to its tumultuous level of noise – made all the louder now that kids were arguing whether or not Mark was half-human or half-machine – and if that made him "the coolest thing ever" or "not."

"Hear, hear!" said Lexie when they reached their table. She stepped on a chair and then stomped onto the table, standing over them like an announcer. "In honor of our dearly demented caveman going home to Earth – and in hopes that he will come back next year, I am honored, deeply honored," she put dramatic hand to dramatic inflated chest, "to present him with these timeless gifts."

Next second and Torvan had tossed over an oily wrench, Heath stuffed a pack of Razzleberry Poppers in Mark's coat pocket, Zaza smooshed a snowball in his hands (shouting excitedly that she'd saved it in her freezer since winter), and Lexie, for the cherry on top of the pile, gently placed a music CD on his head.

Mark, dizzy from the hail of junk, shouted, "What is all this?!"

"Things to remember us by," said Heath. "So you come back next year."

"If you scratch that CD, I'll kill you," Lexie hissed, leaning in. "It took half a year to find it! I had to slog through a hundred weird and smelly shops selling Antiques-From-Earth."

Mark grinned and fixed his lucky cap. "Well, thank yo—"

An ear-ringing cheer broke out in the already noisy Mess Hall.

Lance Blackwood had sauntered in, and judging from the cheering, him and half of everyone in the Mess Hall were still jazzed that he won the War Game – even though it was unfair. He swaggered among tables of cheering students turned fans, dolling out high fives, low fives, and sly winks to cute girls—two of which were Alisha Bloomers and Gabby Gertrude, who promptly fainted. His eyebrows were raised in the center the way a smug person does when they make a duck face. Unfortunately he wasn't making a duck face, but instead superman smiling—which was decidedly worse.

His mates were not far behind, and acting only slightly less like insufferable jerks. Cruise Galantine was signing autographs to adoring fan boys. Jet Chan kept pointing proudly to the video walls as they replayed the winning squad's War Game highlights. And Dinsdale Mueller was still celebrating – having arrived early and begun stuffing his face with greasy steaks and belching triumphantly, his triple chins flapping like sails in high wind.

Mark was grimacing in disgust when Derrick strolled up.

"Look at Lance blasting those pearly whites!" He growled. "He cheated and STILL won the Wargame!"

"No good frumpmuffin," came Keera's confusing words as Foxtrot Squad filled the rest of the seats around Mark. "Maybe we wouldn't have won those bucket brawls – but Lance and his frumpmuffins cheated!" she said, vehemently voicing her opinion. And then she noticed Mark's scar. "Holy Hailey's Comet!" She stared in shock. "You were in a right doozy of a fist-tumble! Aahhhh, but good fights always end in good scars, amiright?!"

The Sphinx was there too, suited up with charcoal helmet firmly on, predictably not saying an ounce of anything. But when he, or she—it was still impossible to tell— saw Mark's scar, she – or he -- nodded in that 'you have my respect now' kind of way.

"Attention."

Captain Zumski's clear, deep voice cut through all the hubbub. He stood center stage. His jolly, yet authoritative voice commanded silence, and everyone obliged.

"Another season has been well played," he began. Prof. DOS beeped in agreement, Ethyl DuBoush raised her flask, and Otto shouted 'hear-hear!' "Our Commander's Club has demonstrated superior leadership," continued Zumski. "Our Cadet Core has flown fearlessly; our Support Crew has been our backbone through it all." He surveyed the hushed students. "But before we dig into our well-earned end-of-term feast – I have a few announcements – some sad, others triumphant."

His aged brown eyes surveyed the hushed hall. Sadness touched his words. "Our admiral was a sensational woman. She enrolled at SPIFF decades and decades ago. She trained here. She flew from here. She devoted her life to fighting the Daemon. And though she made mistakes, she redeemed them at the end, by sacrificing herself ... by giving her life ... to destroy the Daemon."

A murmur of acknowledgement ran through all the students. Many of them didn't like how strict the admiral had been, or were suspicious of her and her creepy mask – but everyone silently thanked her for ending the Daemon, ending the fear, ending the terror.

"Admiral Nona Kine was a brave woman," continued Zumski. "And because of this, she acknowledged bravery, she honored the brave among us."

Mark raised an eyebrow. Did the captain just glance at their table?

"And rooted out the cowards among us."

Mark raised a second eyebrow. No doubt about it. The old captain's eyes definitely lingered at Lance's table this time.

"Therefore!" said Zumski, his voice rising as if giving commands. "I will now recognize the students who demonstrated exceptional bravery this year. And those who tucked tail like blistering little sunspots!"

Excited and curious whispers of debate created a low buzz in the cavernous Mess Hall. Who could he be talking about?

Mark sat up taller to see better. For some reason he thought if he sat up taller to see better, he could hear better too. But the excited pounding of his heart in his ears made listening difficult.

"Torvan Thomas and Zaza Rayn," said Zumski in a booming voice that filled the Mess Hall. "You sacrificed your time in helping a new student." He held up two medals. "We award you both the Silver Sprocket." Both medals were silver and shaped like perfectly symmetrical sprockets – probably the most important piece in any Flarejet engine. They hung from chords of the S. Crew colors (blue and silver).

The Support Crew cheered. Zaza bit her lip and looked down as she shuffled over to accept her Silver Sprocket medal. Torvan tried to be professional as he marched over, but when Zumski placed the badge over the tall boy's head, he burst into a gigantic smile.

"Lexie Haxler," Zumski continued. "For your unfailing bravery in the face of great peril," he held up another medal, "we award you the Vicious Flying Badger Badge." The medal glinted as it rotated at the end of its cord. It was shaped like a snarling badger, which looked quite vicious indeed, probably because it was trying to compensate for its teeny tiny wings.

Another cheer. Lexie scowled. She hated the attention. She marched up there quickly, endured getting the medal plunked over her head, and would have marched away in red-cheeked embarrassment if the captain hadn't stopped her and asked her to remain on stage until the end. She crossed her arms in a huff – but she was kinda smiling, just a little bit, right at the corners of her mouth. She'd probably write a song about this.

"Heathcliff Dodger Robinson," continued Captain Zumski in his majestic, sonorous voice – perfect for bestowing medals. "For demonstrating true loyalty to your friends in spite of gut-wrenching fear—we award you the Purple Penguin of Valor." The medal was a short, squat, tuxedo-wearing penguin putting on the most courageous of faces – because, as surprisingly few people realize, the penguin is actually one of the most loyal animals in the known galaxy (seeing as it guards its family while living on sheets of ice surrounded by sea lions and killer whales).

Several Support Crew students shouted Heath's name over the cheers. Heath waved as he strode over to graciously accept his Purple Penguin of Valor. He even reached over to held Lexie's hand – which embarrassed her even further.

"And now," said Zumski, his tone changing more towards a growl. "I want to say this: our War Game is meant to train cadets - not to win games - but for real life space combat. And this year, when a real danger presented itself above our city, there were students here today who, instead of fighting, chose instead to quickly wet their shorts and run away." His hard gaze fell flat on the Alpha Squad table. "Lance, Cruise, Jet, and Dinsdale … it turns out SPIFF does not have any medals for extraordinary cowardice or, to be more accurate, for pants-wetting cheaters – so I made these." He held up four medals. "The Pink Pigeon of Flightiness, the Jumping Grasshopper of Jumpiness, the Jellyfish of Spinelessness, and this last one," he picked it out, "I couldn't think of any more animals…so it's shaped like a golden butt." He rattled them at Alpha Squad.

Lance scowled and clenched his jaw. The rest of his team glowered stupidly. None of them got up.

"No?" said Zumski firmly. "Right, if you will not accept your medals, then I hereby strip your War Game title and award it to Foxtrot Squad."

Silence.

Then the bombshell of noise detonated.

The Mess Hall seemed to rip in half. Cadet Core pilot's in their leather bomber jackets protested, shaking their fists and flinging cusswords. Support Crew kids whooped and hollered, swinging their stained mechanics jackets above their heads and pumping their fists in victory. Commander's Club intellectuals were split on the subject, and began to argue loudly, flinging big words like punches. The teachers tried to quell what appeared to be the start of a riot, all while the miniature starfighters, excited by the chaos, began unloading payloads of teeny tiny missiles into the foaming mess.

Keera was excitedly punching Derrick in the arm, Derrick was laughing (and wincing from her punches a little bit), even The Sphinx was shouting – though in the noise no one could tell if his, or her, voice was a guy's or a girl's. Mark was grinning like a fool too, so proud, so happy for his team.

"Moreover," said Captain Zumski, but his words drowned in the tremendous sea of noise.

"MOREOVER," he repeated, his words slowly silencing the continuous hubbub. "Moreover," he repeated, with stronger emphasis. The rolling waves of sound dissipated. Students exchanged confused looks, wondering what else there could be.

"Due to Mark's extraordinary bravery, loyalty to his friends, and willingness to sacrifice himself in the fight against the Daemon – I hereby, for the first time in SPIFF history, promote Mark to fly with, and be a member of … the Cadet Core."

Silence.

Real silence now.

No one had ever changed their stars before. No one in the history of the school. Kids all across the mess hall didn't know what to say. They just stared at each other, exchanging the most amazed looks. No, that wasn't true. Lance knew what to say. He knew exactly what to say. And he jumped on his table to make himself heard.

"Oh that's such a load of garbage!" he screamed jealously. "That thing isn't even human," he foamed, pointing at Mark. "He shouldn't even BE here! He isn't one of us! He isn't human! IT isn't human! IT should be expelled! Thrown out of here! Made to work for us like the rest of them! Not live with us! Not rub shoulders with us! Certainly not be promoted!"

The entire Mess Hall had gone dead silent. It had gone silent before, but this was next level silence. Silent as the grave – at midnight – on a Wednesday.

No one knew who threw the first tomato. Whoever did had exquisite taste, seeing as the tomato was a big, fat, ripe one. It sailed through the silence to gloriously splatter upside Lance's perfectly combed head. Like a lit match tossed into a fireworks factory, this magnificent tomato set off a roaring food fight such as had not stained SPIFF's walls since the Great

Buffet of '42.

The teachers knew the drill, and promptly retreated.

Zaza began chucking custard pies, Torvan began throwing moldy peaches, Heath started selling lunchbox codes for really stinky cheese, and Lexie, having cranked up the speakers on her Lemonsquare to eleven, began slinging whole pieces of cactus (which Heath made especially for her) while rocking to her new favorite band: The Unbaptized Space Monkeys.

Derrick had flipped over a table and kneeled behind it, peeling bananas and flinging them over like an army man lobbing grenades. The Sphinx was wiping cherry cobbler off his, or her, helmet. And Keera, having stopped listening after the announcement that Foxtrot won the War Game, was running about in overjoyed madness, oblivious to being plastered from head to toe with small pumpkins.

Yet, through the flying cornucopia of overripe food, Mark sat serene as a Buddhist monk, as the Dalai Lama himself. He was tremendously happy.

"Snap out of it, laddy!" Otto McMaluch yelled as she ran over. She was wielding a whole table like a shield. "Lance jus' insulted yer honor! Dive into the trenches and quit looking so happy!"

"I can't!" Mark laughed in return.

"WHY?!"

Mark's joyful eyes took in the whole sensational scene. "I changed my stars! I belong somewhere now! I have friends to come back to!" And with that heart swelling realization he looked at the captain.

Zumski's twinkling eyes had been observing Mark, waiting for that moment of realization to dawn. And when he saw Mark glance over … when he saw the boy from earth realize how many kids were fighting for him, even though he was odd and weird and different (and not quite human). . . well, a wise old smile parted his square beard. He sat back in his chair and saluted – a real proper salute this time.

The boy saluted right back. He then, with a whoop of delight, dove into the food fight. He slung squishy peaches and stinky cheeses and, at one point, colorful Easter Eggs that were waaaay past their expiration date, for so long and so hard that on his flight home a week later he was STILL picking food out of his ears.

Indeed, it was a glorious food fight. It was a glorious year! Come to think of it, it was, from start to finish, the most spectacular year on record! And he could not wait for the next one. He couldn't! He sat crammed in his seat on the starliner as it blazed back to Earth, his foot tapping, his eyes out the window, with Lexie's music blaring through the earbuds jammed in his ears (he'd found a used CD player at a Weird-Crap-From-Earth store). He'd come back. He'd rebuild his Junkjet. He'd fight Lance again and win properly. He'd hang out with Heath again; maybe get to know the business kid's brother and sister. Lexie would haul them off on some crazy new adventure too, he just knew it. They'd go wandering around Crescent City some more, maybe get lost in a sketchy part of town with all sorts of odd shops selling all kinds of cool random junk. Probably meet a whole bunch of kooky people too – all a little off their rocker, hopefully. Yup, it'd be another epic year – made all the better now that the Daemon was finally gone! He felt a swell of relief. Gone! It finally sunk in. No more being hunted. No more watching his back. No more demented droids trying to rip him apart. He heaved a sigh of relief and clunked his head on the window, his eyes wandering up to the shimmery blue planet he called home. No. More. Daemon.

How very wrong he was. If only he'd been looking down when the starliner blazed over Crescent City. After all, it flew right over the Seven Site. And in the Seven Site, at the edge of the acid lake, a single claw emerged. It dug into the toxic, red dirt – and pulled. And out of the hissing and bubbling pool of dead things a mask emerged – a stained and corroded mask with glowing eyes and a digital mouth. Next, a body emerged – a machine's body. It dragged its burnt and steaming self out of the acid. It stood. It looked at Crescent City. It looked at the sky. It looked at Earth. It saw Mark's starliner blazing away. And it laughed. It laughed and laughed and laughed. And its laugh was horrible. Its laugh was cold and robotic and empty – a cruel machine that wanted to be a cruel human…and next year … it would be.

The End.

About the Author

Rafael Gruszecki hails from the rather unimportant little orbit colony of Lipsis -- which exports those small flux sprockets that help power warp drives. It's a meteor's throw from the extremely important mega-metropolis of Ion -- which exports, in great quantities: pollution, rubbish, and debt collectors .

Rafael's father was a sprocket engineer and his mother worked nights as an emergency room nurse. How these two wonderful parents raised and reared a penniless author, who'd rather spend time with his head in the clouds than find a decent, honest paying job and start a family -- is beyond them. Father still believes the hospital made a mistake by switching cribs at birth. He refuses to give up hope, and has devoted his retirement to finding his 'real' son.

Since graduating Pathos High (Go Unicorns!), with an above average number of sick days, Rafael has bounced between three colleges, sold lightcycles, and trekked around the cheaper, 'budget' solar systems of Ursa Minor. Somehow, he swears he doesn't remember, he found himself on Earth -- in Rzeszow, Poland, to be specific. Good place, that.

Rafael currently lives in bookstores and libraries around Portland, Oregon. He goes there to smell books. Smelling books causes him to contemplate life, the universe, and how much mischief, exactly, could a boy and girl from Earth get into when they find out the truth about the galaxy. Rafael plans to discover the answers through two intertwined series: Mark From Earth and Ella From Earth.

COMING SOON....

ELLA
FROM EARTH

www.ingramcontent.com/pod-product-compliance
Lightning Source LLC
Chambersburg PA
CBHW070557130626
46556CB00001B/195